ONE-SHOT
HARRY

BOOKS BY GARY PHILLIPS

NOVELS

The Jook
The Perpetrators
Bangers
Freedom's Fight
The Underbelly
Kings of Vice (as Mal Radcliff)
Warlord of Willow Ridge
Three the Hard Way (collected novellas)
Beat, Slay, Love: One Chef's Hunger for Delicious Revenge (written collectively as Thalia Filbert)
The Killing Joke (co-written with Christa Faust)
Matthew Henson and the Ice Temple of Harlem

SHORT STORY COLLECTIONS

Monkology: 15 Stories from the World of Private Eye Ivan Monk
Astonishing Heroes: Shades of Justice
Treacherous: Grifters, Ruffians and Killers

MARTHA CHAINEY NOVELS

High Hand
Shooter's Point

IVAN MONK NOVELS

Violent Spring
Perdition, U.S.A.
Bad Night Is Falling
Only the Wicked

GRAPHIC NOVELS

Shot Callerz
Midnight Mover
South Central Rhapsody
Cowboys
Danger A-Go-Go
Angeltown: The Nate Hollis Investigations
High Rollers
Big Water
The Rinse
Peepland (co-written with Christa Faust)
Vigilante: Southland
The Be-Bop Barbarians

ANTHOLOGIES AS EDITOR

The Cocaine Chronicles (co-edited with Jervey Tervalon)
Orange County Noir
Politics Noir: Dark Tales from the Corridors of Power
The Darker Mask: Heroes from the Shadows (co-edited with Christopher Chambers)
Scoundrels: Tales of Greed, Murder and Financial Crimes Hollis, P.I.
Black Pulp (co-edited with Tommy Hancock and Morgan Minor)
Day of the Destroyers
Hollis for Hire
Culprits: The Heist Was Only the Beginning (co-edited with Richard Brewer)
The Obama Inheritance: Fifteen Stories of Conspiracy Noir
Witnesses for the Dead: Stories (co-edited with Gar Anthony Haywood)

ONE-SHOT
HARRY

GARY PHILLIPS

Published by Soho Press, Inc.
227 W 17th Street
New York, NY 10011

Library of Congress Cataloging-in-Publication Data

Names: Phillips, Gary, 1955– author.
Title: One-shot Harry / Gary Phillips.
Description: New York, NY : Soho Crime, [2022]
Identifiers: LCCN 2021035652

ISBN 978-1-64129-457-7
eISBN 978-1-64129-292-4

International Paperback edition: ISBN 978-1-64129-419-5

Subjects: LCGFT: Novels.
Classification: LCC PS3566.H4783 O54 2022 | DDC 813'.54—dc23
LC record available at https://lccn.loc.gov/2021035652

Interior map © Mike Hall
Interior design by Janine Agro, Soho Press, Inc.

Printed in the United States of America

10 9 8 7 6 5 4 3 2 1

For Chelsea and Silas

ONE-SHOT
HARRY

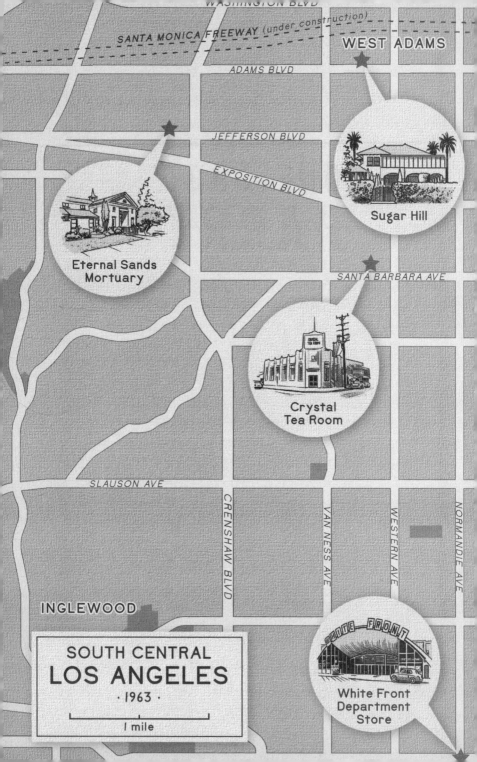

WASHINGTON BLVD

SANTA MONICA FREEWAY (under construction)

WEST ADAMS

ADAMS BLVD

JEFFERSON BLVD

EXPOSITION BLVD

Sugar Hill

Eternal Sands
Mortuary

SANTA BARBARA AVE

Crystal
Tea Room

SLAUSON AVE

CRENSHAW BLVD

VAN NESS AVE

WESTERN AVE

NORMANDIE AVE

INGLEWOOD

SOUTH CENTRAL
LOS ANGELES
· 1963 ·

1 mile

White Front
Department
Store

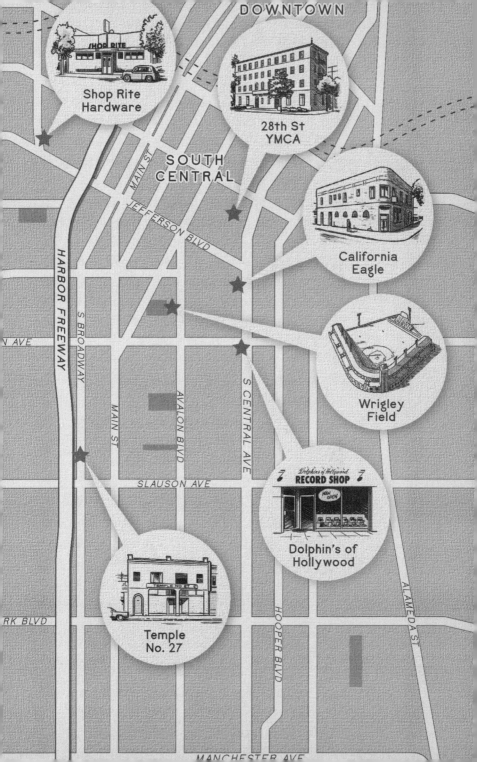

DOWNTOWN

Shop Rite
Hardware

28th St
YMCA

SOUTH
CENTRAL

California
Eagle

Wrigley
Field

Dolphin's of
Hollywood

Temple
No. 27

HARBOR FREEWAY

S BROADWAY

MAIN ST

MAIN ST

AVALON BLVD

S CENTRAL AVE

HOOPER BLVD

ALAMEDA ST

JEFFERSON BLVD

SLAUSON AVE

RK BLVD

V AVE

MANCHESTER AVE

Dolphins of Hollywood
RECORD SHOP
NOW OPEN

SHOP RITE

TEMPLE NO. 27

CHAPTER ONE

"Fifteen." Josh Nakano placed his domino tile on the table with the others.

The raspy voice of comedian Redd Foxx, known for his blue material, issued from an LP spinning on the record player. "Yes, ladies and gentlemen, here we are again for the great racing of the T-bone stakes." An audience tittered in the background of the live recording. The album was titled *The New Race Track*.

"Don't stop writing yet, scorekeeper." Peter "Strummer" Edwards smiled, slapping down a tile. "Ten." He was a tall, dark-skinned man with large hands, several of his knuckles misshaped like a seasoned boxer's.

James "Shoals" Pettigrew marked the points on a lined yellow notepad, then put down his own domino. The hardware store owner didn't score.

Using one hand, Harry Ingram picked up his facedown tiles, turning them toward his face, studying them. Between two fingers of his other hand, a cheap cigar smoldered.

"If you blink three times, they still ain't gonna change," Pettigrew joked.

"Got it, Captain Hook." Ingram put down his choice, hoping this time to block Nakano from scoring again.

"Thanks for nothing," Nakano said, playing after Ingram. He was a medium-built man with thick black hair going gray at the sides. He wore glasses and a colorful Hawaiian shirt over casual slacks. He favored loud sport shirts when not relegated to suit and tie, as befitted a funeral director.

"Always at your service, good sir."

When the LP ended, Ingram got up from the card table and went over to his record player, which was set below several built-in bookshelves. Among the books on the shelves were two police scanners and an AM/FM transistor radio. Ingram put the record back in its sleeve, the photographic image on the front a smiling young woman in modified jockey gear straddling a hobby horse.

"Put on the radio, would you, Harry?" Edwards said, yawning and stretching. "Can't have Redd making me too excited before I go to bed alone."

Pettigrew wiggled his fingers. "Alone, you say?"

Everyone chuckled.

Ingram slotted the Foxx album alphabetically among other comedic, jazz and blues albums he kept in wooden produce crates stacked in a corner. He turned the radio on, adjusting the antenna and turning the dial to bring the station in clearer.

"... and the hunt goes on for the bank robber dubbed the Morning Bandit. But now, my dear listeners," the DJ continued, "we here at KGFJ urge all right-thinking Angelenos to come out and hear what Martin Luther King has to say when he arrives in town less than three weeks from today. As many of us know, his message isn't just for the South, but for what goes on here in the supposedly enlightened north."

"You covered the reverend when he was in town before, didn't you?" Nakano said to Ingram as he sat down again. King had last been in Los Angeles two years earlier to speak at the Sports Arena. The facility had been filled to capacity with thousands standing outside to hear him over the loudspeakers.

"Yeah, I've got a request in through the *Sentinel* to take shots when he speaks this time too. But they'd already got this reporter assigned who takes his own pics." Ingram made part of his living as a photographer for the Black press.

"What about the march later this year?" Edwards said. In the 1950s he'd been the one to look after the interests of gangster Jack Dragna on the Black side of Los Angeles. These days he had his own interests to see to—some aboveboard and others he didn't file taxes about.

"You going?" Ingram asked.

"Thinking about it." Edwards looked up from his dominoes at the other three staring at him. "What? All sorts of people are going, including Moses." He meant Charlton Heston, who was heading the Hollywood contingent to the March on Washington taking place in August.

"You know this is the second time this has been tried," Nakano said.

"Huh?" Edwards lit a cigarette and opened another can of Hamm's he'd retrieved from Ingram's refrigerator.

"A. Philip Randolph threatened a march back in the forties unless Roosevelt desegregated the armed forces and paid the same wages to Blacks working in the war industries. FDR didn't desegregate but did sign a bill about the fair pay. And Randolph called off the march, though some say he was bluffing all along."

"King ain't bluffing," Pettigrew said.

"Damn, how come you always know more about negro history than me, Josh?" Edwards said.

"Maybe he's just a better soul brother than you," Ingram laughed.

"That's probably true." Edwards had more of his beer.

Nakano said, "The Japanese American Citizens League is sending a contingent. A cousin of mine is going to be in it."

"You thinking about going?" Ingram asked him.

"Yep. For sure I'll be at the rally in town." Nakano looked up from his dominoes, a wry smile lighting his face. "Equal rights is equal rights, isn't it?"

"Across the board," Pettigrew said.

The friends played until a few minutes past ten in the evening. After they left, Ingram folded up the card table they'd been playing on, put the dominoes back in their box and cleaned up in the kitchen where they'd made sandwiches. There was a door separating the kitchen from a compact back porch area. In there was a utility sink for use with a rubboard to wash clothes. Ingram had turned this area into a darkroom with lengths of clothesline strung up to hang drying prints. Back in his apartment's living room, he considered putting on one of the scanners but decided to pour himself something stiffer than beer and sit in his easy chair. The window overlooking the street below was cracked open and the sounds of a quieting city drifted in as he sat and drank. The radio was still on, but he'd turned the volume down.

Ingram had taken one of his file folders from a rack of several and had it open on his lap, looking through his photos. He frowned as if this were the first time he was seeing his work from a critical standpoint. There was all manner of mayhem represented in the black-and-whites, from a man laid out on the sidewalk in a nice suit, two-tone shoes and a knife sticking out of his head to a woman in a beret, hands manacled behind her back as a cop led her away. There was a bloody hatchet in another cop's hand and a bloodstain on the lower part of her skirt.

"No wonder *Look* won't hire me," he muttered, enjoying more bourbon. He closed the file and put it aside. As he began to doze off, Ingram resolved to take more happy pictures, like people picnicking in the park and kids laughing as they flew kites.

At some point he woke up and KGFJ, an around-the-clock station, was playing classical music. He got up and went to bed to the strains of Debussy's *Three Nocturnes*.

In the morning after a sound sleep and a trip to the john, Ingram put on his threadbare cotton bathrobe over his boxers and athletic tee. He turned on one of his scanners.

"...suspect, male, white American, twenties, reddish-blond hair heading north on Bronson from Venice on foot..."

With that as his background accompaniment, Ingram fixed a breakfast that included sausage links from the neighborhood grocery store downstairs, Whitehead's Market. Afterward, taking his second cup of coffee into the bathroom, he showered and shaved. The scanner was still going. Monday morning crime, at least in terms of the Black east side, was limited to a purse snatching and a parked vehicle clipped in a hit-and-run. This wasn't unusual. Ingram knew colored fellas were often jacked up by the cops on Saturday night and were awaiting a hearing or still arranging bail at the start of the new week.

Things would be jumping by nine tonight, he reflected as he got his equipment together, including his Speed Graphic camera. There were two nicks from bullets grooved in its casing and Ingram rubbed one of them for luck, as he always did. He'd brought the camera home from the war. Fleeting was the notion of photographing normal people doing normal things. Where was the kick in that? Melancholy moments like the one he'd had last night he invariably washed away with booze.

Tweed sport coat on and no tie, slipping a couple of his cigars into an inner pocket, he quit his apartment, going out the rear door through his darkroom and down the creaking wooden stairs. Behind the building his car was parked in one of the few designated spaces. There was another man downstairs in a plaid shirt-jacket and casual slacks.

"What's happening, Arthur?" Ingram clapped the other man on the shoulder as Arthur unlocked the back door to Whitehead's. Ingram's building was made of brick and wood trim, constructed in the late 1920s. The corner grocery store commanded most of the space on the ground floor. To the south of that was the front entrance into the apartments, stairs leading up to the second and third floors occupied by tenants.

"Same old sixes and sevens, Harry."

Arthur Yarbrough got the door open but did not turn on the lights to cut the gloom. He was a light-skinned Black man about Ingram's height, a little over six feet, though not as solidly built. There was a zigzag of scarred skin along one side of his face that gave him an intriguing as opposed to disfigured appearance. He wore heavy framed sunglasses and the stylish cane Ingram had bought him some years ago leaned near the door.

The store had originally belonged to a Caucasian family named Whitehead. When it changed hands to Black ownership, the name was kept, one, because people were familiar with it in the neighborhood, and two, it was an in-joke.

"Need me for anything?"

"I got it covered, man."

"Yeah, you do."

Yarbrough had been blinded in the Korean War when on patrol he'd stepped on a land mine. It would be another hour or so until one of his sighted employees came to work. In the time between, he'd have gone through the store arranging the items on the shelves, swept the aisles and so forth. There was a blueprint of the store's layout imprinted in his head, Ingram liked to imagine.

Ingram left Yarbrough and unlocked the trunk of his several-years-old Plymouth Belvedere. In here was his traveling photo development setup. When he had to make a deadline and didn't have time to return home to use his darkroom, he developed his pictures in his trunk. He checked to make sure he had enough of the requisite chemicals and that they were secure in their containers.

Trunk closed, he got behind the wheel and backed out of his parking spot into the alley. He righted the car and drove slowly along the rutted, potholed asphalt. He took a left onto Forty-Third Street and headed west, made another left on Figueroa, passing several businesses with a TOM BRADLEY FOR CITY COUNCIL sign in the corner of their windows. He kept on, reaching Imperial Highway, went west again to the municipality of Inglewood and the Hollywood Racetrack. The horse racing venue was miles south from Hollywood. Its name had originated with studio boss Jack L. Warner, who in the 1930s was one of its main backers. Investors included Bing Crosby, Ralph Bellamy and Walt Disney.

The stars still came to the park, but Ingram wasn't here to try for a candid of Doris Day feeding an apple to a thoroughbred. Reaching the track, he turned onto a side road and followed that around a bend to an area most of the patrons didn't venture to, the stables. He parked on an open spot and walked across the hay-strewn ground, taking in the sights and ever-present smell of horse flesh. He passed a teenage stable hand raking up horse droppings and spotted his contact, Dolby Markham. He was washing down a horse in a stall. Ingram aimed the camera strapped around his neck and took a few snaps.

"Hey, Harry," Markham said when he heard the shutter click.

Ingram raised a hand. "Keep working. Looks great, Dolby."

The celebrities who were often photographed in the stands or at the turf club were usually white, though the likes of Nat King Cole and Lena Horne had also had their pictures taken here. The gossip rags weren't interested in the workers behind the scenes. Many of the trainers, stable hands and horse walkers were Black or Mexican American, a few Filipinos too. Ingram had talked with the West Coast editor of *Jet*, who told him he'd pay for some shots of the colored men taking care of the horses. Ingram could also write a few paragraphs to go along with the photos, which the editor figured would be a solid human-interest piece. *Jet* was a weekly digest-sized roundup of news about the Black community. It was published by Johnson Publications, which also put out the monthly full-sized *Ebony* magazine. The digest was not found at newsstands; rather the discerning buyer could find *Jet* on a counter rack at their local market or liquor store. Each issue included a centerfold of a swimsuit-clad young woman as the Beauty of the Week.

Markham took a break as Ingram stepped into the stall. "Don't mind my cold fingers."

They shook hands. "Ain't nothing to it."

The wiry Markham was several inches shorter than the photographer. Once he'd been a jockey. But a particularly bad spill had resulted in his leg being broken in two places. Not the first time he'd been banged up, but what with permanent injuries having piled up over the years, Markham had retired from the racing aspect of the sport. But horses were all he knew, and he had to be around the animals in some capacity.

Ingram said, "Why don't you introduce me to the fellas?"

"You read my mind."

They exited the stall and Markham first took him to the kid who was raking.

"Yo, Tally, this here's a friend of mine, Harry Ingram. A certified daredevil newshawk of the negro in Los Angeles."

The kid stopped raking and glanced over at Ingram. "Say what now?"

"Dolby's funnin' you," Ingram replied, giving his friend a sideways glance.

"I seen you stand up to them peckerwood cops," Markham said. He tapped a thin scar on Ingram's temple, a present from a nightstick a few years ago.

"Anyway, about them shots," Ingram deflected.

"Shots, like from a doctor, because I'm around the horses?" The young man hooked a thumb at the stables.

"Naw, son, Harry's going to make you famous." Markham clapped him on the back.

The teen grinned. "Then let's get to it."

Ingram spent more than an hour taking photos but mostly hanging with the stable hands and other track workers as they went about their tasks, finding out what brought them to horse racing and so on. He'd filled several pages in his notepad. As he finished up, Ingram wondered if this might not be a piece he could interest one of the white slicks in if he fleshed out the story.

"Thanks for spending time with us never-seens, Harry." Markham shook his hand again.

"Like I said, I'll get copies of the prints over to you," Ingram said. He'd used up two rolls of film.

About to head back to his car, Ingram spotted three men

up ahead in front of one of the stalls. One of them was a trainer he'd met briefly when talking with Markham and the others. He wore a sweat-stained hat that once upon a time had a shape. The white man he was talking to was in his fifties, Ingram estimated, tailored clothes and a barbered head of silvery hair. But it was the third one who Ingram zeroed in on. He was standing off to one side and as he got closer, he could see this man lean his head toward him.

"Harry, is that you, home folks?"

"Ben? Goddamn, it is you." Ingram set his camera on a small shelf upon which were bottles of liniment for the horses.

The two rushed at each other and hugged, slapping each other on the back.

"When did you get back to town?"

"A couple of weeks ago. Been meaning to look you up, cousin," Ben Kinslow said. Addressing the silver-haired man, he added, "We were in the service together, Mr. Hoyt."

The silver-haired man nodded curtly. "That's something. Korea, was it?"

"Yes, sir," Ingram said, smiling. He took the older man to be Kinslow's employer, and wasn't going to say something crude if he could help it.

Hoyt and the trainer walked inside the stall, the trainer's calloused hand on the horse's hindquarters.

"I'd heard you're still taking them stills," Kinslow said.

"You still tooting the horn?"

"Now and then."

They'd stepped away from the stall, but Ingram had heard enough to know that Hoyt was the owner of the horse being examined. He said in a low voice to Kinslow, "Look, I don't want to get you in Dutch with your boss. I'm sure he wants you paying attention to every pearl of wisdom spilling from his spoon-fed mouth."

Kinslow smiled, looking over at the other man. "Lay your number on me. I'll give you a shout."

Ingram wrote it down on one of his sheets in his notepad, tore it off and handed it over. "Don't be no stranger," he said in his normal volume.

"Never," his buddy said. "Give me some dap."

They slapped palms. Ingram retrieved his camera and walked to his car. Near his vehicle was a coal-black 1962 Lincoln Continental. He whistled at the swank car. Dispensing with his envy, he got into his car and after turning the engine over for several cranks, the vehicle started. He drove off, stopping at a pay phone on Imperial.

"Hey, Doris. Got anything for your favorite runner?"

"I think I do, Harry," Doris Letrec said. He heard her set the handset down, then papers being shuffled before she came back on the line. "Got a divorce case, a car involved in a cross complaint and some kind of suit involving a truckload of refrigerators." She paused, reading the paperwork further. "Oh, but that one's in Glendale."

He almost cursed. "You might as well have said Mississippi."

"I hear you." Letrec was white but she knew about sundown towns like Glendale. If you were Black, it was best you not be caught there after the sun set—by the cops or by the self-righteous residents. Ingram wasn't going to be there during the day if he could help it. "Okay, I'll swing by for the divorce and car."

"See you." She hung up.

Ingram drove back into L.A. proper and the offices of Galton Process Services and Legal Papers on Grand Avenue, not far from the downtown courthouses. Letrec, the office manager, was at the front desk typing a report when Ingram entered. She was a middle-aged woman who lived with a female roommate, a younger librarian, in a garden apartment in East Hollywood.

Her cat-eye glasses were on a chain and she removed them as she looked up from her Underwood. "I've got them right here, Harry." She handed the paperwork over to him.

"Thanks." He glanced at the addresses, then tucked them away.

The main part of the office contained a row of gray file cabinets, a few chairs, two desks—there was a man who came on for the after-hours trade from four to midnight—and an inner office. This had a door inset with a large glass pane, a set of blinds behind that. As usual, the blinds were drawn.

Ingram pointed his jaw at the door. "Is His Lordship in?"

"He was here before I got in," she said, hunching a shoulder. "He did stick his head out once to ask a question."

"Like the groundhog," Ingram mused.

Tremane Galton, the owner of the business, was of British extraction but had lived in the States since his twenties, some thirty-plus years ago. He was agoraphobic, though he managed to drive from his house in Frogtown to the office at least three days a week.

Ingram started for the exit. "I'll let you know how it goes."

"Keep 'em flying straight, Harry."

"Always above the flack."

Glasses back on, she gave him a last look, then resumed typing.

Driving to his first destination, Ingram passed a sharp-dressed teenager standing on the corner hawking copies of the *Sentinel*.

"'Negro Workers Demand Fair Pay at Bethlehem Steel,'"

the young man yelled. "Get your *Sentinel* newspaper, get your *Sentinel* newspaper."

Serving the divorce papers was not hard. The unshaven man who answered Ingram's knock was wiping sleep out of his eyes. He worked the graveyard shift at a frozen fish supplier out in San Pedro.

"Mr. Efrain Martinez?" Ingram said pleasantly.

"Yes." He regarded Ingram warily.

"You've been served." Ingram held out the tri-folded papers requiring his presence in court.

"That puta bitch," the man growled, taking the papers, muttering in Spanish and English as he slammed the door.

The disputed car was another matter. The address took Harry to a residential street off of north Western Avenue. On his way he passed by the boarded-up Fox Uptown Theater. A few years ago, he'd taken a date there to see Vincent Price in a movie called *The Tingler*. The movie was pretty tame for a horror show. Ingram had hoped to get his lady friend all clingy. Instead, she'd fallen asleep by the second half.

He slowed as he went past a California bungalow, double-checking the address. The car in question wasn't out front, but there was a detached garage at the end of the driveway. First, though, he drove up and down the surrounding blocks, looking for the car whose plate and other details he'd memorized. Having done process server work for some time now, Ingram knew the tricks drivers used to hide cars they owed payments on—including switching the license plates. He rolled up on a Buick LeSabre, but it was the wrong color and plate. He didn't think the driver, a Scott Jayson, had had the vehicle repainted. If he could afford that, he would have tried to come current on the note.

Ingram parked several doors down from the bungalow and walked back to the house. He took a peek inside the garage. The double doors had a chain through where the locks had once been, and this was padlocked closed. But there was enough play between the doors that Ingram gapped them to shine his flashlight inside. The LeSabre was there.

"Hey, what are you up to?"

Ingram turned around to see a white man in jeans, his shirttail out. He was holding a baseball bat and had come out the back door.

Ingram held up a hand. "Take it easy. You must be Mr. Jayson." This wasn't the first time he'd been threatened with violence when he'd been trying to serve someone. The war had taught him how to handle his fear.

"What about it?"

"Your car is involved in a cross complaint and I'm here to serve you papers initiated from Triton Auto Sales." He'd also read the used car lot was run by Jayson's brother-in-law.

"Ain't no coloreds work for Triton."

"I'm being paid to serve you."

"Yeah, then get in the kitchen and get my lunch ready." The man chuckled.

"No reason to not be civil."

Jayson came closer, waving the bat. "What you gonna do if I don't? What if I use this to teach you a lesson about nosing in business that ain't your concern? How would that be . . . boy?"

"That would be a mistake, Mr. Ofay."

Jayson's eyes popped open as if he'd been struck in the forehead. "What did you just say?"

He swung the bat and Ingram turned his body into it, taking the brunt of the blow on his arm. He was hurting but focused. He got his hand on the bat and at the same time punched Jayson with his free hand.

"How dare you, nigger," the other man said, stumbling back but still holding the bat.

Ingram allowed the other man's momentum to carry the both of them backward, muscle memory dredging up the rudimentary jujitsu he'd learned in basic about leverage. Jayson aimed a fist at Ingram's jaw, but he slipped aside, the jab glancing off the side of his face. Ingram got his foot behind Jayson's heel and shoved. This sent them both down to the ground, Ingram landing as hard as he could atop the other man.

"Get the fuck off me."

They both wrestled for control of the bat, rolling around on the ground. Ingram rammed an elbow into Jayson's face, stunning him. An angered Jayson let go of the bat and got both his hands around Ingram's neck, choking him.

"I'll teach you good, Blackie."

Ingram went flat on his back and as Jayson tightened his hands around his neck, the part-time process server got a knee against Jayson's sternum, flipping him over. Ingram bolted to his feet, snatching the bat up from where it lay. The handkerchief pocket on his jacket was torn.

Jayson was getting to a knee. "You better put that down. I'll get you arrested for damn sure."

Ingram was mad enough to strike him, but feared sending him to the hospital, which would send him to jail quick. When it came to the testimony of a Black man against a white man's word, what chance did he have in a so-called court of law? Still. He jammed the opposite end of the bat into Jayson's stomach.

"You motherfucker," the man wheezed, bending over and holding his middle.

Ingram grabbed him by the shirt front and stood him up. "Listen, gray boy, if I have to come back here I'll set that

Buick on fire and you'll never prove it was me. You'll really be in the hole then." He let him go and threw the court order at his feet. "You've been served, asshole."

"What about my bat?'

"What about it?" Ingram started toward him and Jayson flinched. Ingram laughed harshly, then turned, spearing the bat through a bedroom window, shattering the glass with force. "There it is."

Off he went, a tremor in his leg. By the time he got into his car he was shaking all over, tears in his eyes as he gripped the steering wheel. Ingram didn't give a shit about Jayson. It was the violence dogging him he knew. The war wouldn't let him go.

After a few minutes he calmed down. Hand steady, he inserted the key in the ignition, started the car and drove away.

SHOALS PETTIGREW was closing up his store as dusk settled. A late-model, somber-colored Buick LeSabre pulled to the curb and parked. Out stepped a youngish white man in shirtsleeves and tie. He carried an attaché case and stepped inside Shop Rite Hardware.

"Good evening, Mr. Pettigrew," he said.

"Mr. Westmore," the owner said, nodding curtly.

The other man placed his case on the counter. "As I mentioned over the phone, the association we represent is pleased to provide the church another contribution to the building fund." He clicked the attaché's locks open and lifted the lid. He extracted a sealed envelope, placed it before Pettigrew and reclosed his case. "As before, we seek no overblown ceremony. A mention from the pulpit come Sunday is sufficient."

"Yes, sir."

"Have a good evening."

"You too."

The man exited the store and drove away.

Pettigrew, head of the building committee of his church, Ward African Methodist Episcopal, had been tasked by his pastor to receive these particular donations delivered by Westmore. The cash infusion was a one-step-removed protocol being followed. It was understood these funds freed up church monies for stipends and such. These stipends in turn flowed as contributions from individuals to specific previously designated political campaigns in negro neighborhoods. Federal tax law prohibited churches from making outright political donations. Currently the money was earmarked for Tom Bradley's City Council campaign. It hadn't been the pastor who'd explained to Pettigrew how this worked, rather a former church secretary he'd been dating. As far as the books were concerned, everything was aboveboard and legal.

And as far as Pettigrew was concerned, this was how business was conducted in the white world, so why not his church, an entity that was doing right by the community? Bradley was an extension of that as well.

He locked up, taking the envelope with him.

CHAPTER TWO

Ingram heard from his Army buddy Ben Kinslow, who invited him to a party in the Sugar Hill section of West Adams, among the Queen Anne and Beaux Arts homes. The name Sugar Hill, a tribute to the original Sugar Hill in Harlem, had been bestowed on this neighborhood by well-to-do Black folks: doctors, lawyers and those who owned businesses on Central Avenue. Celebrities such as Hattie McDaniel and Eddie "Rochester" Anderson had homes here. They and other actors were often relegated to stereotypical roles, be it maids and manservants on screens large and small, but in Sugar Hill, they were acknowledged for breaking down barriers.

But even here there was no escaping the onslaught of a white-dominated bureaucracy. The Santa Monica Freeway, begun in 1957, would eventually reach the ocean. It had cut a sizable swath through the neighborhood, leveling homes acquired by eminent domain despite residents banding together to try to alter the route.

Kinslow wasn't here yet but Ingram, used to being an interloper, wasn't feeling self-conscious. He was in the spacious kitchen of a three-story Victorian adding chips to the paper plate he'd stacked with a salami sandwich. He winced, his bruised arm smarting where he'd been hit with the bat. On the table beside the snacks were a few bottles of hard liquor, including Old Grand-Dad and Wild Irish Rose. Beer was in a washtub filled with ice on the tiled floor. The rear door was open and there were people socializing in the backyard—though he supposed in a house like this it would be called the garden. He'd once been told by the staid Charlotta Bass, the former publisher of the *California Eagle*, that back in the 1920s, when the residents had been mostly white, that more than one of these fine abodes around here had been the venue for an orgy. Sizing up the racially mixed but sedate crowd chatting away pleasantly, he didn't figure people were going to be letting their hair down that dang much this evening. He had a camera in his trunk just in case.

"Harry, how's it hangin'?"

Ingram gazed at a familiar face. "Johnny, hey, ain't nothin' up but the rent, baby."

"I heard that." They shook hands vigorously.

Johnny Otis was a vibraphonist and bandleader, and had once been co-owner of a nightclub in Watts called the Barrelhouse. He was of Greek origin, but often stated he identified as a Black man and with the negro's fight for justice. The two stepped out of the kitchen to talk.

"I'm doing a fundraising gig for Bradley if you want to drop by and take some shots," Otis was saying, munching on a handful of chips.

"For sure. When and where?"

"The date's still not settled 'cause of the reverend coming to town and Tom's folks are helping to prep the event. But probably no more than a couple of weeks after that." He added, "I'm trying to get King Cole to drop by and perform as well."

"Y'all got a place in mind for this?"

"Oh yes." Otis rubbed his now empty hands together to rid them of his chip crumbs. "The Hotten Tot has agreed to host the fundraiser."

"He's got a chance, right?"

"Should. Hell, he just might be our first Black mayor if he wins this race."

"Sheet, this is L.A., Johnny."

They both laughed. Otis turned his head slightly, scanning the room, then tapped Ingram's arm and pointed.

"Let me introduce you to this chick, she's got it going on."

"The tall one?" The woman had shoulder-length black hair and had thrown her head back, laughing with the man she was talking to.

"Yeah, come on." Otis held up a hand. "Hey, Anita."

The woman looked over as Ingram and Otis snaked their way through a knot of people. As they passed two of the Dandridge sisters, Dorothy and Vivian, Otis said hello.

When they reached the black-haired woman, Otis said, "Harry Ingram, this here's Anita Claire."

"Hello," she said to Ingram. She indicated her companion, an older white man in glasses and boxy sport coat, and said to the bandleader, "This is Frank Wilkerson, who you might know of."

"My man, yes, sir, know of you and dig you." Otis turned to Ingram. "This cat's been out front on housing issues for us poor folks."

"I know. We've run into each other a couple of times."

Wilkerson regarded Ingram. "Where?"

"The equal rights rally at the 5-4 Ballroom," Ingram replied. "It was right after you got out of the joint for facing down Congress, I recall you mentioning. I was there taking pictures." Wilkerson had been one of the speakers at the event. Ingram knew the photographer, like a waiter or floor sweep, was seen but not seen, his face often obscured by the camera in front of it.

"Right, got it," Wilkerson said, but not really.

"Anita's working on Tom's election committee. She's a wiz with numbers, stats, that sort of thing." Otis beamed at her.

"Pleased to meet you," Ingram said.

"Same," she said.

Ingram wasn't going to get caught staring. She struck him as self-assured, and if she knew numbers, she was smart too. Ingram had painful memories of trying to get through algebra word problems in high school, all those trains leaving opposite stations at different speeds. Of course, if he'd had a teacher who looked like her, his mind wouldn't have been on math any damn way.

He orbited back to the conversation that the other three were having about what sort of programs Tom Bradley might try to institute if he got elected.

"Reining in them damn cops of Parker's should be his number-one concern," Otis said.

"Amen to that," Ingram said.

"When Tom made captain in the Department," Wilkerson began, "no white patrolman would tolerate a colored man as his boss. He was put in charge of the graveyard shift, a command of Mexican and Black officers."

"We still got a long way to go," Otis noted.

The other two nodded.

Milling about later, Ingram struck up a conversation with a white man named Eddie Burrows who did freelance reporting for *The Nation* magazine. He was in short sleeves and his longish hair was disheveled.

"I'm going to cover King at the rally," he told Ingram.

"That's great." Ingram hadn't mentioned what he did.

He didn't want to seem desperate to cover the rally, though he was.

"I think the March on Washington is going to be a watershed event, don't you?"

"Maybe. But crackers digging in their heels to preserve the way of life they like has usually been the response to any forward motion us colored folks have tried."

"That's kind of cynical, isn't it?"

"Or just a realistic observation."

Burrows nodded. "So, what is it you do, Harry?"

They wound up exchanging cards, and Burrows said he'd see about getting Ingram into the rally. *The Nation* wasn't big on photos, but this was a special event, a precursor to August.

"'Course this might paint you as a red," Burrows said. "Hanging out with the people I know."

"I've been accused of much worse."

Not long afterward Ingram was out back catching up with Ben Kinslow, who'd finally shown up. From inside the house, riffs from piano keys carried on the evening's warm breezes. He and Kinslow liberally sipped on the Old Grand-Dad from the kitchen.

"Don't think I'm going to be working for Hoyt too much longer." Kinslow winked at Ingram. The two sat near the rear of the walled-in yard in faded Adirondack chairs. Decorative colored paper had been cut into shapes of the Buddha and Day of the Dead masks and hung from a clothesline.

"You taking up the horn full-time?"

"Maybe—that is, maybe I'll have more time to get my chops back."

"What are you going on about?"

Kinslow said, "Jus' talkin' is all. More of those big dreams we had sitting in a foxhole trying not to shit our britches."

"You were gonna have your own club."

"That's right," Kinslow agreed. That had been the reason he'd come out to L.A. before. He'd gotten close more than once to making it happen, but things didn't pan out. Kinslow sat back, arcing his hands in the air as if revealing a title. "How you like the name Club Central? You can be the house photographer, Harry."

"I appreciate that," Ingram said, drinking more. A tall man with reddish-blond hair guffawed loudly. A woman next to him giggled, putting a hand in front of his mouth to quiet him down. The two old friends let the silence linger, staring at the cutouts dangling before them, until Kinslow spoke again.

"You ever wonder what she looked like?"

"Who?"

"Your girlfriend, Seoul City Sue," he said.

"You the one went to sleep at night dreaming of her in your arms, lover boy."

Seoul City Sue was the name for a propagandist broadcast from Pyongyang in the north during the war. She had a velvety voice and lovingly told the GIs how their cause was lost, read the names off dog tags of dead American soldiers, and spun records like "I'll Be Seeing You." Many simply listened to her for her comforting voice, thinking of the girl they'd left stateside. That was the point, of course, but as far as Ingram knew, no one defected because of her.

"She wasn't Asian," he said.

"Yeah, she was. I've seen pictures," Kinslow replied.

Ingram hunched a shoulder. "That was more jive from the reds, man. Not only was she not Asian, she was as white as they come. Whiter than you even."

"You think 'cause I'm tipsy you can bullshit me?" Kinslow drained his glass and set it down beside his chair.

"Naw, she was a Methodist from Arkansas."

"How you know that, Criswell?"

Ingram held his hands up, swaying his upper body. "I see all and know all." He then added, "Read it in the *Saturday Evening Post*."

"For real?"

"For real. She still lives there in North Korea."

"Of course. She came home she'd be shot for treason."

"There is that little hitch."

"She a knockout?" Kinslow asked.

"You'd sell out your country for a pretty turn of the ankle, son?"

Kinslow affected a commanding officer's tone. "Patriotism or pussy, soldier. Which is it?"

"No wonder I could barely get through the war." Ingram's words came out flat, though he meant them to be light.

Kinslow patted Ingram on the shoulder.

Eventually they wandered back inside. Kinslow didn't say anything else about his plans. He'd brought his horn, which he'd stowed on a built-in sideboard beneath an impressionist painting. Joe Sample, a musician Ingram had seen at clubs around town with a group called the Jazz Crusaders, was improvising a tune. Nat King Cole stood off to one side behind some others, hands in his pocket, his snap-brim hat pushed back on his bopping head.

Kinslow had his horn out, waiting and tapping his feet as he discerned the patterns hidden within the seeming non-structure of the music. He held off for nearly a minute, fingering the horn's keys but not putting it to his lips. He joined in when Sample began pounding out a fast tempo. Together they worked their way into a tune that was melodious and involving. Ingram stood on the periphery, digging what the two were laying down. Improvising using spoons on the bottom of an emptied metal trash can, Johnny Otis joined in with understated syncopations. The groove continued for another twenty minutes or so. When they came to a stop, there was energetic applause. The temporary trio took their bows as the din of conversation again rose in the parlor.

"I saw you and the horn player talking earlier." Anita Claire had come up behind him.

What? Was she checking him out? Keeping his face neutral, he said, "Yeah, we were in Korea together."

"I see. I had a cousin who was there."

"How'd he take it?"

"He didn't make it back."

"Sorry to hear that."

"I didn't mean to be so dour."

"Could be the times we're in, Anita. When I came back from over there, figured me and all them other negro troops bleeding for democracy and all that would be appreciated. How could Mr. Charlie deny us our due on the home front?"

"But then it was the same old, same old."

"What a surprise."

"Let's get a drink."

"I'm gonna have something to eat. I might have hit my limit. Me and Ben catching up, I mean. Not that I drink like this normally."

She was heading toward the kitchen. "Do I look like a nun to you, Harry?"

He almost blurted, "No, ma'am, you look like a dream," but managed to stop himself. Instead, he gave an embarrassing chuckle and said, "That sounds like a trick question."

He followed her, noting that he'd sobered up some. Out of the corner of his eye, he spied Kinslow talking with Sample and Vivian Dandridge.

The kitchen had fewer people in it as the evening wore on. There was, though, a white woman in a green swing dress with eyes that matched her attire. Claire put an arm around her waist as the other woman finished mixing a drink.

"This is my running buddy, Judy Berkson," Claire said to Ingram. Both women showed big teeth at each other.

"Good to meet you," he said, sticking out his hand. She shook firmly.

"Here's how." Berkson tipped her glass to Claire and exited.

Claire got a beer out of the tub, which was now mostly full of water. He handed her a church key.

"So, what is it you do when you're not working to elect a candidate?"

"I'm a substitute teacher. I teach algebra and geometry in high schools and at a couple of community colleges. But I'm doing more of the Bradley kind of work these days."

"How does the math work in that situation?"

"I look for the patterns to develop profiles. Frequency of voters in an area—break it down by those who attend church, go to PTA meetings and so on. It's boring shop talk, but you asked."

"No, I'm digging it. You break down how segments of the voters vote?"

"Exactly. Ultimately what excites them to come out and vote. Now them cigar-smoking white fellas overseeing the state Democratic Party figure just running a negro candidate is enough to get colored people to the polls. Which admittedly is accurate to an extent."

Ingram nodded. "But we don't all think alike. A mechanic might have different concerns than a librarian."

"There you go." She smiled at him. "Really it's about compiling data to predict behavior. In a City Council race it's more concentrated, but Kennedy used a computer in his race to glean that kind of information to his advantage."

"He did?"

"Yep. We're all in this together, but we're not always marching in the same direction."

"Like the differences between King's approach and what Malcolm X is on about?" A year ago, the cops shot up the Black Muslim headquarters, mosques they called them, on South Broadway, leaving one man paralyzed and another dead. Malcolm X had come to town and given a fiery press conference in response at the Statler-Hilton. Ingram had covered the whole thing for the *Herald Dispatch*.

"Which way for you, Harry?" Her question brought him back to the present.

"Me, I'm just trying to make the rent."

"Uh-huh."

"Math is not just abstract formulas on a chalkboard?"

"I know, what does it say about me that I find numbers exciting? But you see, working in local politics is kind of a family tradition."

"Your folks work in politics?"

A cagey look came and went behind her eyes. "You could say that."

"Lady of mystery, huh?"

"That's right."

Later, as the party finally wound down, Ingram said good night to Claire, who'd come to the party with Judy Berkson. Her car, a convertible two-tone DeSoto, was parked under a streetlight. She was standing off to one side, pretending to be looking for something in her purse.

"Am I being too forward if I ask for your number?"

"I'm nothing if not numbers, Mr. Ingram."

Making sure to keep expectation off his face, Ingram

waited as she borrowed a ballpoint pen from her friend. Claire wrote her phone number on the curve of his palm. The blue numerals glistened on his brown skin under the light.

"I'll never wash this off."

"I expect you to be shaved and showered when next we meet, sir." With that she turned and took Berkson's arm. They laughed getting in the car.

"You old hound dog," Ben Kinslow said, walking up, his voice clearer that it had been before. "Bye-bye now," he said, waving at the two women as the car pulled away. His face was sweaty from drinking.

"You gonna make it home all right, soldier?"

"Son, I was knocking 'em back when you were still figuring out your wee-wee from your pablum spoon." He dug his keys out of his pocket. His car key held upright, he touched it to his forehead in a salute. "Okay, One-Shot, let's get us some steaks over to Lo Li's soon. Maybe to celebrate."

"Looking forward to it, Ben."

Kinslow slapped him on the shoulder and walked across the street to where his car was parked down the block. It was a '59 black-and-red Mercury with moon hubcaps. Turning the car around, he drove back to where Ingram remained standing. He slowed, the passenger's side window partly rolled down.

"Keep chargin' the enemy. We do what we do to survive." The admonishment from their Sergeant Jefferson faded into the early morning as Kinslow drove away.

A contented Ingram walked around the corner and unlocked the driver's door to his Plymouth. It took several cranks to start the engine. Getting the car in gear, he once again considered buying a newer sled. But then, hoping he might be seeing Miz Claire again, he figured it was best he have folding money available to show her he was no piker. Not that he took her for being a superficial person. If anything she was the sort to zoom ahead, and he wanted to keep up.

He drove past a line of late-nighters at Johnny's, an around-the-clock establishment on Adams Boulevard. The stand served up not only burgers but hearty pastrami sandwiches, fries and tacos. He resisted the garish neon advertising and made it home.

Not ready for bed, he turned on the radio, tuning in all-night KGFJ. This was the time slot for R&B. From a drawer in the kitchen he got out his S&H green stamps and using a damp sponge to wet the backs, put them in their booklets. Enough filled booklets and he could redeem them for an appliance. Eventually he yawned and switched off the radio, T-Bone Walker's "Mean Old World" still playing in his head as he went into his bedroom.

CHAPTER THREE

It was getting to be a hot day and Ingram was in his darkroom, developing shots he'd taken of the neighborhood around Wrigley Field the day before. The facility had carried that name before its more famous incarnation in Chicago, which was originally called Cubs Park. The L.A. Wrigley Field was horseshoe-shaped, with a two-tiered viewing deck. At the apex of the venue's curve was a twelve-story office tower topped with a large clock face. The field was located at Forty-Second and Avalon, not far from Ingram's apartment. The facility had been home to several triple-A Pacific League baseball teams such as the Hollywood Stars who eventually moved to Gilmore Stadium and even the Angels when they went pro—at least until they'd moved to Dodger Stadium in 1962.

This was where Martin Luther King Jr. would be speaking when he got to town and Ingram still wanted to get some compare-and-contrast pictures of the place empty. If he couldn't get inside on his own, he had a contact in the union representing the janitors, mostly Black men of a certain age who cleaned the various municipal buildings around town. Though the stadium was privately owned, its cleaning crew included several who once had been on the city payroll.

Taking his black-and-whites out of the stop bath, he squeegeed off the excess and hung them up to dry. He dried his hands on a rag and clicked off the red overhead bulb. Stepping into the kitchen proper, he was considering whether to fix lunch or go to the Detour diner a few blocks from his apartment. If he wasn't mistaken, today's special was meatloaf. An anemic bologna sandwich didn't stand a chance.

There was a crackle of static over one of his scanners. He'd forgotten he had it on.

". . . repeat, driver, white, male American, went over embankment through the guardrail," the unemotional dispatcher was saying. "Ford Mercury, two-tone, red on black, off of Mulholland near intersection of Outpost Drive. Car smashed against tree, witness reports. KMA . . ."

A policeman in a patrol car responded, but whatever he said, Ingram's impression was as if he were underwater, his voice muffled and incoherent. The car being described over the scanner was Ben Kinslow's car. He rushed down the stairs to his car, consulted his Thomas Guide street map book and took off. His mouth was dry, and he had a hard time swallowing. He drove carefully, though; he couldn't be stopped by the cops until he reached the scene of the accident.

He wound his way up Mulholland in a westerly direction, ascending into the Hollywood Hills. Main thoroughfares branching north off Mulholland led into the San Fernando Valley, the homes of celebrities and the well-to-do. If there were any colored people around here, they were the help.

Approaching the scene, Ingram saw a police car parked on the side of the roadway, another with its nose sticking out into the lane. He went past, looking out his side window but only seeing the broken guardrail.

Ingram parked around a curve. Camera strapped around his neck, he swung a leg over the guardrail and worked his way down the slope, stepping on the plants arrayed across the hillside. It wasn't too steep here and he was able to get closer to the wreck. There was a uniform there poking around the wreckage but one of the other officers called him back to the roadway. Ingram hung back until he left, then moved forward again.

The Mercury was canted at an angle, the undercarriage visible. The vehicle had come to rest against a stout tree. Ingram started taking pictures of the car. He wasn't eager to see his friend dead inside the car, his neck probably broken from the impact. He managed to get several snaps of the undercarriage, some of them close-ups. As he was sighting again, a voice boomed at him from above.

"Hey, what are you doing down there?"

"Press," Ingram called back to the cop.

"My ass." This officer and two others started toward him.

Ingram turned his back to them. It was now or lose the chance. He forced himself to look inside the car. There was Ben Kinslow, his head turned sideways against the driver's wheel, his open eyes stared into the empty nothing.

Choking back tears, Ingram snapped quick shots of his gone Army buddy. A solid cat who was cool around Black folks because he was a sometimes trumpet player. Or maybe he was cool around Black folks and just happened to play the horn.

"Ain't no reason to blow your top," he remembered

Kinslow saying. "We all put our pants on the same way, don't we, Gate?"

A hand latched onto Ingram's shoulder, turning him around. "Who the fuck are you?"

Ingram showed the cop his credentials.

"Shit," this one said, blond hair at the side of his head showing under his cap. He looked at the other two. "This guy says he's a bona fide newshound."

"Yeah, like Clark Kent?" one of the others said, grinning. "He got an *S* on his chest for Super Spade?"

"That right?" The third one had his nightstick out and poked Ingram with it.

"You can't do that," the photographer said.

Blondie leaned into him. "We can do whatever the fuck we want, Ingram."

"Give us that camera," the one with the nightstick said. This time he tapped the end of the billy club against Ingram's chest.

Ingram handed the camera over. Blondie opened its back roughly.

"Hey, goddammit," Ingram objected.

"Shut up." The nightstick slapped hard against his body, causing Ingram to groan.

The cop pulled the film out of its canister, exposing the roll. He tossed it aside and regarded the camera. "This sumabitch needs to be taught not to nose around in police business."

"He do," the second one agreed.

Blondie said, "Ah, the meat wagon is coming and probably real reporters. I don't want to have to explain why this darkie was all beat to shit, crumpled on the ground whimpering and carrying on."

The other two snickered.

"Have them burr heads in the N double A Coon Patrol all upset and getting them preachers to harangue the captain like last month." The other two laughed some more. Blondie threw the laminated press credentials on the ground, followed by the camera, hurled with force. Several pieces flew off the frame. But the cop wasn't through. He kicked the Speed Graphic, bouncing it off the crashed Mercury.

Ingram wanted to cuss the bastard out but knew he'd get a beating or worse. He'd brought that camera back from the war.

Staring at Ingram evenly, the cop said, "Now get the fuck out of here before I change my mind."

Ingram picked up his broken camera, stuffing the pieces he could find in his pocket, as well as his press credentials.

"Hurry up." Blondie rapped the end of his nightstick against his open palm. "We got important shit to attend to."

Ingram worked his way back up the slope, getting a look at the fresh skid marks where Kinslow's car had taken out the guardrail. He got in the Plymouth. He had half a mind to march back to those crackers swinging a tire iron like Josh Gibson. He could see the headline now in the *Sentinel*: "Crazed Photographer Shot Down Like a Mad Dog."

Angry and sad simultaneously, Ingram wiped tears wetting his face. But he had to hold it together. He started his car and drove back to his place. There was one bit of satisfaction. When he'd had his back turned to the police, he'd switched out the film in his camera for a blank roll. The one with the shots was in his coat pocket. This wasn't the first time Ingram had been braced by the cops over taking snaps where he wasn't invited. Nor was it the first time his favorite camera had been banged around.

Back home, he put the Speed Graphic on the kitchen table, examining the damage with a practiced eye. The front standard was cracked, the lens was broken, a few knobs had been snapped off and the shutter release arm was bent. From a kitchen drawer he took out needle-nosed pliers, a steel screw extractor and several other tools. From the darkroom he came back with a medium-sized cardboard box containing various parts of cameras he'd salvaged over time. Putting on a Nat King Cole Trio album, he got busy repairing the camera. It took the length of playing the A side of a second record, but he got the Speed Graphic back together. To test it he took some shots of his bookshelf, a chair and out the window of passersby on the street below. He even set up the timer to take a couple of shots of himself. The camera was functioning again.

He regretted not getting a shot of one of the cops, especially the one with the billy club. Or, as he'd heard cops referring to it in the past, my "Nigger Be Good Stick." What a great shot it would be, him aiming up from a low angle as a nightstick came thundering down on his face. Now that would get him on the front page of the *Herald Ex* for sure.

Afterward he developed those photos and the ones taken from Kinslow's crash. By habit he made a brief notation on the back of each shot using a soft leaded pencil so as not to create markings in relief on the other side. Often when he made pictures he knew he was going to sell, he'd make two prints. The shots from the accident were for him, though he might try to get one in the *Eagle*.

Sitting at his kitchen table, he used a magnifying glass

to look more closely at the shots he'd taken of the Mercury's undercarriage. When they were in the service, Kinslow, who at one point had been the driver for a general, got the two of them out of an ambush. His friend had been behind the wheel of a jeep and he handled it like he and the vehicle were one. Bullets whistled by them, pinging off the vehicle, but Kinslow didn't lose control as he ducked and dodged mortar holes and ruts in the road. Yeah, that was a decade ago, and maybe Ben had been drinking, but Ingram recalled how Kinslow had handled the Mercury the other night.

Ingram would find out if booze had been in his friend's system. He knew an attendant who worked in the city morgue, prepping bodies for autopsies.

Peering through the magnifying glass, he zeroed in on the brake line where it originated from one of the rear wheel brake drums toward the front of the car and the master cylinder in the engine compartment. He looked closer at a break in the line. Was it severed, or had it pulled apart, causing the crash after the fluid was expelled? Ingram kept staring, unsure of what he was looking at. He needed an expert's eye on this. He might be wanting to see foul play where there was none. He'd show this to his mechanic, Jed Monk.

Staring at Kinslow's face, for the first time he saw the trickle of blood trailing from the corner of his slightly open mouth. It was dark against the stark black-and-white composition. He glared at this for some time, then went to his cupboard and took out a bottle of Jim Beam. It was past four, late enough in the day to have a blast, he reasoned. Hell, he'd earned it. He drank until the sun went down and decided he'd better get something to eat. He walked to a hamburger stand and got a cheeseburger with extra onions and fries. Rather than walk back with his dinner he sat and ate at one of the open-air tables.

At one point a police car rolled by, the white officer in it eyeing him and the other Black patrons. Ingram chewed away as the cop rolled on past. It was then Ingram made up his mind to find out if he was imagining things or if his friend had been purposely silenced. Maybe the police would do a thorough investigation but he owed Kinslow his life; he owed it to him to find out the truth. That time Kinslow had driven them away from certain death, he'd pointed out later, he'd been saving his own butt. That didn't make any difference to Ingram. Because now he was the one left standing. He couldn't bring Kinslow back, but he could find out what happened.

Balling up the paper his burger had been wrapped in, he tossed it away and started back to his apartment. He lit a cigar and puffed as he walked along. The evening was turning cool, but Ingram barely noticed. He paused at a campaign poster for Tom Bradley pasted on a wooden fence.

BRADLEY, THE ONLY CHOICE was in large red, white and blue letters, a semicircle of stars crowning the words.

"Yeah," Ingram muttered, "the only choice."

THE NEXT day Ingram went over to the *Eagle*'s offices on Central Avenue. The newspaper was across the street from the Elk's Hall, where Ingram had enjoyed sets by jazz musicians over the years. He had a fond memory of being lubricated there before shipping out to the Army, listening to long tall Dexter Gordon coaxing bittersweet ballads out of his sax. Ingram had written up a brief piece to go with a few of the shots of the crash he showed to the managing editor, Wesley Crossman. The middle-aged bachelor worked at the newspaper and did freelance work for various publications such as *Jet* and a magazine called *Dapper*.

The latter publication was white-owned but intended for a Black male readership. The articles ranged from the lurid—"Mary Had to Pistol Whip Her Deaf Husband"—to ones about the appointment of a Black judge or a profile of the teacher of the year. Ingram had done words and pictures for *Dapper* as well. Though it was by no means as rugged as *Stag* or revealing as *Playboy*, Ingram had done a few cheesecake pictorials of pretty Black women for the magazine along with other work.

"I don't know, Harry. It's not like we don't run pieces about white people, but you know it's usually about our allies, like Governor Brown or Supervisor Hahn."

The two sat at Crossman's compact desk in his compact office off the equally modest newsroom. Several reporters clacked away on typewriters, the smell of stale cigarette smoke hanging in the air.

"I understand he was a friend of yours," Crossman was saying. There was a well-used pipe in a worn pipe rack along with several piles of edited copy and file folders on the desk.

"I get it, Ben was unknown," Ingram said flatly.

"Look, if we need some filler, maybe I can run this photo." His finger tapped the shot Ingram had taken from above the tipped-on-its-side Mercury. "But I'm not promising anything."

Ingram stood. "I appreciate it, Wes. Whatever you can do."

He left, then set out to locate where his dead friend had been staying. He called the musician's union pretending he wanted the horn player for a gig. But Kinslow hadn't re-registered upon his return to town so that got Ingram nowhere. That also meant it was unlikely he'd be able to get a piece run on Kinslow in their newsletter.

Ingram then drove over to the Crystal Tea Room on Santa Barbara, where Kinslow had played a few times back when last he lived in L.A. That was about four years earlier. The club wasn't open yet. Next he drove out to Mission Road, where the morgue was located on the same grounds as General Hospital. His contact, Somerset, was on duty, and for a five spot told Ingram that Kinslow's body was there. He was an older, gray-haired white man with stooped shoulders.

"Any arrangements for which mortuary he'll be sent to?" Ingram asked.

"So far, none that I know of."

"Can I see what was in his pockets and glove box?"

"Christ, Harry, ask much, do you?"

Ingram produced another five.

"Make it quick. I ain't losing my job over your amateur hour Dick Tracy foolishness."

Somerset led Ingram past several corpses on gurneys lining the hallway to a plain room. Inside were file cabinets. They had index cards taped on each drawer in alphabetical order and he pulled open the appropriate one.

"Don't try and leave with nothing. They'll know." With that Somerset walked out.

Ingram understood if he was caught, he was on his own. In a paper bag, neatly folded over like it held a lunch, Ingram looked through Kinslow's effects: keys on a ring, an assortment of papers. There was a small key, like for a padlock, and Ingram slipped it off the ring and put it in his pocket. He found a rent receipt with someone's name other than Kinslow's on it. No address but it was better than nothing. He wrote down the name and considered taking the rest of the keys but sure enough those cops who rousted him would remember putting them in the bag. He closed the drawer just as an attendant in a blood-smeared smock entered.

"Hey, how you doing?" Ingram said off-handedly as he headed toward the door.

The attendant frowned at him as Ingram kept going.

CHAPTER FOUR

Ingram looked through the For Rent section of the *L.A. Times* going back a month, searching for the name signed on the receipt, Ernestine Morrison. Scanning the past issues on the library's newly installed microfiche reader, he didn't find the name related to a property. He then figured he might as well try the *California Eagle* and *Sentinel,* given his deceased friend's open-mindedness. Kinslow might have wanted an apartment that was walking distance to a couple of the Black-oriented clubs where he could sit in on a jam session or two. Those archives couldn't be found here but at the respective papers' offices. Nor were they preserved on film but bound hard copies he had to leaf through. He headed back to the *Sentinel.*

"Find what you're looking for, Harry?" Margaret Hutson asked him. She was a small-boned light-skinned Black woman with gray eyes who, Ingram knew from experience, could curse with the best of them if provoked. She ran the paper's Want Ads department.

"Not yet, but ... hold on, looks like you brought me luck." He tapped a listing for a room for rent on Van Buren Place. The contact name was E. Morrison.

Hutson laughed good-naturedly. "Tell that to my two exes."

Ingram wrote down the address and phone number and drove over to the house, a two-story clapboard affair that needed a paint job but looked comfortable and homey. Seems his friend had been rooming in a Black neighborhood. Now the question was how could he get in to look over Kinslow's room? Had the police already been here? Would the lady of the house be on guard?

He walked up to the front door as a man was exiting.

"Is Miss Morrison around?" he asked.

"It's Missus and she works until six or so. You want to rent a room?"

"I do," he lied. "I guess I'll come back later."

"I can take your name and number if you like."

"That's okay, I'd like to see the room first."

"They're nice, plus Sunday dinner is included. She makes a mean fried catfish, friend." The man adjusted his fedora and shut the door behind him, walking away.

Ingram also pretended to leave but circled back to try the front door. It was locked. He went down the driveway to the kitchen door on the side of the house. That was also locked. But behind the building, a window had been left cracked open. He used his penknife to carefully remove the screen and pushed the sash up. He climbed in, wondering who might be in the house at this time of day and what the hell he would tell them if he got caught.

Ingram had let himself into a bedroom, but a quick glance told him this was an older man's room, what with small round tins of Doan's Pills and bottles of Ben Gay on the dresser. He quit the room, entering a short hallway, several doors on either side. He tried one and it was locked. At another, he heard someone snoring on the other side.

Instinct suggested he try upstairs. Here was what he was looking for.

There was a police padlock and hasp on the door, with a posted flyer warning not to enter. Just to make sure, he tried the padlock key he'd found on Kinslow's ring, but it didn't fit this lock. From his car, he got a screwdriver, and using the kitchen door he'd unlocked, re-entered the boarding house. He unscrewed the hasp enough to allow him entry. The door itself wasn't locked.

Standing upright on the dresser was the horn case Ingram remembered seeing the other night. He eased the door shut and began looking around. He wondered, had the police gone through Kinslow's digs? It seemed in addition to the horn, his other items had been left here. But then, if they'd already concluded it was an accident, what would they take? Ingram would check with Somerset about the possibility of liquor in his friend's system.

On the dresser was an opened envelope with the name Shirley Kinslow and a return address in Kansas City. Ingram was pretty certain this was Kinslow's mother. The police would have informed her of what happened. He wrote down her information, intending to call her. He went through the drawers, coming up blank. The closet contained only a few of Kinslow's jackets. Inside one of the pockets he found two handwritten notes on index cards, contact information for the clubs the Totten Hot and the Crystal Tea Room.

He kept nosing around. At one point he opened the horn case, taking out the trumpet. He looked it over as if it might contain a vestige of his now-dead friend. If somehow he were capable of coaxing music out of the instrument, the melody might conjure up the spirit of Ben Kinslow.

Except for the door, there was nothing that had a padlock on it.

There on the nightstand was a photo of the squad from back in Korea. It was leaning in an inexpensive drugstore frame. Ingram picked it up, a rueful smile on his face as he looked at the dogfaces in the shot. Were they really that young then? Every battle, every push to take higher ground, had aged them years in weeks. Looking at the photo he realized it must have been taken by Milo Costas, the man from *Look* assigned to document various squads. But Costas didn't make it to another detachment. He died right next to Ingram on a winter day, snow up to their calves and a blinding white sheet of an icy wind tormenting them along with enemy fire.

Sitting on the bed, Ingram was carried back, the only clear sounds the howl of the wind and ice tap-tapping against their helmets. That gale increased in his ears and Ingram got lost in grief and fury.

"Pardon me, but what are you doing here?"

He looked up to see a woman in a crisp linen outfit and a hat at a clever angle standing in the doorway. He must not have shut it properly. Shit. Be cool, baby, he told himself.

"I was a friend of Ben Kinslow."

"Is that right?"

"It is. I'm trying to find out a few things about him."

"You just said you were his friend."

"We were in the service together. He lived out here for a while, then went away about four years ago. I saw him again in town just a few days ago."

"Before the accident," she said. "I overheard the policeman talking to Mrs. Morrison."

Ingram didn't respond. He rose, holding out the photo for her to take. She did. "That's me, second from the left."

She looked from the picture to Ingram then back again. "Yeah, that does look like you. And I recognize Ben too."

"You were friends with him?" Ingram asked.

"He was a friendly guy."

"Yes, he was."

"Look, I've got to get to work and I probably shouldn't leave you here."

"Sure, I understand." As he edged past her, he took the photo back.

"What did you say your name was?"

He told her who he was and what he did for a living.

"Would I have seen your work in the *Sentinel*?"

"I covered that incident on McKinley recently."

Her eyes got wide. "Oh my, you're that kind of photographer. Showing that man's head caved in after his wife hit him with an iron." She shook her head. "Don't you want to take more, I don't know, civilized sort of pictures? Like graduations and successful people being honored?"

He shrugged. "I don't know, I guess I find that sort of stuff ordinary. Anybody can take those kinds of shots."

"You seem like a nice fella, but have you considered that the kind of death and mayhem you shoot further brings our race down?"

"I don't just take shots of colored folks cuttin' up. Plenty of white people show up in my pictures too."

By her expression it was clear that wasn't a satisfactory response.

"I'm looking to cover Reverend King when he's here," he added.

"That's a start." She snorted. "May God guide you on the right path, Mr. Ingram."

"Yes, ma'am."

As he walked back to his car, it occurred to him he'd sold two publications those pictures he'd taken of the aftermath of the domestic squabble on McKinley. The *Sentinel* had run only one, the wife who'd brained her husband being led away in tears by the police. The more gruesome photos, including the laid-out husband after the iron had gone upside his head, those had run in *Dapper*. Ingram's shots were included in their Crime Calendar section. Since the shot she referred to only ran in the magazine, could be she wasn't as proper as she put on, he surmised.

He drove over to the Four Aces auto repair and showed the shots of the Mercury's undercarriage to Jed Monk. Monk was also over six feet, solidly built with a trim mustache and a baritone voice. He wore a grease-stained gray work shirt and matching khakis. His shop was called Four Aces on account of the fact that he'd won the lease in a poker game.

They sat in his office off the service bay. Monk had also been in Korea but the two didn't know each other then. Ingram told the mechanic about Kinslow as the latter peered through a magnifying glass he'd gotten out of his desk drawer to examine the pictures.

"Honestly, Harry, I can't say for certain I see what you see." Magnifying glass set aside, he put a finger on the photo where the brake line had separated from the rotor. "If you look closer, you can see some frayed trailings from the end of the line. The line could have been ripped loose on impact."

"Could the line have been partially cut into? Whoever did it knowing it would eventually pull apart because of the pressure of the brake fluid pumping through it?"

Monk shook out a Lucky Strike, first offering one to Ingram, who declined. "Yeah, but there'd be a leak from the line when the car was parked. Maybe not big drops but still."

"You being a mechanic, you might notice that, but what if you weren't a mechanic?"

Monk blew smoke out. "Plus, there's the brakes themselves.

I mean you go to apply the pedal and they wouldn't hold, or you'd have to pump the pedal several times to make them hold. You don't have to be no grease monkey to know something's up. And if you knew that, you sure as shit wouldn't be taking that car up a climb like Mulholland with those curves." He sat back with his cigarette, watching the smoke climb toward the ceiling. He then said, "But if I wanted to take out the brakes, figuring I couldn't be crawling up under a car parked somewhere, I'd pop the hood and use a screwdriver to punch a hole in the master cylinder."

Ingram nodded. "So even if you put on the emergency brake, you still might lose control."

"Maybe." Monk pushed the pictures back toward Ingram.

"I hear you, Jed. I appreciate this."

"Why do you think there was something funny about how he died?"

"I guess it was what he told me. That big things were about to happen for him."

Monk shook his head. "That could mean anything, like he was going to get a better job."

"Yeah," Ingram agreed. "But from the way he talked, it didn't seem to have anything to do with music. At least, not directly."

"I don't know, man. I do know a good driver is only as good as his vehicle," Monk said.

Ingram was on his feet. "I hear you, thanks." They shook hands.

"Let me know when you got your next domino-and-beer night going on. I haven't played any bones in a month of Sundays."

"I will."

Back home Ingram got listings for two Shirley Kinslows from the directory and called them. The first one wasn't Ben's mother. The second number rang several times but wasn't picked up.

He called the morgue and found out Somerset wasn't on duty today. He paced about in his front room, feeling stymied, out of sorts. Maybe he was making this all up in his head to what, avenge his friend when in fact his car hadn't been tampered with? He stopped, hands on his hips, trying to recall the name of the man Kinslow had been driving for. Hoyt, was it? Had there been a first name mentioned? No, there hadn't. Who was he and could he be tied into this, if there was anything to be tied into?

Ingram rubbed the back of his neck. Was he jumping through hoops of his own making? Certainly he could be, but that didn't mean he shouldn't be thorough. He'd try to find out who this Hoyt was if only to satisfy himself that he hadn't ignored any possible angles.

He tried to occupy his mind by fixing an elaborate lunch—elaborate by his standards, meaning more than just a sandwich and a bottle of beer. But halfway through preparing a dish of macaroni and cheese to go along with a pork chop he meant to fry up, he lost interest. He needed to get out, to do something to get at whatever it was that was eating at him.

It occurred to him he knew who could find out about the disposition of Kinslow's body. He supposed he'd put off asking because he didn't want to seem like he was taking advantage of a friend. But then what were friends for? He dialed Josh Nakano.

"Eternal Sands," said a woman's modulated voice.

Ingram asked for his friend and she asked who he was. He was then connected.

"What's up, Harry?"

Ingram explained what he wanted. "If it means I have to

pay to have his body picked up by you, Josh, that's okay, but see if you can find out what the coroner's report says."

"You mean like alcohol or drugs in his bloodstream?"

"Yes, and was there any, you know, bruising on his body."

"He was in a car accident, you said."

"I mean inconsistent with the crash."

"I'll see. I think I've got all the particulars I need. I'll be back in touch."

"Thanks, man."

After hanging up, Ingram sat there for a few minutes, but he couldn't relax. He got up and turned on one of his scanners, listening. He stood there, slightly hunched, ear toward the speaker in anticipation. Various alerts from dispatchers were made, and responses to them came in from patrol cars over the airwaves. The incidents were ordinary, a traffic bang-up with two vehicles, a man locked out of his house and so on. He turned the scanner off.

With nothing else to occupy his mind, he took up his favored Speed Graphic and went out. He walked around his neighborhood, taking a few snaps of people going about their everyday activities. Ingram continued walking for several miles and eventually was in the Crenshaw area around Exposition and Muirfield Road, near Dorsey High School. Ingram recalled meeting a fellow vet, a man named Julian Dixon, at a function not too long ago. He was a few years younger than Ingram and had been in the service toward the end of the fifties. Dixon had mentioned he'd attended Dorsey and was contemplating a career in elected office to better advance the negro agenda.

Maybe that's what he should get, Ingram thought. An agenda—a more defined plan for what he wanted to do. Not that he was going to give up taking pictures, but if he wanted to crack the white magazine market, he should work more toward what they wanted to see. Or could be what he should do was put together his best shots and try to get a deal to do a coffee table book.

Contemplating this, Ingram was mid-block on Hillcrest when he saw a man in well-used coveralls heading toward a modest house, carrying lumber under an arm. His battered Ford pickup truck was parked at the curb. There were all sorts of materials and tools in the bed of the pickup.

"Hey you," said a voice. It came from a police car that had pulled to a stop in the middle of the street. A white cop was addressing the Black repairman.

"Yes, sir," said the handyman.

"Put that shit down and come over here," the officer demanded.

The man did as he was told, laying the studs on the lawn. Standing several feet away, Ingram began taking pictures. He kept the camera down on his torso, sighting through the viewfinder from above.

"What are you up to?"

"Fixing a few things in Sister Armar's home."

"Sister? You her brother?"

"We belong to the same church is what I mean."

"There's been some burglaries around here. You could be faking this repairman business. Good cover a shifty colored like you could use to get away with who knows what." He glared at him up and down. "You got some ID?"

"Yes, I do." He began to reach for his wallet.

"Hey, what the fuck you doing?" The cop shoved his car door open, nearly hitting the other man with it. He was out on his feet, hand on the butt of his holstered revolver.

"Getting my identification like you asked, Officer."

"You were reaching for that hammer."

"What? No." There was a claw hammer in a loop of the coveralls.

The gun was out now, aimed at his chest. "Don't you back talk me, boy."

"He wasn't. He was answering your question."

Both men turned their heads, seeing Ingram for the first time.

"Who the hell are you?" demanded the cop.

"A member of the press." Ingram couldn't help but hear the cop's drawl. Police Chief William Parker actively recruited white officers from the Jim Crow South, running ads in various regional newspapers down there. The better to keep the natives in line, he reflected.

"Yeah, you look just like Edward R. Murrow," the cop huffed.

"Want to see my ID?" Ingram held his hands away from his body, the camera hanging around his neck. "As you can see, I don't have a hammer."

The cop's lips puckered like he was sucking on a lime. "Goddamn, is today negro sass day?"

"The man was just doing his job is all," Ingram said.

The cop still had his gun out, but it was down at his side. Coming closer to Ingram he said, "I suppose you take a lot of pictures with that thing, yeah?" He tapped the barrel of the gun against the camera.

"Everywhere I can, Officer."

"Get printed, do they?"

"In the *Eagle* and the *Sentinel*."

"Figures." The cop sneered.

"Even in the *Herald Ex* from time to time."

"That right?"

"It is."

The officer now tapped the gun against his uniformed

thigh. "Both of you, let me see those IDs. Put them on the hood of my car." The cop took another position so as to be behind both men as they complied with his orders. Ingram and the handyman looked at each other silently.

"Now go sit there, on the curb. Make sure you sit on your hands and don't neither of you fucking twitch."

Ingram was about to object but followed the command, like the other man.

The cop unclipped his microphone from the car's two-way radio and called in the particulars on their driver's licenses, asking of course for any wants or warrants. He replaced the microphone, waiting for the reply. He leaned on the driver's side door, arms in front of him, holding the revolver. In this way he kept his eyes on the other two. A few people walked by. Eventually came the reply from dispatch.

"Are you sure?" the officer said upon hearing neither one had an outstanding ticket or other matter involving law enforcement. He replaced the microphone after the confirmation was repeated. He walked over, looking down on them. "Guess you two got lucky today." He tossed their licenses at them, the paper cards fluttering in the wind. Instinctively the handyman was about to make a sudden move to try to catch his. Ingram clamped a hand on his arm for him to remain still. He looked up at the cop who glared at him unblinkingly. The driver's licenses lay in the roadway several feet away.

"Keep your noses clean." The cop got back in his car and drove away.

Finally Ingram and the other man stood, dusting off the seats of their pants.

"Mister, if you hadn't been here with that camera, things sure could have gone worse with that cracker. I'm Deon but they call me Deets."

"Hell of a way to live, ain't it?" Ingram introduced himself as they shook hands.

"I'm just glad I can finish what I started." He picked up the wood and went back into the house.

Ingram felt elated, having achieved a minor victory in his confrontation with the cop. He took a bus back to his apartment and made a double-decker sandwich for his late lunch, early dinner. He then went back out, this time with a specific destination in mind. He stepped inside the Lucky Clover tavern on Broadway. The bar was originally built here as the location was a terminus for the Yellow Car trolley. Unlike the Red Car, which served the interurban area, the Yellow Car operated inside the city, with downtown the center. There were a few trollies still in operation but the transportation department had announced those too would be mothballed by year's end. The name of the watering hole was straightforward. But as the freeways came to dominate and define Southern California, patrons who'd been coming to the bar for years routinely called it the Cloverleaf, as in the crisscrossing patterns of the region's many elevated freeways.

Sam Cooke's "Twistin' the Night Away" was playing on the jukebox as Ingram sat on a stool at the bar. People laughed and conversed. Ingram liked the place. The atmosphere was inviting, as a neighborhood joint should be.

"Haven't seen you in a while, Harry," the barman, Clyde Hampton, said. He was a barrel-chested man with salt-and-pepper hair. Hampton wiped down the bar with a flourish. "You been on the wagon?"

"Not hardly. Gimme a beer—no, make that a rum and Coke."

"Been that kind of day?"

"Damn right."

"Cuba libre coming right up."

Soon the barman returned with his drink and Ingram drank slowly, realizing there was tension in his shoulders, a residue of his encounter with the cop today. There were Black cops on the force but why the hell was it the white ones he always seemed to encounter? Surely, sitting here in a bar with "Luck" in its name, some of that had to rub off on him, didn't it? He sniffed, having more of his rum and Coke, relaxing some.

"Hey, GI, you lonely tonight?"

Ingram had been staring at a napkin with the bar's name on it. Now his head jerked up.

"Who said that?"

He glared at men and women, couples and those sitting by themselves. Little Eva was singing "Loco-motion" on the juke.

But that woman's voice.

He wheeled back around on his stool and chalked it up to his nerves. The welcome alcohol warmed his insides. He had more, already considering another round.

"I know you're cold out there."

Ingram bolted off the stool, nearly knocking it over.

"Hey, man," the customer next to him blared.

"Goddamn, that was Seoul City Sue," Ingram muttered. He wiped his wet tongue over his dry lips as he went in search of the voice that used to broadcast to tired soldiers on those bitter-cold winter nights by the Naktong River. He looked hard at various female faces, some of them staring back at the possessed man. But this was a Black bar. Occasionally there might be a white or Asian person in here; it wasn't unheard of for city department clerks or typists to come in here with coworkers. But there were no white faces in here tonight, and, as he'd told Ben Kinslow,

Ingram had seen a photo of the woman they'd called Seoul City Sue.

Though what if those pics he'd seen in the magazine had been more propaganda from the enemy? What if it was a trick by the Red Chinese, the backers of North Korea? They might have set the whole thing up, duping the press as part of their plan. Hadn't they perfected what was called brain-washing, using psychological methods to break the will? Making a person do things they wouldn't normally do under their own steam? It wasn't so crazy to think the commie might have a reporter or two in their pocket. White bread–eating white Americans who'd been given the whammy and even they didn't know they were under orders from Peking. Wasn't that the plot of the movie he and Strummer had seen last year, *The Manchurian Candidate*? POWs reconditioned to carry out deep-seated orders planted in their minds. There had been a scene where one of the GIs was ordered to strangle another captive.

Ingram sat back down at a different position at the bar. He was aware eyes were on him, including Hampton's. Be cool, he advised himself. Don't blow your top. If he next started seeing that child from Chorwa village walking up to him, they'd carry him off to the loony bin for sure.

"Everything okay, Harry?" Hampton was there in front of him.

"Yeah, just winding down is all." He shook his glass, knocking the ice around. "Give me another, would ya?"

"Coming up."

On alert, Ingram was poised to hear Sue speak again but there were no other words from her. Must be a screw loose in his addled brain. Was he under too much strain? Cobbling together a living chasing photos of people doing bad things to each other with the occasional process server job sprinkled in, always unwelcomed when he showed up bringing unwanted news. Maybe he ought to sell shoes or refrigerators. A job bringing smiles to faces.

What had that guy Deets said? If Harry hadn't happened along today, it might have gone way different with the police. Ingram nodded. That was something to hold onto.

After finishing his second drink, ignoring the nervous glances of the other patrons, he paid his tab and left the Lucky Clover. On his way home, he hunched his sport coat around his shoulders against the cool of the evening. Seoul City Sue didn't call to him from an alleyway or from a passing car. The ghost of a hungry and scared nine-year-old didn't materialize in front of him. Even the cops left him alone. A weariness from more than the day's activities had overcome him by the time he got inside his apartment. He sat in his favorite chair and fell asleep.

Sometime past three in the morning Ingram awoke. He pulled a bottle from his cupboard and poured a drink. He stripped down to his boxers and A-shirt and stretched out in bed, yawning. Try as he might, he couldn't get back to sleep. He turned on his portable GE transistor radio, the one item in his apartment purchased in this decade. He didn't find anything of interest on the AM band, so he switched over to FM. He turned the dial with the precision of a safe cracker, its glow on his fixed features the only illumination in his bedroom. Ingram came upon a soothing woman's voice. She didn't remind him of Seoul City Sue, therefore he didn't turn away. This was on a station at the end of the dial with the call letters KPFK. It was run by a bunch of peace lovers and vegetarians, Ingram recalled, amused.

The woman was talking about Eastern religion, in particular something called the chakras. Apparently there were seven main ones in your body, invisible wheels of energy you could enliven with proper meditation techniques. It was all gibberish to Ingram but as he lay there sipping cheap whiskey, he did enjoy the music she started playing once she was done talking. It was from an album called *Hypnotique* by a man named Korla Pandit. He was playing exotic music with a soulful resonance on a Hammond B3 organ, accompanied on a few of the numbers by a guitarist. Ingram knew a secret about the so-called Pandit that Johnny Otis had told him once. Pandit was really a Black man, John Redd. Otis became Black and Redd became the exotic other, both crossing a color line for their own reasons. He chuckled softly, floating along with the melody, not quite awake but not asleep either. Whether he got in touch with one or more of his chakras, he couldn't say.

CHAPTER FIVE

An informal repast for Ben Kinslow was held at the Crystal Tea Room. His mother didn't attend. She and her sister had made prior arrangements, and his body was taken back by rail to Kansas City, where there'd be a service and burial.

"Mr. Ingram, we want to thank you so much for all you've done," Winnifred Stewart had said to him over the phone two days earlier. She was Kinslow's aunt.

"It was the least I could do for him, ma'am."

"Yes, I understand you two were in the war together, the same squad. He'd mentioned you more than a little when he was back here visiting. He always was, I don't know, interested in a lot of things. Like that horn of his. Nobody in our immediate family can play a note yet he'd sit there when he was a kid listening to those jazz musicians. It is a kind of tradition around here, I guess. The jazz, I mean. Anyway, one day I came over and he was sitting in a chair figuring out notes on a secondhand horn Shirley bought him." She paused, remembering her nephew. "He kept at it until he willed himself to get good."

"He was one of a kind, that's for sure. Did he mention anything to you about this Mr. Hoyt he was driving for?"

"No," she drawled on the other end of the line, then added, "oh wait, hold on, will you?" She returned a few moments later, picking up the handset. "I thought I recognized the name when you said it," she said. "A Winston Hoyt sent a lovely wreath for Ben. I wrote down the names of people who sent flowers to thank them. Do you know him?"

"No, I don't. I was just asking is all. Did he have a return address?"

"He did not. In his case it was through the florist. Did you want to talk to him about Ben?"

"Just filling in the blanks. It's not important." They'd talked for a few more minutes and she'd promised to send him a program from the service before they ended their call. After he hung up he took a moment, glad about this gathering honoring his friend.

Ingram milled about, the conversations ranging from the three Black men running for City Council to a recent occurrence in which a mixed-race couple had their home shot into in Santa Monica—an incident covered in the Black papers but which got no mention in the *L.A. Times,* and only a paragraph in the *Herald Examiner.* Given that those gathered today were Blacks and whites, who not only hung out with each other but in some instances dated across racial lines, what happened in the beach town of Santa Monica was of keen interest.

Ingram had come early to help set up. Strummer Edwards was there, as he'd known Kinslow through Ingram. Arthur Yarbrough was also in attendance. He'd been in a different company than Ingram and Kinslow, but part of the larger battalion. Ingram had one of his cameras with him, a compact Canon model he could wield effortlessly.

Several local musicians attended, including Johnny Otis and bass and tuba player Red Callender, who did a goodly amount of studio work. Ingram and a few others had chipped in and there was a spread of light foods and beverages, including wine and beer. Along the walls were candid shots of the various musicians who'd performed at the venue, including the six-foot-six saxophonist Dexter Gordon, an L.A. native, and pianist and singer Carmen McRea. Ingram proudly noted more than one of those pictures had been taken by him.

"Nice turnout." Edwards munched on a handful of peanuts.

"What are those lyrics by Cab Calloway in 'St. James Infirmary'?" Yarbrough asked. The three sat together at a small table.

Edwards swallowed. "Something about laying him out with a twenty-dollar gold piece on his watch chain so the boys know he died standing pat."

"And a Stetson hat on his head," Ingram added.

Yarbrough smiled. "That's how I want to go, gents. I got one with a red feather. Use that one on my head, okay?" He had two pairs of dark glasses, one set he wore around the store and this pair, the lenses in a more stylish frame, which he wore to occasions such as this.

Ingram patted his shoulder. "I'll make sure, Arthur."

"You do that."

At some point Ingram and Edwards wandered over to where a few of the musicians who'd brought their instruments along were discussing what songs to play at the wake, or whether they should just go for an improvisational set. Yarbrough too was up and talking to a woman in high-waisted toreador pants and pale silk top.

"Hey, Strummer, in your various travels you ever run across a white man named Winston Hoyt?" Ingram described the man briefly. "Ben was driving for him and he owns a racehorse out there at Hollywood Park. That means he's got dough."

"You know the name of the nag?"

"No, but I can find out."

"Not necessary, just wondering. Let me ask around. Why you interested in this cat?"

Ingram was reluctant to share his notions about Kinslow possibly having been murdered. Far as he could tell, the police had closed off any further investigation, ruling his death an accident.

"I could be just barking at the moon, Strummer, but Ben dying so soon after he got back to town, I don't know." He lifted a shoulder.

"Okay, let me see."

"Righteous."

The afternoon progressed. As the musicians were ready to begin, Ingram asked if he could say a few words.

"Go on, man." Edwards clapped him on the back.

"Yeah, Harry," Yarbrough added. The woman in the toreador pants stood next to him.

Ingram breathed in deep, placing his camera atop a built-in shelf.

"Well, look," Ingram began, stepping onto the raised stage where the musicians waited. He held several index cards with his notes on them. "I'm nobody's preacher who can sermonize, sending off the dead properly. I could talk about going to hear Ben wail on his horn at the clubs around here or just having a beer together. But I wanted to talk about how we became friends. Like what me and Arthur there went through"—he indicated the grocer with a nod—"Ben and I didn't know each other before we were drafted and thrown into the police action, they called it. But once the shooting started, we damn sure had to depend on each other to get out of there with the skin on our backs or"—acknowledging his friend's blindness—"as whole as we could manage it."

The woman touched Yarbrough's arm.

"Now that's not that unusual for a colored man and a white man to know each other, as you all know in here. But we also know in the bigger world, well, a lot of times you got second and third looks. And not just from the ofays," he said, earning some nervous laughter. "For a whole lot of reasons most of you know, Truman integrated the armed services a couple of years before Korea jumped off. And even then when the fighting started, there were still all-Black units like the Twenty-fourth Infantry Regiment, the Buffalo Soldiers going back to the Civil War days." A few heads nodded among the assembled.

Ingram paused, studying his cards. "Look, I'm not going to go on about how it was between the Black and white soldiers. Some of you were there even before, in World War II. Hell, a lot of times more blood was spilled in the fighting in the barracks or in the mess hall than on the battlefield."

"Tell it," Edwards said.

Ingram tucked his index cards away. "The thing is, me and Ben went through the meat grinder and came out the other end. Stuck in the same foxhole or icy trench, crawling on our bellies trying not to freeze up from fear as the shooting went on all around us, you get to know a cat. Hunkered down in the dark together, smoking and talking or running for your life as bullets whizzed by, or eating lousy C rations and waiting for the next blastoff." He saw Kinslow in uniform, smiling. "It was tooth and nail, baby. We went in strangers and came out as two guys who respected each other as men, as soldiers. I can't say that's equality, unless you count the reds as equal opportunity killers. But for us, for then and now it was enough. Here's to Ben." Ingram raised his cup.

"To Ben," was said in unison, raising their cups too as the gathered toasted the deceased.

"To the soldiers who sacrificed," Edwards said, tipping his glass toward Yarbrough.

"Amen," Ingram said, also tipping his glass toward the grocer.

"Way to go, brother," Johnny Otis said as Ingram came off the stage.

"Thanks, man."

"You knocked it out the park, Harry," Strummer Edwards told him, grabbing him by the shoulder. "Straight from the heart."

"Too bad it ain't like that the country over," Yarbrough said.

"I heard that."

After several more congratulations, Ingram stepped outside to light a cigar. People were smoking cigarettes inside, yet he'd found ordinary smokers were often offended by stogies. Imagine that. He stood in front of the club facing Santa Barbara Avenue. Pedestrians and cars and trucks came and went. Ingram began walking, blowing streams of smoke on this warm, clear day. He had a destination in mind, and he went into the Owl drugstore to use the pay phone.

"Hello," he said when the line connected. "Is Anita Claire available?" At the party she'd given him both her home number and the one to the Bradley campaign offices. It was only a moment before she came on the line.

"Hello, Anita, it's Harry. I hope I didn't catch you at a busy time."

"It's always busy getting out the vote, Mr. Ingram. You sound upbeat."

"Funny that I do. I'm at a sendoff for a buddy of mine from the war."

"I'm sorry, Harry."

"No, it's okay. I feel good even though he's gone. I think part of it is he was the first white man I got to know as a person, not just some joker staring at me for being Black, about to try and put me in my place, you know?"

"I know exactly what you mean."

"Look, I don't want to hang you up at work. How about dinner Thursday night?"

"I'd say yes but sometimes they got us on the chain gang late."

"Sure, I understand."

"Call me around five on Thursday and we'll figure it out."

"For sure. See you soon."

"Bye, Harry."

She rang off and Ingram got off the seat in the booth, buoyed by the possibility of seeing her again. Maybe there was a hink in his head. A bullet had unknowingly ricocheted off his thick skull back in Korea, short-circuiting his thinking. He should be melancholy at his friend's wake yet here he was, eager to make time with this dynamite chick. What if, he reasoned as he sauntered back toward the Crystal Tea Room, it was death that made you embrace life so much stronger? You needed to connect to someone to know there was more to you than a few words said over your corpse.

Ruminating on this, Ingram happened to look across the street, noting the Dodge Polara parked there. He'd seen it on his way into the drugstore but hadn't paid it any attention other than noting he liked the car's styling. He'd looked at a used one not too long ago on a lot, thinking about trading in his Belvedere.

This time, though, he checked out the two white men sitting in the car. The windows were halfway down, and cigarette smoke trailed upward from the interior through the gaps on either side. There were a few smoked butts lying on the ground below the driver's side door as well. They weren't no musicians. Cops, he wondered? Yet as he moved past, his instinct was they weren't cops either. The fancy hat the driver wore had him thinking this. But cops wore nice hats, didn't they? Was he again fantasizing there was more to Ben's death than the obvious?

Whatever, he memorized their license plate and went back inside the club. Onstage the musicians were playing and in the spirit of Ben Kinslow, one of them was taking a trumpet solo. People in the crowd were smiling and bopping their heads.

"Got a pen?" Ingram said to Edwards, who stood off to the side.

"Here." He produced one with a tire company logo on the barrel.

"Thanks," Ingram said as he wrote the plate number down on a napkin, tucking it away afterward.

"What's that about?"

"Nothing, maybe."

"Man, you getting all Johnny Dollar?"

"Not sure. Could be chasing my tail."

"As long as you don't catch it. Then you'd really be going in circles."

Ingram picked up the camera he'd left on the shelf and headed toward the kitchen, which was closed down for this afternoon, and let himself out the back into a small parking area. His car was here and rummaging in his photographer's leather bag in the trunk, he got a telescopic lens out and attached it to the Canon. He then walked along the alleyway and came to a break between two buildings. Down this snug passageway he went. As he'd mapped out in his head, he was now back to the avenue a few cars down from where the Polaris was parked.

He didn't step out onto the sidewalk as he didn't want to be seen. He sighted and took several clicks of the two sitting and talking in the car. A dark shape loomed, blocking his shot.

"What are you up to?" It was an older woman in a sun hat, tugging a cart with groceries in it.

"Just taking a few snaps is all, ma'am."

"Yeah, you a peeping Tom? A pervert? God will judge you, young man." She wagged a finger at him.

If this kept up, she was sure to attract attention. "The Lord sent me on this mission," he blustered. "Pastor's worried about one of his flock falling in with the wrong company."

"What, is that so?" She looked over her shoulder.

He pointed across the street. "In that window up there, on the second floor."

"Is that so?" she said in a hushed tone. She turned around to look where he'd indicated. By the time she turned back he was walking away. "Hey, wait, I can help you. I've delivered many a sinner," she called at his back.

Ingram returned to the club and got a beer, sat and listened to the music until the repast broke up about forty-five minutes later. "All right, thanks for coming out," Ingram said as he shook hands with the trumpeter. "Great set."

"Man, it's what he deserved," the musician said.

Ingram and Edwards helped put away the folding chairs and straightened up the place before they too went out front. The photographer saw that the Polaris was gone.

"Okay, Harry, I'll see what I can find on this guy you asked me about."

"Thanks, Strummer. Catch you later, Arthur."

"For sure, Harry." Yarbrough exchanged a good-bye with

the woman he'd been talking to. She kissed him on the cheek and walked away.

Yarbrough left with Edwards. The blind man had his white cane with him but held onto Edwards's upper arm as the two walked to the Chrysler parked on the next block. The vehicle was a late-model 300G with modest fins, white wall tires and fender skirts. Edwards piloted the dark blue automobile past the Crystal Tea Room, waving at Ingram, who stood out front.

Ingram remained where he was for several moments, wondering who he might ask to get a name to go with the license plate of the Dodge. He knew a few lawyers. They would probably have to file some sort of paperwork—how would he justify it? Well—he crafted his argument as he got behind the wheel of his car—there were a couple of suspicious ofays out front of this here colored jazz spot and we wanted to know what they was up to, Your Honor. He supposed, as he pulled out into the light traffic, he could go to Motor Vehicles and claim it was a hit-and-run. A bystander had given him the plate number and he was trying to locate the driver for insurance purposes. If he did that, it probably also meant signing a piece of paper.

He didn't flinch when it came to putting his camera in a cop's face or duking it out with chumps like the one he'd served, but once you put your name to some sort of official paperwork, man, that could come back to bite you in the ass—who knew when or how. If it was proved or even suggested he was lying, could be a reason to pull his press credentials and that meant no steak or chops in his freezer. And he'd gotten in the habit of eating what he wanted. No, the more he could do this on the hush-hush, the better, he concluded. Because it could be those were cops in the Dodge, the drug squad looking to bust a few spades with their reefers. The "tea" in the name of the joint did have a double meaning. All this was amusing to consider, Ingram noted as he drove along, but not helpful in getting results.

Back at his apartment, he developed the shots of the two in the car as well as the ones where the handyman Deets had been confronted by the patrolman. Those he set aside. The photos of the two in the car weren't anything definitive but did suggest he wasn't simply inventing all this.

At his kitchen table he laid out three selected photos of the undercarriage of the Mercury and the new photos of the men staking out the club. He made notes on a pad of paper though nothing materialized as an answer or a lead to anything else. He did, though, have the padlock key he'd gotten at the morgue. He took it out of his pocket and put it on the table. Somewhere in the city there was a lock the key fit. For all he knew Ben might have tucked away old shoes or a magic trumpet. For now it seemed real clues were mirages shimmering in the distance. As he got closer, whatever he imagined it was could well disappear, evaporate like smoke through his fingers. Still, the key was real.

Okay, he figured, getting up and getting a beer out of the fridge. If he was going to play Johnny Staccato, then he better come at this like a hawkshaw. What would an actual private eye do? Why, he'd woo some dame, right arm around her waist, and use his mighty left hook to beat the truth out of a thug. Or like Peter Gunn, he'd have a bunch of oddball types he would visit in the middle of the night, slip them a five, get the address of where they kept the padlocked goods. Sadly he lacked any such resources.

The fact, though, was Ben Kinslow did go to the trouble of securing something he hadn't kept in his room. Could be the lock was attached to a footlocker but that meant it would have to be at a storage facility. There was no way Ingram could determine which one if that was the case. He folded his arms, wishing like in those half-hour detective shows he could get to the bottom of this before the next cigarette commercial.

Ingram got up, staring out the window, working out where else you could rent space and use your own lock. The YMCA, of course. Now, getting in there was doable.

He took hold of the White Pages next to the phone and sat down again, paging through the thick directory. He checked to see the exact address of the 28th Street Y, which was known as the colored branch, given the clientele it catered to, even though the national Y after World War II had established a policy to desegregate its facilities. In practice this varied widely from city to city, Ingram knew, from the velvet glove application of Jim Crow in Los Angeles to the more overt methods in nearby sundown towns like Maywood. In general, the Y was where a young negro from out of town could rent a dorm-style room for cheap and not be worried about being turned away like he would from a white motel. Examining the street map in his Thomas Guide, he double-checked its location against his friend's last known address. As he'd already estimated, the branch wasn't too far from where Kinslow had been staying. There was another one within the arbitrary ten-mile radius he'd established from Kinslow's rooming house and he wrote down that address as well.

From his bedroom closet he took out his gym bag, which had last seen use a year or so ago. He put in his workout clothes and set off for the 28th Street location. First, though, Ingram stopped at Shop Rite Hardware on Hoover. Shoals Pettigrew's store was sandwiched between Satellite TV and Radio Repair and a secondhand store selling reconditioned appliances. There was a stacked display of various blenders in the store's window.

"Hey, man," Ingram said to Pettigrew as he entered the establishment. Metal trash cans, rakes, shovels, pipe fittings and so on were neatly arranged in the compact shop, which contained several narrow rows of the varied tools repairmen and do-it-yourselfers required. Pettigrew was behind the front counter talking to an older man in faded dungarees. Ingram recognized this individual as one of the regulars who hung around here, a retired janitor who dispensed useful tips on fixing this or that to the customers when they asked for a light switch or some such. He nodded at this man, not recalling his name.

"What brings you to my den, Harry? Need a set screw for one of your cameras?"

"No, a padlock."

Pettigrew pointed at one of the aisles. "Got combination ones and keyed ones as well. You locking away your archives?"

Ingram was already looking in the row. "Not today. Just something for a locker." He soon placed his selection on the glass counter, under which was a shelf of vise grips, some as big as Ingram's hand, which he found dismaying.

"You should think about doing something with all those photos you've taken over the years, you know," Pettigrew said. "You got 'em, what, stacked in boxes in your closet, right?"

"You know I do."

"What am I saying then?"

He shrugged. "A lot of my prints are over in the newspapers' offices."

"But that ain't preserving 'em. You should talk to a college about that."

"Why all of a sudden you worried about my photos? You know something I don't know about me checking out?"

"What I'm saying, Harry, is the negro people need to be the keepers of our history, need to pass on what we've learned

and what we experienced to the next generation." Pettigrew swept a hand through the air. "For sure no one else
will do it."

"That's right," the older man said.

"Can I buy the padlock, Shoals?"

"All right, brother, but don't disregard my words." He rang
up the purchase on the register. "Did you get the okay to
cover the King rally?"

"Yeah, for *Jet* and for the *Nation*."

"Those reds? I thought you took care of all of them in
Korea, Sergeant York," Pettigrew cracked.

"Apparently some of them slipped through," Ingram said
dryly.

Pettigrew chuckled.

"I was going to attend even if I didn't get an assignment."

"I hear you." Pettigrew handed him his change and a
receipt. "But it's nice to have somebody legitimizing you. Let
alone get your name associated with covering the event,
which is gonna have the white press there too."

"See you," Ingram said, nodding at both men.

Resuming his trip to the 28th Street Y, he recalled it'd
been designed by a Black architect, Paul R. Williams, a man
who designed homes, some for celebrities, in areas of town
where Black folk couldn't buy. Ben would have dug what all
that meant. The façade was done in the Spanish Colonial
Revival style, its whitewashed walls reflecting the afternoon's
bright sunlight on rough-hewn surfaces as if the building
had been transported to the present from a century ago. He
parked and went inside.

"May I be of assistance, sir?" the bespectacled man at the
front desk asked. He was a tan-colored individual on the wiry
side, not so tall, with a set of piercing dark eyes behind the
thin lenses of his rimless glasses.

"I'm considering joining."

"Looking to keep in shape, are you? Wrestler, huh?" He pointed at Ingram, a clear-polished nail at the end of a tapered finger. "Those arms, I mean."

Ingram had taken off the sport coat he'd worn earlier and was in short sleeves and a snap-brim hat. "Naw." He laughed. "Want to keep my middle from spreading even more. Okay to take a look around?"

"Sure. I'll give you a tour. We have a full gym outfitted with the latest equipment, locker room that's kept sparkling, a pool and a handball court. Hold on a second."

"Okay." Ingram didn't want a guide but there was nothing he could do about it but go along. The desk attendant stuck his head through a doorway behind him to ask whoever was in there to watch the front.

"Come along," he said, stepping out from behind the inlaid marble counter. "Say, I didn't get your name."

Ingram told him.

"I'm Brian, Brian Gonzalvo."

"Dominican?"

He brightened. "Why yes, most people don't pick up on that. And I'm Haitian on my mom's side. Seems you've been around, Harry."

"Maybe I'm just a good guesser."

"Whatever you say."

As they stepped into the gym, Ingram asked, "You give a veteran's discount?" Several men of varying ages and body types were working out, including a muscular man strenuously exercising on the rowing machine.

"Oh yes, sir, indeed we do." Gonzalvo regarded him for a beat. "Korean War was it?"

"Right."

"Had an uncle over there. He was in World War II as well."

"And he volunteered to go back?"

Gonzalvo shrugged. "He's that kind of guy. Career Army all the way. Said if things keep heating up in South Vietnam like he figures they will, he'll jump into that too."

"He must have a chest full of medals." They were now in the locker room. Each locker had a number in a circle on it.

"He has, and because he never married and has no hobbies, he lives for the next call-up."

"Just in case I go out of town and leave my lock on a locker, is the policy to cut it off after a week or so?"

"Well, some of the men upstairs keep items down here, so what we usually do is post a notice if we see a lock has been on for a time and seems to be unused." He took a quick scan around. "We've got a few like that now. I'll get up a new reminder."

They completed the tour and Ingram paid for a membership. You had to commit the money for the first three months and thereafter could go month-to-month. Ingram wondered if playing detective might wind up being too expensive an undertaking.

Back in the locker room, he took his time getting into his sweatpants and top. There weren't that many guys currently using the gym in the afternoon on a weekday. At one point he was alone in there. Water echoed off the tiles in the nearby showers. Ingram tried his key on a few padlocks spaced away from the others, figuring maybe they'd been in place the longest. No dice. Hearing bare feet padding into the room, he went to his locker, getting a cross look from the man who'd entered with a towel wrapped around his lower body. Ingram finished dressing and headed toward the gym, aware the man's eyes were on him. Last damn thing he needed was to be reported to the front desk, suspected of trying to steal wallets from the members. He could imagine the shame of such a headline in the *California Eagle*.

In the gym he did jumping jacks, several push-ups, running in place as well as sit-ups. He was huffing and sweating profusely by the time he'd gone through his series of calisthenics. He bent over, hands on his legs. He was more out of shape than he'd figured. He straightened up, patting his stomach and using his towel to wipe his face. Next, he used the barbell with a moderate amount of weight on it to do a set of curls. In all, Ingram spent more than an hour exercising and was proud of himself that he actually got into it.

The locker room was empty when he returned, and he tried the key again on a few locks. Then someone else came in from working out and he got busy stripping down for the shower. The other man also went into the showers. Ingram hurried washing up. Dripping with a towel around his waist, he was again momentarily the only one back in the locker room. He tried two more locks to no avail. As he was chancing a third one, he heard voices getting nearer. Two men entered in street clothes as the key snapped the padlock open. Ingram grinned.

The men carrying gym bags passed behind his back while Ingram removed a soft-sided leather attaché case with twin clasps, like what a lawyer might use to impress clients. He didn't dare open the case in here and paw through it. Casually he put the case in his locker and got dressed. One of the newcomers raised an eyebrow at this but said nothing. Ingram finished tying his shoes and left with his prize.

In his car he opened the case and took out a glassine envelope and a single piece of lined paper with handwritten notes on it. In the glassine envelope were several shots taken close-up and others from what he determined had been medium range using a close-up lens. They were pictures taken through windows, some of them through a gap in heavy drapes and others where diaphanous curtains had been drawn. Had Kinslow taken the shots? A few were out of focus or blurry from shaky hands.

The pictures were of men, all white, from youngish to old, in suit coats and sleeves as they laughed and drank with women, also mostly white. There were a few Black and Asian women among the white women as well. To the one, the women were in lingerie or racy underwear and laughing up a storm—paid to do so as part of their services, he concluded. Once more at his kitchen table, Ingram used his magnifying glass to zero in on those male faces. He put aside one of the pictures, a color film shot. Then he picked it up again and put the glass back over it, peering closer.

This was one of the shots taken through a gap in the drapes. He was looking at an older balding man sitting on a couch as one of the party girls was swaying before him, holding a martini in one bright-red-nailed hand. The grin on the old boy's face was as big as a crescent moon as he reached out a hand. Under the outstretched arm was what made Ingram take a second look. A white woman was also sitting on the couch, though not in her skivvies. She was wearing a dress, her legs crossed. Her face was obscured but he could see the end of her arm and a sparkling bracelet on it. He stared at the image through the magnifying glass but couldn't make out her features.

He looked for the woman in the other pictures. He didn't spot her or any other regularly dressed female. From what he could tell, given the recurring skimpy attire of the good-time girls, the pictures had been taken on at least two separate occasions but at the same location. This he determined from glimpses of the abode's eaves and style of the windowsills. Two different dates and two different windows, he also surmised. He got a beer from the fridge and opened it with his church key, stood while he took a pull. If Ben Kinslow had taken these incriminating shots, he'd probably driven a couple of these birds to the location. Wheeler-dealers like Hoyt, he hedged, and for sure a judge or politician in for the fun as well. The image of the older smiling man on the couch tickled at a memory in Ingram's head but wouldn't crystalize. Maybe this was a usual get-together Hoyt threw.

Obviously Kinslow planned to blackmail them. These men had position, were married and had kids, even grandkids for some of them. Had he confronted Hoyt with these and thereby earned his untimely demise? Hoyt wasn't in any of the pictures. That didn't mean he wasn't there, of course. Had Kinslow taken the pics on Hoyt's orders? Ingram also wondered where the negatives from the photos were. Those were the gold tickets.

He sat down, sipping and thinking. He studied the piece of paper. There were three fractions on it and words in script. He could make out "vein" and "application," but the rest remained unintelligible. Kinslow must have written this in a rush. Transcribed, Ingram guessed, from another source—a source Kinslow got a look at but couldn't remove from where it was. A notebook in Hoyt's study? Did Kinslow double back on one of the party evenings to write this down? Or was it kept at wherever the sex palace was? For sure it had to be a mansion with a lot of bedrooms for the real partying to happen. Though for all he knew, there could be one big room for an orgy. Imagining such had him chuckling.

Well, however Kinslow had a peek at these numbers, why write them down, and why keep them with the candid shots?

Ingram noted the physical characteristics of the pictures. They weren't developed commercially—not like Kinslow could have dropped them off at an Owl's drugstore, what with the subject matter. Who would Kinslow have found to develop the pictures? Ingram wasn't the only photographer, professional or amateur, to take shots in the jazz clubs around town. Kinslow would know a few of those cats and could have gone to one of them.

As to why Kinslow hadn't come to him, Ingram figured he knew the answer to the question. If this was about blackmail, Ingram would have told him to drop it. Blackmail was a sucker's bet.

Ingram supposed his friend thought of him as a goody-two-shoes. After all, Kinslow had said he'd been back in town for a couple of weeks, yet hadn't looked Ingram up. Had Kinslow been avoiding him as he worked out his scheme? Afraid if he told Ingram what he was up to, his old foxhole buddy would have tried to talk sense into him?

Ingram had more of his beer. Was there a point in trying to hunt down how Kinslow had gotten in with Hoyt? There had to be someone who'd been a connection. Ingram doubted Hoyt had placed an ad in the paper for a driver. Working out the steps, Ingram also had to wonder: was it merely coincidence that Kinslow took the job with Hoyt and stumbled onto the potential payday? Or had he been put in place purposefully?

He sat back in the chair, too many "what ifs" and not enough certainties. Those two men outside the club, now that was a reality. He recalled asking Strummer to inquire about Hoyt. He called him at one of his offices, this one located in a two-story cinder-block building on Western Avenue near Adams. The bottom floor was taken up by an exterminator service. The door to the office was marked

RENARD ENTERPRISES, a catchall for Edwards's many activities. He reached his answering service.

"Please have Mr. Edwards call me when he can," he told the pleasant-voiced woman on the other end. "He has my number."

"Give it to me just in case, shugah."

He smiled as he did so and hung up.

Glancing at the shots of the men he'd taken outside the Crystal Tea Room, it occurred to Ingram he best tuck the good-time pictures away. He didn't think those two had been following him but then again, he hadn't been paying that much attention. He would from now on. He also realized with a degree of calm that Hoyt didn't know he was a photographer. When he ran into Kinslow at the racetrack, the silver-haired man hadn't seen him with his camera. He'd set it aside. Except for the initial exchange with Hoyt, the moneyed man had been preoccupied discussing his horse with the trainer. And dollars to donuts, Kinslow hadn't told Hoyt what Ingram did and for sure Hoyt hadn't asked.

Because if Hoyt did know Ingram was a photographer, and he'd had Kinslow killed, he would logically conclude Ingram was Kinslow's accomplice.

For the time being, Ingram was an invisible man to him. He gathered up the photos and put them in a large manila envelope, which he taped closed. Then he went downstairs to Whitehead's.

"Harry," Arthur Yarbrough said as he stepped inside.

"What it could be," Ingram quipped.

Yarbrough was sweeping along an aisle, his back turned toward the front door. He knew Ingram from how he walked. There were two women from the neighborhood in here shopping. None of the other workers were around.

"I'm just stepping in back for a second, Arthur."

"Okay." He bumped into a bin filled with oranges. One of them rolled off the top and Yarbrough stuck out his hand, catching it before it hit the floor.

In the back office behind a section in the wood paneled wall was a safe. Ingram undid a hidden latch and removed the panel. He bent down and dialed the combination on the safe. He then opened the heavy door and put the envelope inside and locked it up again. He replaced the panel and went back out front. Strummer Edwards was a part owner of the building. Through him, Ingram, Nakano and Yarbrough each owned a piece.

"Yes, Miss Rose, I should have fresh rhubarb in on Thursday," Yarbrough was saying to one of the shoppers.

Ingram was heading toward the door, then double-backed to the canned goods. He took a can of peas and carrots off the shelf and put a dollar on the counter.

"See you, daddy-o."

"You overpaid," Yarbrough said.

"You sure you can't see?"

"I know the sound of money."

"Wish I did."

Back upstairs Ingram tidied up and got some ground round out of the fridge. This he put in a skillet and browned, cutting the meat to scramble as it cooked. He drained the meat and added the vegetables and a couple of other items from the cupboard, including a small can of tomato paste, to concoct his hobo stew. He was feeling good having found the photos. While they presented more pieces of the puzzle, he was elated to be making progress in finding out what had happened to his friend.

At his kitchen table he ate while Ella Fitzgerald sang on the record player. He had a second helping and when he was done, he sat in his favorite chair and lit a cigar. He turned on his black-and-white television, bought secondhand. Fooling with the rabbit-eared antenna, he cleared the fuzzy picture. *Petticoat Junction* was on and he watched the comedy show to the end, laughing a few times at the goings on. After that a doctor drama started and Ingram got up, clicking away from this to the next channel. He came upon a game show in progress. He left it there, mildly interested in the contestants vying for space-age cookware.

Ingram sat and puffed away, his smoke trailing out the window he'd opened overlooking the avenue. Out there a dog barked, and two men could be heard discussing who was the better boxer, that loud-mouthed Cassius Clay, who'd recently beat Doug Jones in New York, or the bear, the heavyweight champ, Sonny Liston. Each man effusively argued for their respective fighter, their voices fading into the night as they sauntered along. Getting more comfortable in the chair, Ingram started to doze, having stubbed out what was left of his smoked cigar in an ashtray. Just before going under, he looked at the TV screen. The point of view was through a windshield as a vehicle bounced along a dirt road in a village. His breath caught in his throat as he hauntingly recognized the humble dwellings of Chorwa. He gaped, staring as Korean peasants went about their daily chores. A plane buzzed over the village. The aircraft dropped a bomb. People screamed and ran as it exploded and gunfire erupted.

Ingram was leaning forward but couldn't get his legs to work to get him out of his chair as the devastation unfolded. He blinked and swallowed, trying to surface from the miasma. Now the TV showed a bucolic middle-class street as jaunty theme music signaled the beginning of another comedy program. He could make his legs work now and he got up, clicking through the channels with a dry mouth. There was no village destruction to be seen. Ingram rubbed a hand over his face, worried he was becoming unmoored. He had a blast of whiskey before going to bed, afraid he'd have a nightmare. But he slept soundly, untroubled.

CHAPTER SIX

"How's your sandwich?" Ingram asked Anita Claire.

"Fine, thank you. Sorry I couldn't get away."

"Ain't nothing wrong with honest work, as my mama would say." She'd called him earlier today to tell him she had to work late. He'd suggested he'd bring her dinner and she'd agreed. Not exactly four-star, getting sandwiches, potato salad and two slices of apple pie from the Detour diner. They ate at her desk, which was tucked in a corner of the storefront campaign office on Pico Boulevard. There were three others working, calling people from voter lists to reaffirm they were voting for Bradley and seeing if they needed a ride to the polls.

"Does your mom live in town, Harry?"

"No, she went back to Atoka in Oklahoma. My dad was gone several years by then. This was when I was drafted."

"You were born here?"

"Well, no they're both from Oklahoma. I was only there until four when the family moved to L.A. We came out here because my father had a job waiting for him through a cousin. He was a trolley man."

"Did your mom stay home?"

He shook his head, grinning. "She was and is an

independent sort from a long line of those kind of women. She worked part-time as a secretary at Golden State Mutual, then eventually sold policies."

"Wow, impressive. Any brothers or sisters?"

"Kind of," he said. "Pops left us for another woman, and he had two children with this woman back down in Texas. Boy and girl."

"Have you met your steps?"

"Yeah, but there's an age difference so we're not exactly what you'd call close." He made a feeble gesture. "Same goes for my dad. Although he did write me a couple of times when I got out of the Army."

"Sorry to hear that, about your dad I mean."

He ate more of his sandwich, setting it down on a square of unfolded wax paper.

"What about your folks?" he asked.

She cocked her head. "Go ahead and ask."

"What?"

"You know what, smart guy." She said it sharply but was smiling.

"Okay, fine, your mom is the one who's white?"

"Good guess."

"Don't go all shy now."

She forked down a bite of potato salad before speaking again. "They're both lefties, Harry. That's how they met, on the picket line."

"I see," he said.

She slapped the back of his hand playfully. "What do you see?"

"You can't help yourself, indoctrinated to help the downtrodden and be the Wonder Woman for equal rights."

"You damn right."

They had more of their food. Then, taking a gander at

her coworkers, Claire eased open a drawer in her desk. A finger to her lips, she extracted a flask and unscrewed its attached top while also holding it in the same hand. She poured a shot for Ingram in his coffee cup.

"My mama warned me about you big-city women." He tipped his cup toward her and took a sip. "Are your folks here in L.A.?"

"They are," she said. "They're divorced yet have remained friends. They went through some hard times, which put a big strain on the marriage. Had me and my sister coming and going when we were teenagers."

"How do you mean?"

"They were involved in a lot of agitation around housing covenants and don't shop where you can't work campaigns. They know Charlotta Bass." The *Eagle* and the *Sentinel* regularly took bold stands against discrimination. "That always meant they got grief on the job, both of them being public school teachers. Loyalty oaths, getting followed, that bullshit took a toll."

"I can imagine."

She studied him a moment, sitting back in her chair. "It just occurred to me. How is it you were fighting them commie Asian devils over there yet don't miss a beat working for somebody like Bass when you first got back?"

"She hasn't taken a shot at me. And by the time I came on, she'd already sold the paper." Lawyer and one-time reporter for the paper Loren Miller owned the *Eagle* these days.

Her lip curled. "You know what I'm talking about."

"I didn't volunteer, Anita. But yeah, like I said at Ben's send-off, once I was over there, I decided I should do my duty. I guess I hoped like a lot of negroes, we'd show Uncle Sam we were good at soldiering, fighting for democracy and all that."

"I suppose Black troops in the Civil War figured the same," she said. "Look at those fellas who came back from the First War and got lynched in their uniforms in their own hometowns, they must have counted on a goodwill for their sacrifices that never materialized."

Ingram had more of his spiked coffee. "We can only do what we can do. Not ignore the past, but don't let it shackle us either."

She folded her arms. "You're just full of surprises, aren't you, Mr. Ingram?"

"No more than you it seems."

Claire poured from her flask into a paper cup she'd had water in. Raising it to her mouth she said, "Maybe we'll keep surprising each other."

"Pie," he said, pushing a slice toward her on a paper plate.

She patted her hip. "One bite is all you can tempt me with. Any more than that, and I'll have to be shopping for a new dress size."

He made sure his eyes didn't linger on her hip, and avoided the temptation to make a Redd Foxx–like remark. He wasn't looking to get slapped for being fresh. They finished their meal and she walked him out. Claire's coworkers were still making phone calls.

"Don't you think I'm not shouldering my load," she said as they stood next to his car.

"What are you talking about?"

She notched her head toward the campaign's storefront. "The phone banking. My shift is tomorrow morning."

"Nobody's thinking you're a goldbricker."

She pointed at him. "That's right."

He unlocked his door. "See you again?"

She put her arms around his neck and kissed him. "See you soon."

Wistfully he watched her walk back into the office. Driving home, he rolled down his window halfway to let the cool air of evening blow across his warm face.

The following morning he got up and as was his custom, put on the scanner as his coffee brewed. But as a report of a domestic squabble came over the airwaves, he turned off the device. Ingram decided he had other matters to attend to this morning. Not in a rush, he made breakfast and had two cups of coffee, leafing through a copy of the *Herald Examiner* from a day ago. He washed the dishes and headed out for the library.

"Where would I find books on the body, particularly the heart?" he asked the librarian.

"Like how the heart works?"

"Yes."

"That would be in the three-hundreds, down that row." She indicated.

"Thanks."

Ingram stood in the aisle and pulled various books about anatomy and internal organs off the shelf, glancing through each one. He carried several to a table and sat there to regard them more thoroughly. He'd brought along the page with the hurried scribbles and the fractions and unfolded it, smoothing it out on the table. He was sure now one of the words was "heart." He read sections about how the heart functions, but no lightbulb went off in his head. Was one of these scrawled words a name for a chemical? Was it referring to something the body produced? He looked through the indexes and tried comparing what he found there with what he guessed the word was, but no match. He also looked through a high school chemistry text but found no match there either.

He slumped, imagining walking into his neighborhood

drugstore to show the word to the druggist, some guy in a white smock who looked like Boris Karloff. The cat would take a look and say, "Wait right here, will you?" Then would go away to call the cops on him. At least Ingram would know he was onto something. Like maybe this was some kind of stuff used to make an explosive.

He could show the fractions to Anita but what could she make of them? Best to keep this to himself for now.

He left the library and spent time back at his apartment cleaning his gear and straightening up in the darkroom. Ingram took a handful of photos from a bottom shelf of a rickety table he'd rescued from the trash. In his bedroom he opened one of his file boxes and tossed them in. He paused before closing the closet door. What had Pettigrew mentioned about preserving his legacy? He hardly considered what he had as gallery quality but here he was running around playing snooper and there could be consequences. If he died, who would take care of his thousands of photos?

He sat heavily on the end of the bed and lay down on his back. He'd been going at this since he'd come back from the war. Damn near ten years now. Rushing out in the middle of the night to take snaps of a drunk man on his knees crying over the body of the wife he'd just stabbed to death, or some poor mother devastated after her little girl was killed in a hit-and-run. That lady in Kinslow's rooming house was probably right about him. He'd spent a lot of time and energy capturing those petrified looks of horror, stark in the white glare of his exploding flash bulbs. The unmistakable defeated slump of the shoulders, the head hung low. Humanity at its worst and most vulnerable. Ingram had seen and photographed a city full of misery and gruesomeness. There were plenty of pictures of picket lines too, cops wailing on brothers and white guys just because, rallies for equal rights and on and on. There was a breadth of subject matter he'd shot over the years, albeit not for the tea and crumpets crowd.

"Fuck it," he muttered as he sat up. He wasn't about to burn his pictures in a backyard incinerator like they were garbage. He'd made an honest living taking these pictures. He'd never staged anything like he knew more than one photographer in town had. For good and for ill they represented his work, and he shouldn't be so cavalier about caring for them. But first, time for a sandwich and a beer.

Ingram went into the kitchen to fix his lunch and try to figure out where he could archive his photos. Some of the boxes were organized by gunshot, woman-on-man crime, man-on-woman crime and so on. Ingram got calls from time to time for such a photo where an editor determined they wanted to illustrate a point in an article, and it didn't have to be of current vintage.

Fortified by two hot dogs weighted down with onions and relish and half a bottle of Eastside Old Tap, Ingram got the boxes out of his closet and from under his bed. He wasn't about to go through them to put order to everything. That would require setting aside days to get done. Rather a brief shifting through the contents in each box reminded him generally which contained the tamer shots, like those taken backstage at the Crystal Tea Room, and which had the more lurid material. Good thing he always made a notation on the backs of each as to where it was taken and date.

One of the boxes wasn't full of photographs. This one was metal, designed like a miniature steamer trunk, and stashed behind another box on the top shelf at the rear. He took it down to look through it, placing it on the bed. He undid its flaps and opened the lid. Aside from his service weapon, in here were souvenirs Ingram had brought back from Korea. He took out his service medal, an embroidered silk scarf he'd gotten on leave in Ashiya, Japan, and a bayonet from a Garand rifle he'd coated with Cosmoline to prevent rusting. He'd wrapped the blade in an inexpensive cotton handkerchief. Ingram hadn't looked in this box since he'd first packed it away after getting back.

He also took out a particular type of can opener the soldiers would dangle from their uniform's flapped breast pocket. The device was used to peel back the lids of their C ration tins. You wolfed that grub down because you were perpetually hungry, and it seemed half the time you got diarrhea from the chow. That is, until he'd learned from other dogfaces if you put a dent in the tin, then set it on an open fire until the dent popped back out, you were good to go. Having an upset stomach also reminded him of General MacArthur, who was in charge of the United Nations Command over there. The troops included Canadians and Australians but were mostly US personnel. Even though President Truman had officially integrated the armed services a couple of years before, MacArthur was of the studied opinion that Black soldiers were inferior in every way to their white counterparts. When the president fired him in '51 for insubordination, General Matthew Ridgeway, who took over, put the integration orders into effect. Not that there was a bunch of psalm-singing and roasting marshmallows after that among the white and Black enlisteds. Far from it.

Also, in the metal box was a deungsil, a typical Korean lantern hung outside a home, or from the rafters in a barn. It was designed to hold a candle. The lantern was made of thin metal and glass and was in fragile condition. He turned it over and over in his hands, his eyes tearing up. Countless lanterns like this could be found in villages and towns all throughout the country, north and south. Like in Chorwa, when his patrol had marched through on their way to reconning the Hambone Ridge. Where the KPA, the Korean People's Army, aided by a contingent of Chinese soldiers, opened fire on them from huts and hidden foxholes. In the onslaught of bullets and screams and bodies blasted apart, Harry Ingram accidently shot that nine-year-old. He'd tried later to find out the boy's name, but he hadn't been able to. Nor find his folks.

Ingram closed his eyes, and it took him several minutes to compose himself. He put everything back in the metal box, closed it up and put it away.

Ingram got back on task. He separated out his negatives, many of which were inserted between piles of photos. By the time he'd finished, he'd had a second Old Tap and it was late in the afternoon. The phone rang and he picked up the handset.

"Hello?"

"Harry, it's me."

"What's up, Strummer?"

"I'm coming by to pick you up," he said in a rushed manner.

"Where we going?"

"You'll see. Be downstairs."

Edwards soon arrived in his Chrysler.

"Why all the hush-hush?" Ingram asked his friend as he got in on the passenger side of the bench seat.

"Kind of a delicate situation, you might say."

"The hell you talking about, Strummer?"

"I forgot to mention it—did you bring a bat?"

"Negro, where the hell are we going?"

"Watts, son."

"Yeah?"

"You told me there was a couple'a colored gals in those ofay party pictures."

"I did." Edwards had called him back, having gotten his message.

"That helped narrow down who I was asking around about." Edwards glanced over at him. "Better than asking around about some silver-haired ofay who procures or has procured for him the darker gals for their mysterious hoodoo ways." He bugged his eyes at Ingram.

"This chick packs a rod?"

"Seems the company she keeps can be a bit obstreperous. Least that's what I've been told. Open the glove box."

Ingram did. Except for a few papers in there and a nearly depleted roll of Life Savers candy, it was empty. "Okay, so?"

Edwards reached under the dashboard on his left side and pressed a button. The back end of the glove box swung inward. "In there," he said.

Ingram reached in and took out a snub-nosed .38 with a taped grip.

"Just in case."

His friend shook loose a cigarette from a Lucky Strike pack he plucked off the dashboard. The cigarette was bent but held together. Edwards pushed in the cigarette lighter. "Let me do the talking when we get there." The cigarette bounced up a down in his mouth as he said this.

"Sure." Ingram put the gun in his jacket's outer pocket, aware if the cops stopped them, he and Edwards might not live to see jail. This gave him a weird sort of calm, like when he was in the heat of battle, scared but eager.

"We're not going in there guns blazing, okay?" Edwards said. "The gat is, you know, insurance. No reason to be trigger happy but be on guard."

"Yeah, I got it. I'm not thrill crazy."

"Just saying, One-Shot Kid."

"Fine."

On they went. Eventually they reached a street in Watts that looked to be more country than city. What sidewalks there were existed in brief spans of concrete interspersed with sparse lawns that gently sloped all the way down to the uneven asphalt, grass tendrils stretching across as if trying to join with the lawns on the opposite side. Here and there were chunks of what had been curbs, cast aside as if the road crews had lost interest.

By now it was dusk and what streetlamps there were had come on, pale yellow glows like fading stars. They parked and Ingram heard chickens clucking from not too far away. This under the hum of steel on steel as the Southern Pacific railcars went by on the tracks also not far from where they were.

In the low horizon behind the houses at the end of the street was the silhouette of the top of the spires of the Watts Towers. Ingram had done a photo layout of the towers a few years ago for an assignment for a French jazz magazine whose name he couldn't recall now. There were three main spiraling structures with plumbing pipe, and various other minor structures including arches compacted on a triangular piece of land. This had been erected by a cantankerous man named Sam Rodia. Mortar, tiles, the bottoms of glass bottles, wire mesh and rough concrete he'd used, material scavenged from all over to construct his wonder. Often Rodia, who began the construction in 1921, would change his mind and tear down a section after months of putting it together. It took until 1954 for him to say it was finished. Ingram had interviewed him, and recalled learning Rodia's third wife had left him due to his obsession with its construction. Rodia had dismissed her splitting on him with a wave of his calloused hand.

"Over here," Edwards was saying. He pointed at a modest

house with a large palm tree on a circle of dry lawn. A 1940s-era Hudson pickup truck was parked in the driveway. Judging from the lumpy bodywork, the vehicle had seen a lot of miles. There was a light on inside the house. A screen door hung haphazardly over the front door and as they got closer, Ingram noticed two rough-hewn symbols staked in front of the house. They were made of what seemed to be plaster embedded with rebar like lollipops. They looked like Rodia's handiwork. One was a cross painted in silver; the other symbol, which he didn't recognize, was painted gold.

"That's an ankh," Edwards said.

"How you know that?"

"That teacher I used to date."

"Must be the one who taught you what 'obstreperous' meant."

"Forget you." He nodded toward the gold symbol. "It's Egyptian, fool, and it symbolizes life."

Edwards knocked lightly on the screen door. As the inner door creaked open, still no shape could be discerned. A pungent order came from within, clinging to the screen door's mesh. Ingram half expected to hear the organ of Korla Pandit but there was only the sound of a television program.

"Yeah?" came a rough voice.

"I'm a friend of Rochelle's. Strummer's my name."

"Good for you."

"We came to see Hanisha."

"That right?"

"I'll make it worth her while. We're here to talk is all."

"About what?"

"That's for her to share with you if she wants."

"Let 'em in, Clovis," a female voice said from behind the man at the screen door.

There was the shuffle of feet on carpet. Edwards and

Ingram exchanged a look. The one called Clovis had walked away. Edwards pulled the screen door open and both men stepped inside.

The interior of the home was spare in its furnishings but tidy. Sitting on the couch was a woman in white jeans, sandals and a man's dress shirt, tail out. Her hair was stylish, and she was pretty in a natural way. She was chestnut colored and smoky-eyed. Ingram was positive she wasn't the Black woman he'd seen in the picture. There were several heavy bracelets on one of her wrists. The television had been turned off.

"How you doing?" Edwards offered his hand, and she shook it. "This is my buddy, Harry Ingram. He wanted to ask you a couple of questions about a white man named Winston Hoyt."

There wasn't an overabundance of religious artifacts, at least not in the front room Ingram catalogued. On the carved mantel over the fireplace were several items including a statuette of a deity he'd seen in an article in *Ebony*. It had been about a religion called Santeria from Cuba that had found its way to the States, particularly back East. If he recalled correctly, it was a combination of religious practices from the Yoruba peoples in West Africa and Catholicism.

The man she'd called Clovis straddled a chair he'd set backward in an archway. He must have been six-four when standing, Ingram estimated. His large muscles strained the white T-shirt he wore. To his back was a kitchen and there was another woman in there, humming as she prepared food. The savory aroma of simmering collard greens filled the house.

"You're a journeyer," she said. There was a gray cat lounging at her feet, indifferent to the newcomers.

"Huh?" Edwards said.

She lifted a dark red nail at Ingram. "You go in and out of people's lives."

"Yes, ma'am. I take pictures for the newspapers."

"Not just any pictures." Before he could answer, she added, "Sit, why don't you?"

They both looked around and Edwards took hold of a chair and brought it over to sit close to Hanisha. There was no other chair, and it wasn't like Clovis was going to offer his up. Ingram sat on the other end of the couch.

The woman in the kitchen said, "Clovis, get in here, will you?"

"What you want?"

"I want you in here, what I just say? Get this jar open for me and take down this big bowl I need on top of the icebox. Use them muscles 'sides showing 'em off to silly girls down there at the record shop."

Clovis sighed and rose, moving into the kitchen fluidly for a man his size.

"What can I do for you, Mr. Ingram?"

"Harry, please. I'm interested in what you might know about this Hoyt."

She folded her arms. "Why you want to mess in white folks' business, Harry?"

"You mean I should be afraid?"

"I mean I don't want no shit coming back on me and my practice." There wasn't a coffee table in front of the couch but on an end table with a lamp on it, there were two books lying on their sides. One spine read *The Kabbalah Explained* and the other *Practical Ancient Alchemy.* Each had several torn strips of paper for bookmarks in them.

"What is it that you do exactly?"

She held out her hands. "I see and I provide."

Ingram chanced to ask, "Would that be colored gals for his parties?"

She grinned. "What is it you're really trying to find out? Knowledge is a key, but it can be a burden."

Clovis returned to his post.

Ingram said, "Your name will never be heard from me or Strummer."

"Not even if you were offered money? Far more than thirty pieces of silver."

He was getting irritated about this 'round and 'round, but he had to be cool. "I just want whatever information you can give me. I can pay."

Clovis spoke from his chair. "How we know these spades can be trusted?"

Edwards glared at him.

"Yes, we should see if they are men of their word," Hanisha said.

"Some kind of proof," Clovis said with relish.

"Exactly."

"Now wait a minute," Edwards began. "What Harry said is on the level, we ain't no tattle tales. You can ask Rochelle. She knows me."

"Okay, go on your way," she said, shrugging.

"What kind of test you talking about?" Ingram said.

Irritated, Edwards grimaced.

Clovis said, "This here is real what we're talkin' about. You two strokes look like you ain't up for it."

"Fuck," Edwards said, "this is some bullshit."

"We getting to do this tonight?" Ingram asked, wondering if Hanisha had a pit of hot coals in the back and expected him to walk over them barefoot. Or like in the western he watched on TV the other week, cross a branch over a pit of spikes blindfolded.

"We'll let you know what and when," Hanisha said. "It'll be soon enough."

A cat slinked out of the kitchen at the sound of food frying in crackling oil. The cat walked between Clovis's legs, stopped in the middle of the front room and sat on its haunches, pale green eyes on Ingram.

Harry stood and so did Edwards. "Here you go." He gave Hanisha one of his business cards. It had his name and phone number on it along with a reproduction of a generic camera with a flash lamp attached. The two started for the door.

"I'll tell you this for free, Mister Photographer," she said as Edwards pushed the screen door open. Ingram turned his head back toward her. "Winston Hoyt is a member of the Association of Merchants and Industrialists. Them's the peckerwoods who decide such things as having a freeway cut through colored folks' neighborhoods like Sugar Hill, even though they be highfalutin. But they had to be reminded what they got is only nigger money to fool with. Now you could have found out what I just told you in the library. It's what you can't find out there is why you'll be back."

Ingram said, "I suppose so."

She and Clovis exchanged a look. The cat rolled onto its back.

"WHAT IN the holy hell was that about?" They were back in Edwards's Chrysler, driving away.

"You the one brought us out here, Columbus. Shit." He chuckled nervously.

"I wouldn't put it past her or Clovis making you drive over to Maywood to fetch some damn thing or another."

Maywood, the sundown town not too far east of South Central, was home to a white gang called the Spook

Hunters. They'd fought Black gangs such as the Slausons and the Del Vikings.

"I need to find out what I can, Strummer."

"Why? He's a rich white man who can squeeze you by the nuts, Harry. What else is there to know?"

"The more you learn from recon, the better prepared you are for the battle."

"Yes, sir, General Patton." He'd gotten out another cigarette and lit it. Again, it dangled from a corner of his mouth as he talked. "Man, are you so shell-shocked you think everything's a mission?" He looked over at him.

"I only want answers."

"Brother, listen to me when I tell you I've had more experiences with cats like your boy Clovis. Whatever that robust negro and the voodoo queen come up with, you can be sure it's some shit where you might wind up with a bullet in your gut. And that might be a lucky outcome."

From out on the avenues, the various-colored neon glare of liquor store and motel signs reflected off the car's glass as they rode past—businesses that were the staples of the ghetto.

"You the one that said they could be obstreperous."

"More like mumbo-jumbo. Her practice." He snorted. "You know she wouldn't be the first chick to be a pimp. All that hooey jive she spouts, a glorified way to mesmerize some greenhorn country girl fresh off the turnip truck. Power of the pussy is what."

"You might have something there," Ingram agreed. They rode along some more, then Ingram asked, "If it went bad back there, you expected me to blast our way out?"

"What kind of friend you take me for?" he said indignantly. "You wasn't gonna be the only one fillin' his hand. I got a rod strapped to my ankle." He tapped his lower leg.

"Good to know."

"Yeah, well, if you want my advice and I know you don't, ignore that call when you get it from that hoodoo dame."

"If I do, she might put a curse on me."

"You can outrun a curse, not a bullet."

"For a cat who does what you do, you're kinda bent out of shape over this, ain't you?"

Edwards finally took the cigarette out of his mouth. "Dude come at me with a knife, fine. He's mad 'cause I tried to make time with his girl or he wants to take my bankroll, okay, that's normal. I can handle that action. But a mother-lover wants to carve me up because he had a vision of Ooma-Gooma who ordered him to do so. Now that fella is always gonna come at you. He's operating on another level, trying to get his seat at the table in the great by-and-by."

"But that's only if you believed in that sort of jive."

Edwards tapped the dash with his index finger. "You're missing the point, Harry. It might not be an act, them two could believe in their ghost in the sky like, you know, the followers of Malcolm X. Selling bean pies on the corner and preaching about Yakub. Ready to stand shoulder to shoulder against the cops if Malcolm said so."

Yakub was supposedly a Black scientist who lived on an island thousands of years ago and created the white race to bedevil the Black man. Ingram didn't believe this yarn, but he got the point. Members of the Nation of Islam, many of them culled from the ranks of prisoners and addicts, had been cleaned up and reformed. They'd embraced the cause deeply and wouldn't hesitate to defend the faithful.

Ingram nodded. "A lot of that has to do with Malcolm's charisma."

"Oh yes, that man can speechify. Stronger than King in some ways," Edwards admitted.

"With God on our side, how can we lose," Ingram intoned. He then added, "Anyway, I don't figure Clovis as no true believer."

"Yeah," his friend drawled, "he's her man or bodyguard or enforcer or whatever. Anything he's on about, it's on her orders." They drove more in silence. At some point Edwards glanced over at him again, snapping his fingers. "You know what your problem is, you're too damn curious is what. See what you really want is the story, isn't it?"

"That's not what this is about."

"Uh-huh. A juicy story about the sex lives of the rich. Murder and blackmail brought to you by your ace negro reporter." Edwards grinned.

"Could be I can accomplish both things. Find out who killed Ben and write about it." This was the first time the notion occurred to him—or at least the first time he was willing to admit that he might have a dual purpose in trying to find out what happened. A true-crime piece he could for sure sell to a white slick.

"You don't deny you want to be whatshisname, the one who blew his brains out, Hemingway for the colored crowd."

"You learned a lot from your teacher, didn't you? All I want to do now is get home and put my feet up."

"Yeah, well, best be practicing on some bottles and cans with your pop gun, son. If'n you intend to deal with them again." He grinned. "Probably stealing the gold teeth out of some old rich dame in Beverly Hills while she sleeps."

"They'll be in a glass on her nightstand. Piece of cake."

"Sure you right." Edwards dropped him off at his place. Ingram had put the gun back in its hidden compartment.

"See you, Harry."

"Later." Ingram tapped the side of the car as his friend drove off.

Upstairs he had a pour of whiskey and turned on the radio in his bedroom. There was a news report about a suspect who was cleared as the Morning Bandit, a bank robber who'd struck yet again two days ago, robbing a bank in Venice, an area of surfers and beatniks called the slum by the sea. He dialed in KBCA, a jazz and blues station on the FM band. A John Lee Hooker number was playing, "Boom, Boom." The Mississippi Delta native's raw baritone was unmistakable as he sang about desire over the licks he laid down on his electric guitar. Ingram poured another drink. Having stripped off his shirt down to his athlete tee, he lay in bed, propped against the headboard, sipping, and worried about what Edwards had said about him. Was his eagerness to look into Kinslow's death really about him being selfish, seeing it as a way to further his career? That could very well be the lens through which he was viewing the death, which could be an accident after all. He was trying to will it into being a murder because he needed a crime in order to make the story interesting.

Ingram took his pants off and got under the covers but couldn't fall asleep. It bothered him his motives weren't pure, but more so that he hadn't recognized this himself. He could look in the mirror and see a familiar face, yet those he knew saw his true self.

"Shit," he muttered, resisting having another belt, though he could rationalize the liquor would help him sleep. He lay and brooded. He got out of bed and, cotton robe and slippers on, went back in the living room, where he leafed through a stack of magazines. He was like a patient in the dentist's waiting room, quietly dreading the root canal to come. He looked through *Ebony*, *Time*, *Dapper* and so on going back months. He'd kept the back issues, planning to read this or that article but usually never getting around to it. He came upon a piece in *Los Angeles* magazine about the state's restrictive housing covenants and the ongoing discussion in the California legislature about the matter. There was a mention of the Association of Merchants and Industrialists and several of its members. Hoyt wasn't mentioned but Ingram wrote those names down. He yawned. Eventually sleep came as Ma Rainey sang "Bo-Weavil Blues" from his bedroom radio.

The following morning, he awoke early, groggy yet restless to be in motion and not anchored with a bunch of introspection. In his front room he turned on one of his police scanners. By the time his coffee was ready a call was coming over the airwaves that got his attention.

"...unit 1-A, see the woman corner apartment second floor, Hoover and Fifty-third Street. Male, negro American burglary suspect. Description tweed pants, silk shirt, repeat..."

Ingram got dressed quickly and was out the door with his camera. He arrived at the address shortly, but two prowl cars were already parked there. There was also a white reporter on the scene he knew slightly from the *Herald Examiner*, Mike Piedmont.

"Harry," the man said as he walked up. Piedmont had been talking to one of the uniforms. He was the sole policeman in view.

"Mike," he answered. "What's going on and why is your paper interested in what us natives are doing down in the jungle?"

Piedmont was a two-pack-a-day man and reeked of the Pall Malls he enjoyed. "Crime is everyone's concern, Mr. Ingram."

"Uh-huh." Ingram began walking toward the apartment building. From around the corner of a house two doors down came two officers with a Black man in handcuffs. The suspect was dressed as the dispatcher's description had indicated. The officers were on either side of him, one of them holding him by the arm. There was a splotch of blood on the man's silk shirt, which was partly untucked. As they got closer, Ingram saw the fresh bruises on his lumpy face. He sighted his camera and took several rapid clicks. In the doorway of the apartment house stood a middle-aged woman in a housecoat, her hair up in rollers and a handkerchief tied around that.

"The cops do this to you?" Ingram said to him as they got closer.

The captured man had a blank expression on his face, as if not quite aware of what was happening to him. The woman went back inside as he was marched past Ingram.

Ingram was mildly surprised the cops didn't tell him to buzz off or try to stop him from taking shots. They barely acknowledged his presence. Piedmont moved in to try to talk to the arresting officers and got nothing out of them except stony silence. The police loaded the prisoner into one of the cars and drove away, one by himself and the other two with their captive.

"I'll see you," Piedmont said. He hurried away to his car, no doubt to drive over to Newton Division, which covered this area. Ingram had another idea. He went into the apartment building. From the vestibule he took the stairs to the second floor, where the apartments began. No response came from his knocking softly at the first door. He tried a second door.

"Yeah," a male voice said on the other side.

"Sorry to disturb you," he said. He went to a door on the opposite end of the building and knocked. This time he got a female voice in response.

"Yes?" she said.

He told her who he was. The door opened on the chain. She was the woman he'd seen downstairs.

"You have identification, young man?"

He handed her his press credentials through the opening and after she gave it the once-over, she handed it back. She undid the chain and opened the door more, but not so much he took it as an invitation to step inside.

"Did you know the man the police arrested?"

"Yes, he's my stepson, I guess. That is, his father is dead a few years now. The only one he really listened to," she said wearily.

Recalling the stepson's lost look, he said gently, "Is there something wrong with him?"

"He needs help, the kind you get in a mental hospital, mister. He lives in a group home, but he'll put on his dress clothes and come around here. He gets it in his head his father is going to drive up in a big Cadillac to take him . . . I don't know where. If he would just come to see me, that would be fine. I could talk to him. But he'll go to other people's houses, even sometimes try to get in through their windows." She sagged against the doorframe. "I saw him outside and called to him, only he ignored me. Somebody sicced police on him but Lord help me if they shot him."

"They beat him a piece."

"Yes. I'm sure they asked him who he was and Stevie being Stevie, he might have told him he wanted to see *Captain Kangaroo,* one of his favorite programs. He don't have no driver's license. I should have gone out there, but I suppose I wanted him to go away and not bother me. So tired of dealing with his mess," she said in a small voice. Straightening up, she drew in a breath. "Let me get dressed and go on down there and bail that child out 'fore anything else happens to him."

"Sounds good," Ingram said. He got her name before he left.

Her door closed quietly and he walked down the stairs, going over how he would write the incident up. Normally he'd go with a shot of Stevie worked over by the cops and get the few particulars from the station house. He would contrast the dry facts he'd get from the cops with how the man looked, emphasizing the rough treatment of yet another negro in cuffs. And this time it was a man who lacked certain mental capacities. Maybe even get a longer piece out of it if he did it for the *Eagle*. Driving back home, though, he considered the angle should be on the woman. He wouldn't ignore how the police had treated Stevie, but wasn't it more about how for guys like the stepson, it shouldn't be the cops handling this sort of situation? Of course cops weren't social workers, he could hear them saying. They would claim he was resisting arrest, the old catchall to excuse the use of nightsticks.

Damn Hanisha must have put a spell on him. Had him thinking about his work in a whole other way. Getting all up about people's lives and wants and whatnot, rather than just take his pics and move on.

He arrived at his place and brightened upon seeing Anita Claire sitting on his front steps. He pulled to the curb, putting the car in neutral. He leaned across the bench seat and rolled down the passenger-side window. She walked toward the car.

"Hey, young lady, you want some candy?"

"What kind you got?"

He patted the seat. "Get in and find out."

She slid in beside him.

He gave her a peck on the cheek. "What brings you to my neck of the woods?"

"You had breakfast yet?"

"No, I was out on a shoot."

"Then I'm buying."

"In that case, anything for you."

"We'll see." She looked straight ahead.

Ingram put the car in gear and pulled away. For a change from his usual, he took her to Lovejoy's Broiler on Vernon near Central Avenue. The couple got a table and sat opposite each other. They ordered coffee as they perused the menus.

"Feeling kinda famished," Ingram said.

Claire fooled with her spoon.

"I can wait, I got all morning."

"I need a favor."

"This a test?"

"What?"

"Nothing. Go ahead."

"You remember Judy from the party?"

"Sure."

"She kind of grew up like I did. Her father wasn't in the Communist Party, but he might as well have been, given who he associated with. He was a plumber who became an organizer for the Boilermakers union. Her mother was more of the stay-at-home type, but she got involved too, especially by the time Judy and her brother were teenagers."

"Her dad was in San Pedro with the ships?" Ingram said. He'd done a photo story about several equal rights organizations pushing to have more Black workers hired on the docks.

"Yes, though in his case that meant talking to those men in the bars where they drank and socialized after their shifts. He was involved in quite a few strikes and work actions, as they called them."

The waitress came and they ordered. Claire continued

once she was gone. "When I mentioned that business about the loyalty oaths, her parents went through that too. Fact we'd met at a summer camp for youngsters like us when we were kids."

"Indoctrinating y'all to be the beachhead of the revolution, huh?" His joke only made her look graver. He touched her hand. "I'll keep my big mouth shut."

"A lot of these people were scared, Harry. Eisenhower had signed the Communist Control Act. At that time California had the most Party members outside of New York State and the largest number were in Los Angeles. Papers like the *Mirror* whipped up the fear, talking about housing areas as communist operating divisions. And not too many years before that the Rosenbergs had been sent to the electric chair at Sing Sing."

"I remember the day I heard the Rosenbergs were executed," he said.

"It was bad all over. People my folks knew had their jobs threatened and the authorities told them they could get their children taken away. The pressure was unrelenting. In that regard some turned their backs on their friends and what they believed in. Marriages broke apart. Others ratted out a good friend to a school board or what have you to save their own skins. Even the ones who stayed the course tried to hide their"—she searched for the words—"political persuasions. Secreting away what kind of books and pamphlets they had on their shelves in case the FBI came knocking."

"Your folks do this?"

"They did," she acknowledged. "I helped move boxes into garages and rented spaces all over town, and out of town too."

"And this gets us to Judy?"

"That's right. Her folks also participated in hiding their

books. Mind you there were a few, and only a few, who kept records of what was put away where. One of them in particular is a man named Emil Freed, an electrical engineer by training. He was a main organizer of this effort."

"Didn't want to see this stuff get thrown away."

"Right," Claire said. "Obviously then these lists also had to be hidden away as they would be a propaganda coup if the authorities got ahold of one of them." She spread her hands wide. "Have a big ol' televised bonfire of book burning on Main Street."

"Yeah," he said, agreeing, "the commie hunters would make a show of it."

Their food came and Claire went silent again. They each had a forkful of their breakfast. Claire then continued. "Okay, skip forward to now. While it isn't the workers' paradise long envisioned, there's been a degree of loosening the vise."

"Meaning these books have been returned to their owners?"

"In some cases. But a lot of the books at Freed's urging have been donated to what will be a library, an archive of this kind of material. To keep this history alive, 'cause it's not the kind that will be taught in our schools."

Ingram had more of his catfish and scrambled eggs.

"About a month ago, Judy and me and her folks gathered up their boxes from where they'd been tucked away. We took them to their place to go through to determine what they wanted to give to the proposed archive." She stopped to have another sip of her coffee. "One item in particular wasn't in any of the boxes. A diary really."

Ingram said, "I'm guessing this diary contains sensitive information."

"Yeah, it's her dad's. The one her mom kept they have— several, actually."

"Sounds like his was misplaced."

"Maybe," she allowed. "Both sets of diaries name names. Not in a malicious way, but people he knew and worked with. There are those who are or were in the Party or had other radical affiliations they want—rather, need—to keep such hush-hush."

"But if it was stolen, why not take the mom's too?"

Claire said, "The crazy thing is, Judy's mom, Ester, never hid her diaries, despite being advised to do so at the time. She always said she would burn them before she'd let them be confiscated." Claire added, "But if the information her dad has in his gets out, a lot of people would be . . . uncomfortable." She leaned forward. "Like there are a few he knew who were tasked with burrowing from within."

"What does that mean?"

"For instance, their job was to get hired at a factory and talk up the benefits of being in a union."

"That include sabotage?"

"Not so anyone would get hurt. But yes, striking a blow for the workers against the bosses was sometimes called for."

He said, "After y'all went through the boxes, Judy's folks looked for the diary other places too?"

"Nobody was in a panic. They figured they must have put it elsewhere. Given to a friend out of state for safekeeping, like certain other items."

"But they checked around and they came up dry."

"Mm-hm."

"What do you want me to do?"

"Aren't you curious as to why I'm coming to you?"

"You mean from among your many male friends?"

"Yeah," she said, "you figure since you're a man, you can take command and help us silly women out." For the first time, her mood lightened.

"I was thinking that, but it sounds wrong when you say it out loud."

"I ought to reach across and slap you."

"Please." He offered his chin. "What does Miss Judy do, by the way, for a living?"

"Works at a tile factory in Huntington Park."

"Really?"

"Operates a machine that cuts them down to size."

"Damn."

"Oh, you're impressed by her, are you?"

"Not at all like I am by you, baby."

"Good answer."

He grinned and ate more. "You asked me not for my manliness, which I find disappointing, but 'cause I'm with the press."

"There is that, and you being a stranger to these folks." She seemed to have more to say but stopped and instead had more of her food.

Ingram studied her. Taking his time, he eventually said, "You ain't so slick."

"What, Harry?"

"Are you working your wiles on me?"

She batted her eyes theatrically. "Whatever do you mean, darling?"

"You and old buddy Judy have come up with a few suspects and you want me to interview them like I was doing a story about bringing the books out of hiding. What with me having a press credential for legitimacy, not to mention I'm covering the rally for the *Nation*."

She crooked her head to the side, smiling.

"But these are some white folks, isn't it?"

"Two are and the third is Black. And anyway, the white people are all about equal rights, they'll go for a colored man interviewing them."

"You should be ashamed of yourself, Miss Claire. Playing on their good intentions."

"This is for a greater good, Mr. Ingram. Judy's folks aren't getting any younger, and they want to use their diaries to write a book about their times. A joint memoir. One missing diary isn't that critical to them writing their book."

"It's the fact that it's missing."

"Right," she said.

"No blackmail note sent?"

"Nope. And as far as we can tell, the diary remains tucked away. The G-men haven't busted in the door of anybody the family knows lately."

"It could just be lost, Anita."

She shook her head. "He has an exact memory of which box he'd put it in. We checked all the boxes. Even a few still in the closet."

"When do you want to start doing this?" He liked that he was useful to her.

"Let me talk to Judy first and we'll get it set." She held up her cup, signaling the waitress for more coffee.

"Naturally I'm in. But you counted on that, didn't you?"

"You think me a tease?"

"Of course not."

The waitress came with more coffee and filled Claire's cup.

Over the rest of their meal, they discussed the matter more and Claire gave him a list of names. Written out too was brief information on who these people were.

"Freed isn't on your list of suspects." Ingram tapped the paper with his finger.

"Judy's dad, Jacob, insisted that he was above reproach."

"That's not being thorough."

"Me and Judy argued that, but he wasn't budging."

"Doesn't mean we can't talk to him."

"I don't know, Harry. Her dad wouldn't dig us going behind his back because I'm pretty sure Freed would call him if we did."

"Them being good friends shouldn't be a blinder. Sometimes it's the ones closest to you could be up to no good. Could also be Freed put the snatch on a few things like this diary. Figuring he knew best where to hide or even destroy this stuff 'cause as you said, it could do too much damage if Hoover's boys got ahold of these accounts."

She crossed her arms. "And what do you suspect me of, Harry?"

"Well, since you asked, you said this happened a month ago." He stopped talking and had more of his food.

She said pleasantly, "I see where you're going, hotshot. Us meeting at the party and what if I was reeling you in all the time like a sucker."

He showed even teeth.

"But it was only a few days ago Judy brought this back up. Like I said, her folks did some searching and came up with nothing. And it was only when she'd asked them if they'd found it, they told her. Then she and I got to talking and we sort of cooked up the idea of asking you all on our own."

He sat back, holding up his hands. "I'm cool."

"Uh-huh." She sipped more coffee.

"You figure me questioning the folks, tripping them up on their answers, will get one of them to break down, confess like they do every damn week in court on *Perry Mason*? Blubbering and carrying on."

"Uh-huh, just like that, knucklehead."

They both laughed. Claire had to get to the campaign office as sets of people were going out door-knocking this afternoon, "canvassing" she called it. She and others had prep work to do before then. Outside the restaurant, he stood with her near her car, a Rambler.

"When you and Judy talk, think about what questions I should be asking these people," he said. "Can't just come out and say, 'Hey, what about that diary I heard talk about.'"

"You're right."

"We'll figure out something."

"Oh, you mean I come over to your pad and we put our heads together to figure out how you approach the ones on the list? Maybe over a glass or two of wine?"

"Exactly." He leaned in and gave her a quick kiss.

She touched his chest. "See you soon, Harry." She kissed him back, not too quickly.

She got in her car and he watched her go. He then walked up the block and used a pay phone to make a call. Afterward, he drove to the Eternal Sands Funeral Home on Jefferson a few blocks west of Crenshaw Boulevard. He went inside and was ushered into the office of his friend Josh Nakano. He was dressed in a dark suit and somber tie, much different than when Ingram had last seen him at their domino game. They sat opposite each other in the compact space. As befitting a business with a high degree of Japanese and colored clientele, there were no religious trappings in here, though he knew Nakano was a Shinto Buddhist. Among several framed photographs on the wall behind the desk was one of Nakano in uniform as a radioman. He was posing with other members of the 442nd, the all–Japanese American "Go for Broke" regiment from World War II. Another was of his smiling nine-year-old son, Chris, on the beach in Hawaii where the child lived.

"This have to do with your Army buddy?" Nakano asked him.

Over the phone Nakano had told Ingram what he'd

obtained from the coroner's report, which listed Kinslow's death as caused by "misadventure." That could mean any number of things or, as the cops were saying, that he'd gone too fast around the curve and lost control of his vehicle. An accident plain and simple.

Ingram had asked Nakano what he knew about the Association of Merchants and Industrialists. "Ben was working for a man named Winston Hoyt and he's part of this association."

"Don't know nothing about this Hoyt, but I do know the association is all-white and I'm sure that's no surprise to you."

"Your invitation probably got lost in the mail," Ingram said, deadpan.

"Yeah, well, the association is very interested in not seeing the Rumford Act passed."

"Naturally," Ingram said, nodding. Currently being debated in the state assembly was a measure barring discrimination in housing—technically the California Fair Housing Act, sponsored by Assemblyman William Rumford.

"The original wording targeted public and private housings," Nakano continued. Both knew that meant eliminating housing covenants.

"Let me guess, buddies of the group are trying to make sure private housing isn't part of the measure."

"That's right. They're rallying members of the assembly, mostly Republicans but several Democrats too, under the notion of freedom for property owners."

"No sense calling a spade a spade," Ingram quipped.

"On the other hand, the association is giving money to the Bradley and Billy Mills campaigns for City Council."

"What?"

"It's true."

"How do you know this?"

Nakano spread his arms wide. "Why'd you ask me if you didn't think I knew what I was talking about? It's in my interest as a businessman to know who might be representing this district."

"I hear you, Josh." He wondered if his lady friend knew about this, her being tied in to the lefties.

"And there's my cousin I mentioned the other night. The Japanese American Citizens League keeps tabs on groups like the association. I called him after you called me. I remembered he'd mentioned them before." Noting the eagerness on Ingram's face, he held up a hand. "Now don't go off all half-cocked. Way I understand it from him, they're using a beard, a front to make the donations. They're being coy."

"A Stepin Fetchit supposed to be representing some kind of equal rights for us colored folk organization."

"Yes, sir, something like that."

"Ain't that some shit? Why are they playing both sides against the middle?"

Nakano said, "If I were a dime store headshrinker, I'd say they see themselves like old-world patricians. Sitting around smoking their expensive cigars, not them owl feathers you light up," he added quickly. "Sipping their expensive whiskey surrounded by their Renaissance art pontificating on what's best for the hoi polloi. Got to keep the natives happy but have to grease the wheels for the white man's progress too." He checked his watch. "I need to get to this meeting, Harry." He rose. "But over here at the library branch on La Brea are bound back issues of *Fortune* magazine. I bet if you looked through them, you'd find an article or two on the AMI. Nothing that revealing but probably worthwhile to look at."

Ingram was also standing. "What would I do without you, Josh?"

"Stumble around not knowing which leg of your pants to put on first." He clapped his friend on the back and the two walked toward the rear of the establishment. They passed by the sample room where there were various styles of coffins across a wide price range. A young woman in a business skirt and matching jacket was showing a model to an older couple.

"The gold and ivory handles really make this one a premiere choice." She lovingly touched one of the handles. The two murmured in agreement.

Out back was a parking area reserved for Eternal Sands employees. Nakano unlocked the driver's door to his pearl-black Ford Galaxie. Its red leather interior was immaculate as befitting a funeral director. "See you at the rally, Harry. I'm going with the Little Tokyo contingent."

"Righteous."

They shook hands and Ingram walked back around to the street and his car. He then went to the Baldwin Hills branch of the library as his friend had suggested. Perusing several back issues of *Fortune* magazine, he found an article about the history of the Association of Merchants and Industrialists, which was founded in the city at the turn of the last century. Its membership had included such men as Harrison Gray Otis, veteran of the Civil and Spanish-American wars and publisher of the *L.A. Times*; Elias Jackson "Lucky" Baldwin, real estate speculator for whom this area was named; and William Mulholland, the man who essentially stole water from Owens Valley in the transformation of the city from pueblo to metropolis. All influential white men, as Nakano had pointed out. As predicted, there were no secrets revealed, but Ingram took notes and placed the magazines back in their collector's boxes and returned them to the reference desk.

"Did you find what you were looking for?" the aging, handsome librarian asked him.

"A few more pieces of the puzzle. Still have a ways to go."

"Research can be so demanding yet rewarding when you make a breakthrough," she said.

"Amen."

Ingram left and ran a couple of errands, including turning in his filled green stamps booklets for a four-slice toaster at a redemption store. Afterward he returned home and heated up some leftover spaghetti and meatballs he'd made two nights ago. His stomach full, he then went back out on foot and walked to the Lucky Clover bar for a beer or two. This time there was no whispering from Seoul City Sue, and he drank in peace.

CHAPTER SEVEN

The following morning the jangling phone woke him up. He rolled over, one eye open to see by his clock it wasn't quite five minutes past seven. He plucked the handset free, clearing his throat.

"Hello?"

"Sorry to call so early, Harry," said the voice on the other end of the line.

"Doris?"

"Yes, sorry again. Guess I'm a bit flustered."

"About what?" It was Doris Letrec from Galton Process Servers and Legal Matters.

"What do you know about the Nation of Islam?"

"I know not to mess with them."

"I was afraid you were going to say that."

"What's up?"

"An attorney we've done work for previously has called us. He's out of state."

Ingram rubbed a hand on the side of his whiskered face. "There's a Black Muslim he wants to serve a subpoena on in town?"

"No, not a civil action. Apparently the individual in

question is named in a will." She lowered her voice conspiratorially. "A man owning a lot of acres named Fordis Royal has died in Athens, Georgia. He was white. And Mr. Jones is said to be one of the ones requested to be there for the reading next week. Really it's just a letter from the lawyer requesting his presence."

Ingram laughed harshly. "His momma was this old bird's nanny or could be, you know, the other thing."

"What other thing?" Letrec asked genuinely.

"This old Confederate who croaked wouldn't be the first gray boy who had hisself a Black kid or two out of wedlock. Forcing himself on the help." Now he was getting angry, reflecting on how many times this had happened over how many decades.

She took in a breath. "You think that's what it is?"

"I don't know and probably don't want to know. But since this is good news, why doesn't he get on the phone and tell this guy?"

"That's part of the hitch," she said. "His name is William Jones and it's known he converted or whatever they call it about four years ago."

"And the lawyer doesn't know his Muslim name?"

"He's not sure," she said. "It could be William 2X, William 3X or William Muhammad. Or it might be something different. He is pretty sure he's here in Los Angeles, though."

Ingram yawned, covering his mouth. "Excuse me. Look, Doris, like I said, I don't much truck with the Nation except buying a bean pie now and then. But I get it, having a white face show up at the mosque trying to see Brother Jones could be a problem. But even a Black face of an outsider only goes so far with them."

"It's two hundred dollars if you can serve him."

"That's my end?"

"Yes."

"Damn. You drive a hard bargain, Miss Letrec. You have some particulars on Mr. Jones the Mystery X to help narrow down my search?"

"Of course."

"Okay, I'll swing by." He hung up and went into the bathroom to get ready for the day.

He drove over to the Galton offices and got the papers and what information she'd been given by the attorney on the former William Jones. Ingram didn't know anyone in the Nation of Islam, but the money was an incentive to get to know someone, somehow. Though he wasn't about to go up to a dude selling those bean pies or their tracts on a street corner like they did and ask did they know the man in question. It didn't take much imagination to see how such an approach could deteriorate quickly.

Back in his car Ingram considered how strange it was that he was so much in demand. Sure, for Anita he'd run barefoot over broken glass to fetch her purse to impress her, but he was fascinated by these radicals she hung around with. In the war it had been drilled into the soldiers to "get those dirty chinks," and kill the "commie gooks," but it never got under his skin like it did with others he'd known then. To him the war had been a matter of survival more than fighting the red hordes. Not that he was building a statue of Uncle Joe Stalin in his backyard, but once he got back, things hadn't changed here. Negro GIs had sacrificed just like the white ones, but it wasn't as if any of that really mattered once the conflict was over. And it wasn't like they'd won. The goddamn truce drew a line between the north and south, the 38th Parallel.

Picking up Milo Costas's camera had literally given him a different perspective. Sighting through the viewfinder had allowed Ingram to take a step back and see his surroundings as a man removed. As if the pictures he took of his fellow soldiers in the thick of it were a stage upon which he'd been set. He knew the lines he was supposed to say, but events changed the script drastically. By the time he accidentally killed that kid, his head was already coming apart. After that there was Harry the dogface and Harry the dispassionate photographer who documented an upside-down world. Was he trying to make sense of the chaos by capturing his stills?

Hunting for a red's diary or running down a would-be heir, he wasn't giving up on Ben Kinslow. Not by a long shot. But a job was a job.

Ingram paid a visit to Resolution Blueprint Services, an outfit he did regular business with, to get a photostat made. Leaving, he stopped at a pay phone and called the Bradley campaign office asking for Anita. Given her circles, she might know a Black Muslim.

"She's out at the moment, can I take a message?"

"That's okay, I'll call her back. Thanks."

Leaning inside the phone booth, the door open, he took out one of his cigars from an inside pocket and lit it, contemplating his next steps. He went back to his car and drove over to Wrigley Field, puffing away. He hadn't tried his janitorial contacts yet. This time of day the park was closed, and he expected to walk around its perimeter to get a lay of the land before the rally. Yet when he got to the venue, there were a number of cars in the parking lot which wasn't blacktopped but oily dirt. The main gate was open. From his trunk he took out his camera and strolled inside. A boxing ring had been set up on the field. There had been several pro bouts at Wrigley in the past, even one at Dodger Stadium as well. As Ingram got nearer, he could see one of the fighters was former welterweight champ Emile Griffith. Last year Griffith had regained the title after defeating Benny Paret in a very brutal fashion.

Ingram had seen the match on television. In the twelfth round, Griffith got Paret in a corner and went to work on him something fierce. He rained blows on him, several to the head. Paret was so out of it he stopped defending himself, his arms lifeless as if the bones in them had melted. The crowd yelled for the referee to halt the fight. He finally did but it was too late. Paret was carried off to the hospital on a stretcher and never regained consciousness. Griffith tried to visit but was turned away. Ten days later Paret died. The pope himself denounced the fight as an example of a barbaric practice that should be banned.

Last month Griffith lost the title to Luis Rodríguez. Observers said Griffith didn't have the killer instinct anymore given the terrible outcome of the Paret fight. Yet here he was giving an exhibition bout. Unusual, too, as he fought out of New York City. Ingram took shots from various angles. Satisfied for the moment, he went into the stands. Everyone was sitting in the lower rows.

"Hey, Harry," came a greeting.

"Brad," he said, shaking the bespectacled man's hand and sitting next to him. Brad Pye Jr. was the sportswriter for the *Sentinel* and also did public relations for the Angels, the first Black man to have such a position in the majors.

"Who you covering this for?" he asked.

"I just happened to roll by. Figuring to do a bit of reconnoitering before the big event."

"Right, right." Pye had his attention on the match. Griffith slipped a blow and landed an uppercut on his sparring partner that got heads nodding. Ingram estimated the majority of people in attendance were connected in some way to the boxing game. He recognized a reporter from *Ring* magazine and the sportswriter from the *L.A. Times*.

As Ingram watched he asked Pye, "Who's the guy Griffith is sparring with?"

"Local kid, Michael Hodges. He chose him 'cause he's got moves like Rodríguez and he wants to be in tip-top shape for the rematch." He made more notes on the yellow pad he had on a knee.

More punches were exchanged. Ingram said, "Brad, you know any Black Muslims?"

Pye gave him a sideways look, a sly grin on his face. "You talking about the rumor?"

"What rumor?"

"About Clay."

"Cassius Clay?"

"Shh, be cool, keep you voice down. You want these Jesus-loving white folks in here to run us out on a rail?" His smile turned into a wide grin.

"Clay is one of them?"

Pye wagged a finger. "Not yet he isn't. But Malcolm X has his ear."

"I was wondering for a different reason."

"You thinking of joining?"

"Please, I like pork chops too much."

"Amen, brother."

Ingram was a fan of boxing, but he needed to be attending to why he'd come here. "See you, Brad. I'm going to take a walk around."

"Okay. And keep the Clay business to yourself. I'm angling to get an exclusive."

"Remember me for the picture of you and him shaking hands."

"You can bet those pretty little green ones I will."

Ingram walked through the arena, taking several pictures from different angles as the sparring continued. It was only five rounds and drawing to an end. He ascended the steps to a higher position and noted places in his steno pad he might stake out when he returned for the Freedom Rally to capture the sweep of the crowd. As he made his way back to his car in the parking lot, he passed two sports writers smoking and talking. One leaned on a car.

"Yeah, the Tellis Group is backing that middleweight kid Aguirre from Lincoln Heights."

"That's that grocery store guy, Stockworth?" his companion said, a tall man in short sleeves.

"Him and a few other businessmen, including a guy who owns a couple of strip clubs."

Both snickered. Ingram walked over to them. "You said Stockworth, that would be Howard Stockworth?"

"Uh-huh," said the man who'd mentioned the boxer. "You figuring to get a piece of the action?"

"You never know."

"Sure," the other one said, blowing a stream of smoke toward the sky.

Howard Stockworth was one of the names Ingram had written down from the *Los Angeles* magazine article about the Association of Merchants and Industrialists. Hoyt liked the ponies and apparently this grocery chain man liked the sweet science. There was some sort of symbolism there, he considered. He turned away and was pleasantly surprised to see a hot dog vendor had set up outside the gate with his cart, steam rising from it. He walked over and ordered two chili dogs, extra onions.

Post lunch, Ingram drove over to see Shoals Pettigrew at Shop Rite Hardware. It occurred to him his friend interacted with a cross section of people coming through his door.

Everybody had to take a trip to the hardware store at some point, didn't they?

When he walked in, Pettigrew was selling a woman two cans of paint and assorted items. She was in a pinafore dress, turtleneck and ragged tennis shoes. She was noticeably pregnant.

"Be right with you, Harry," he said.

"Take your time."

Pettigrew carried the items out of the store for the woman and loaded them in her car. He returned. "What can I do you for today?"

"Ever get any Black Muslims in here?"

"You looking to do a story on them?" He stood in front of the counter where the morning mail was stacked. A letter from Pettigrew's bank on top.

"Need to find one of the true believers here in town."

"Shit, you trying to get your head caved in? You gonna lay a notice on him getting a paternity suit by some chick? Man." He shook his head in disbelief.

Ingram told Pettigrew what it was about.

"Oh, well," he said, moving back behind the counter, "that's different. A time or two a couple of gents in blue suits and bow ties have been in. Mostly getting rat traps or drain cleaner, stuff like that. You can't forget 'em 'cause they always say that greeting, a salaam . . . however the hell it goes," he said dismissively. Pettigrew was an active member of his Methodist church.

"Is there a mosque around here?"

"Not that I know of."

"There's a dry cleaners a few blocks over them fellas run."

Ingram turned to see the retired janitor who hung out here emerge from one of the aisles. He was dressed as usual, holding a box of nails.

"Where?"

He pointed east. "On Main, can't recall the exact block but not far from the Boys market."

"I appreciate that," Ingram said.

"My pleasure." The older man put the nails on the counter. "Catch you later, Shoals."

"Not if I see you first."

Ingram checked the address for the Boys supermarket at a pay phone with a White Pages chained to it. He then drove to the address. Using that as his starting point, he went south then north and soon spotted the business he was looking for. A large sign over the front door announced SHABAZZ DRY CLEANERS NO. 2. He parked and walked into the establishment. At the counter was a man in a dress white shirt, buttoned at the wrists and wearing a tie, steam-pressing a pair of pants in a work area behind the front counter. Despite the heat and steam rising around him, he wasn't sweating. A man dressed similarly was also behind the counter. His glasses were ovals over a keen set of eyes.

"What can I do for you today, brother?"

"I'm looking for a man who used to be named William Jones."

"None of us go by our slave names anymore thanks to the Honorable Elijah Muhammad."

"Yes, sir, I'm aware of that. I'm representing a lawyer."

"A white lawyer?" he asked without rancor.

"Yes. But it's not trouble. It's for a good reason."

"From a devil lawyer?"

From his inside jacket pocket he removed the folded-over photostat he'd had made. This was part of the letter referring to the disposition of the will. Purposefully it did not include the name of the attorney nor his location. No sense cutting out his fee as middleman if he could help it. He laid the photostat down on the counter, facing the man so he could scan it.

"As you can see, this is the second page from a two-page letter from the lawyer. There's to be the reading of a will and Mr. Jones—the former Mr. Jones—is requested to be present." He tapped his finger on the date. "It's taking place next week."

"Where?"

"I can tell that to the man in question. I can say it's in Georgia."

"There's a lot of Williamses from Georgia in the Nation, brother. Even out here in the land of plenty," he said, sans irony.

There had been physical characteristics listed for Jones in the other paperwork Ingram had been given. "I do know the man in question is about six-one and missing a piece of his earlobe." He tugged on his left ear. He had no idea how this had come about.

The counterman's expression didn't change but he picked up the photostat and read it carefully. "Is there money or land involved?"

"I can't divulge that." He didn't know. Gently Ingram took hold of the photostat and folded it, inserting it back in his inner pocket. He then put his card on the counter. "Time is of the essence."

The counterman looked from the card to Ingram. "I'm not promising anything."

"Of course. Thank you on this. Good day, brothers." He nodded to the man in glasses and the presser who'd been looking on. Walking to his car, Ingram understood the counterman's question about land or money involved hadn't been an idle query. The one thing he did know about the Black Muslims was they espoused the separate nation idea:

three states including Georgia set aside for Black folks to be left alone by the white devils. If William the former Jones was a conduit to helping make that happen, the counterman, like Ingram, had incentive. He figured the man would talk to whoever it was he reported to in the chain of command.

The following early evening Ingram and Anita Claire had a date at Pacific Ocean Park on the beach in Santa Monica. Given the breeze off the ocean, he wore an aviator-type leather jacket and she a button-up cashmere sweater.

"What, the big tough Army man is scared of a roller coaster?" She delicately inserted a single kernel of popcorn in her mouth.

"I'm just saying, wouldn't you prefer the diving bell or the Skyway ride?"

"After we go on the Sea Serpent, tough guy."

"Fine, me Tarzan, you Jane." He thumped his chest with his fist. "But you know that monstrosity was built before electricity was discovered."

She chuckled. "Stop being such a worrywart, you sound like my mother." Claire guided him toward the line for the ride. It was a weeknight but there were plenty of people out to enjoy the amusement park. There was a threadbare quality to the whole thing, like shoes worn too long but too comfortable to get rid of. They stood close in the line, Claire feeding him the occasional piece of popcorn. At one point her finger came to rest on his lip and she left it there, looking into his eyes. They kissed.

"Ahem," said the roller-coaster operator. "You getting on or not?"

They sat in the car. Right behind them two teenage girls got on, giggling and whispering to each other. Once the cars were full, the retaining bars were lowered and off they went. Per the protocol of roller coasters, the first part of the ride was a slow ascent to build the tension and anticipation among the riders.

"Nervous?" She pinched his arm.

"Ha ha." He tried to blot out the constant creak of wood as the steel wheels of the cars rode over the rails supported by aging struts and beams. He didn't recall hearing about any fatal accidents happening on this particular coaster, so he supposed that was partially reassuring. Even when he was a kid he'd never been fascinated by roller coasters like his friends were. His grade-school friend Shoals Pettigrew, for instance, loved them. A few years ago the two had driven to Galveston, Texas, to fetch a car a recently deceased uncle had left Pettigrew, who was also getting over a divorce then. Making sure to map their route using the *Green Book* so as to avoid unfriendly towns, Ingram had reluctantly made a couple of stops along the way. This so Edwards could ride a specific roller coaster in a particular town. A grown man giddy like the teenagers behind them now, Ingram recalled.

The train of cars crested the first loop then speedily plummeted, riders screaming with joy. Claire latched onto Ingram's arm, squeezing hard. She laughed at his stoic expression. His stomach was in his throat, but he was determined to show her how manly he could be. She laughed more.

"Oh, hold me, you big strong hunk, hold me."

He had to laugh too as he put his arm around her shoulders, squeezing tightly as they whipped through a turn to ascend once more before a steep drop. When the ride was over, the teenagers hopped out laughing and ran off to the next thrill. In the last car had been a burly man with a crew cut and his date, a petite brunette with hoop earrings. His face was florid from too many beers and hot dogs, Ingram estimated. With the help of his companion, he weaved to a trash can and bending over the rim, threw up.

"What next?" he asked Claire, smiling.

"The one that takes you out over the water."

Off they went hand in hand to the Ocean Skyway. Bubble-shaped gondolas rode passengers on a cable seventy-five feet over the Pacific for half a mile out then brought them back to the docking area. After a short wait, they sat close together in their gondola on the bench seat. The doors to each vessel were secured by the operator and off they went. They swung gently to and fro as they were carried out over the dark water. Claire stared down into the depths.

"Can you imagine we were swimming in that millions of years ago? Creatures that one day decided to get out of the muck and came up on land to check things out. Then who knows how many other millions of years it took to develop legs to move off the shore and the lungs to breathe in the air."

"You mean it wasn't like on *The Flintstones*? Riding dinosaurs to work and eating giant barbecue ribs the size of a Mack truck?"

She nuzzled his cheek. "When I was a kid in school I got in trouble with Mrs. Hempel in the fourth grade. The subject of how people came to be was asked and, being a nice Christian lady, she naturally said that God created Adam and Eve in the Garden of Eden." She narrowed her eyes. "Until that ditzy Eve was tricked by Satan and she bit into the apple of knowledge. We got kicked out by an angry God, she told us, but that's why we had dominion over the animals and had planes to fly through the air." She shook her head at the memory. "I sat there frowning."

"You being a precocious sort with commie atheist parents," Ingram said.

"Yep. I blurted out evolution was the reason we walked

on two legs and our brains—which had grown along with our bodies—told us how to use our opposable thumbs. Now Mrs. Hempel tried to give me the benefit of the doubt. Asking me didn't I mean God made evolution happen?"

"And you said?" The gondola began its round-trip back.

"I said maybe, but nobody so far as my parents were concerned could prove God or Heaven or Hell existed and that's what they'd told me when I'd asked about where you went when you died. I told her they'd also said as I got older, I should investigate these ideas for myself. On their shelves were science books, naturally, but also a copy of the Bible and the Talmud, or they would assist me in whatever else I wanted to learn about in terms of seeking to achieve inner peace."

"Did her head explode?"

"I was escorted to the principal's office and my mother was called. I remember clearly he didn't say much to me but had a worried look on his face. I guess he was concerned about the fate of my immortal soul."

"Did she yell at them when she got there?"

The gondolas stopped. The couple automatically looked around. Both were relieved the cable was still intact.

Claire said, "Mom was a seasoned organizer, used to confronting screaming bosses and cops itching to bust heads. Particularly this race traitor, a white woman married to a Black man. When she got to the school, she quietly asked what the problem was. By then the vice-principal was in the office too. He was a hard-ass, ex-Marine, was at Guadalcanal and all that old mess."

Their ride ended and they stepped out and started to walk back along the planks toward the main part of the venue. The ocean broke against the pilings beneath them. Nearby a child squealed with delight.

She continued. "I found out years later he was not on the front lines. He was a supply clerk. But he terrified us kids. Anyway, Mom began with a reasoned approach. She said wasn't school the place where thinking and asking questions should take place? The principal answered that was true but there were underlying notions, shared beliefs as to how learning took place. One of them being we were a Christian nation. That's what we affirm in the Pledge of Allegiance, he said."

"Your folks tell you not to do the Pledge?"

Claire said, "Sounds like a teacher drilled that into you."

"Yes, ma'am. Mr. Lakefield and his icy glare."

"Well, just so you know, my parents remain loyal Americans. They had big arguments with their friends over the Rosenbergs. It was one thing to work for equality and certain socialist ideals, but giving up secrets to the Soviets was a line they wouldn't cross. They would never sell out the United States," she said proudly.

"But to answer your question, yeah, there's that part about 'One Nation Under God,' but they said I could ignore that in my head if I wished. My dad always said the part to really pay attention to was the liberty and justice for all. Nonetheless I stood, hand on my chest and all that."

They wandered through the amusement park with no particular destination in mind.

"I bet at some point your gung-ho Marine got excited at this meeting with your mom."

"Very perceptive. Mr. Ingram. Yes, things soon deteriorated, and the two so-called educators pretty much accused my mother of being a bad parent, and asked if she was even born in this country, her with her Brooklyn accent."

They'd stopped in front of the ring toss game. Ingram asked, "Did they kick both of you out of the office?"

"I got suspended for a week. Now of course my parents knew a few firebrand lawyers who'd gotten them and their comrades out of hot water over the years. When Mom returned to school with one of them, a tall woman partial to pearls, threatening to sue in violation of my folks' free speech rights and saying that this had been settled in the Scopes Monkey Trial and so on and so on, I was back in two days."

Ingram paid for three rings. "You and Mrs. Hempel avoided the subject for the rest of the semester?" He made his first toss.

"Only two more, friend, and you win the lady a teddy bear," the man in the booth said. He was reedy and balding, wearing a rainbow-patterned vest and straw hat.

His next toss was good too, landing on the neck of one of the upturned milk bottles assembled together in the middle of the booth.

"Way to go, dead-eye," Claire encouraged.

Ingram did a few practice moves with his arm and let the third ring fly. It bounced off the neck of a bottle and fell onto the dirt floor.

"Aw, too bad, friend. The lovely lady goes home empty-handed."

"No, she won't." Claire gave him a quarter and got three plastic rings. She made all her tosses.

"There you go, ma'am." The attendant handed her the teddy bear. As he did that, he bestowed a quick sneer on Ingram.

"My dear." Claire handed the small stuffed animal to Ingram as they walked away.

He gladly took it. "Thank you, darling."

By the time they left the amusement park they were happy and hungry for more than amusement park food—at least Ingram was. The teddy bear on the seat between them, he drove them from Santa Monica, taking Olympic Boulevard east. They went past the Olympic Drive-In, "Enjoy Movies in Your Car." At several intervals parallel to the car, they could discern the dark forms of graded earth, heavy machinery and the skeletal framing onto which concrete would be poured to form the lanes of the upcoming freeway. He arrived at La Cienega and pulled onto the parking lot of the Ships Coffee Shop on the southeast corner. It was a twenty-four-hour Googie futurist-designed building suggesting the promise of space-age efficiency. Anita Claire dozed on the seat next to him. Light from inside the restaurant colored her in soft ambers and yellow. She seemed to him a living painting. He touched her shoulder.

"Want to eat?"

"Yes." She opened her eyes and turning her head toward him, pulled him close.

The two kissed passionately, but eventually went in. Occupying the counter and booths were the denizens of the night, including hotel clerks just getting off work in nearby Beverly Hills and Black and white men in bus-driver uniforms eating prior to their early morning shifts.

The waitress deposited two menus at their booth, as well as several slices of white and wheat bread on a saucer. Each booth was outfitted with its own toaster, the same for the counter.

"Coffee?" she asked.

"None for me," Claire said, a hand in front of her yawning mouth.

"Orange juice for me, please, and we'll be getting food."

"Sure. Be right back."

Claire took a slice of bread and put it in the toaster. She dialed the timer and plopped it down. "Think we'll beat the Russians to the moon like the president wants?"

"Sure. You worried we won't?"

She frowned. "I guess I'm torn. I know full well the horrors of Stalin's reign and what might be an unsure fate should they get there first. But all that money to reach a hunk of rock and we got starving children in this town, Harry, let alone down in Alabama and Mississippi."

The waitress returned. Claire ordered half a grapefruit as compared to Ingram's plate of two pancakes, scrambled eggs and bacon, crisp.

He said to her when the waitress left, "If I can't win you a prize, at least I can eat like a man."

She laughed and continued where they'd left off. "But the race is on, ain't no stopping it now. Maybe some of what gets developed for those rockets and space suits can have practical applications for us stuck on this mudball."

"I know you don't mean ray guns like in the Flash Gordon comic strip. 'Cause say what you want, them generals with the fruit salad on their chests are looking to come out of this with better missiles to reach your poor Russian people and take them out of their suffering in a mushroom cloud."

"Believe me, I know. But did you know there are several colored women mathematicians working at NASA?"

"What?"

"Yep, they're fondly called the human computers. Figuring out complex trajectories, working navigational charts for theoretical flights and so forth."

He whistled. "Somebody ought to write about that."

"I think there was an article about one of them, Katherine Johnson, in an alumni publication."

"Yeah, well," he said. "You and four others saw that."

"There's a lot about us we should preserve for our future generations. All generations really."

"Meaning I should do more to broaden my subject matter?"

"I wasn't trying to be sly, Harry. Now don't you worry, comrade," she began, affecting a theatrical Russian accent, "one day you and your images will inspire the vanguard of the lumpenproletariat."

"Damn right, whatever it is you said."

After they finished their meal and got back in the car, she put her head against his shoulder.

"Home next stop, ma'am."

"Okay." She placed a hand on his thigh and kissed and nuzzled his neck.

As he reacted, she wasn't shy about rubbing her hand in another area as well.

Back at her apartment they made love and finally found sleep in each other's embrace around four in the morning. He awoke to the sounds of a shower going. Ingram was momentarily disoriented, as if he'd had a carnal dream about her but hadn't really been with her. Claire's bedroom was compact and neat. On a wall were several framed photographs. Getting into his boxers, he walked over to them, recognizing Karl Marx, Ida B. Wells and Charlotta Bass speaking at a podium. There was also one of a Black man in a gray suit and glasses. It wasn't Malcolm X, as this individual was dark and had dark hair. But he reminded Ingram of the charismatic leader.

"That's Patrice Lumumba," she said over his shoulder. "An African freedom fighter who was assassinated a couple of years ago. The Central Intelligence Agency is complicit in his demise. He was the first prime minister of the so-called newly independent Congo."

"Them whites making sure the darkies didn't take that business about being our own bosses too seriously, you mean."

"The power-hungry puppet they helped install is named

Mobutu, from the military." She was standing in the doorway to the bathroom in a terry cloth robe, drying her hair with a towel. "Sometimes," she sighed, shaking her head, "we can be our own worst enemies." She wrapped the towel around her wet hair.

There was a lone photo on another wall of a Black man and a white woman. She was sitting and he was standing behind her, his hands on her shoulders. They were dressed in everyday clothes and smiling. Claire looked to be a darker-hued version of her mother.

"Your mom's a good-lookin' chick."

"Shut up, idiot."

On a tidy bookcase were the types of books he expected to find, nonfiction works such as *The Souls of Black Folk; Fear, the Accuser; Anarchism and Other Essays* and several textbooks about math. There was also a book called *The Second Sex* and several fiction paperbacks he was surprised to find with titles such as *Women's Barracks, The Midnight Blade* and *The Long Wait.* Their covers were salaciously intriguing, living up to their exciting titles.

He had one of the paperbacks in his hand when Claire came up behind him, putting her arms around his middle. Her fingers on his flesh reminded him that while he'd already found Kinslow's pictures at the Y, he should make working out there a routine.

"I like it that you have a wide variety of interests in reading," he said, turning his head to kiss her.

"Blame it on my curious parents. There were always all kinds of books lying around the house when I was growing up. My mom could read three or four of them at a time. Still does."

"Lucky I can read my name," Ingram muttered, overjoyed to be in her arms again.

She'd undone the robe and her hand slipped inside his boxers' waistband as they swayed together. Sometime later they were dressed and having coffee and sharing a sweet roll in her kitchenette. Ingram ate most of the pastry. Claire had two small pieces at the end of her fork. They were staring at each other when her phone rang. She got up to answer.

"Yes," she said, listening. "Right, okay, why don't we meet there in about half an hour?" There was a response, then, "Yes, I know where he lives. See you there." She hung up and came back to the table but didn't sit down.

"What's up?" He finished off the sweet roll.

"There's a meeting at Reverend Brookings's house. Hollingsworth has a new ad on the radio touting himself as the negro's best friend. Actually using the fact Tom was a policeman to hint he's in the pocket of interests outside of our community." Joe Hollingsworth was white and when the midterm opening on the City Council occurred in 1961, he'd been appointed among several candidates, including Bradley, who at the time was still on the police force. Hollingsworth had an inside track with certain elements in City Hall. He'd been a construction supervisor working on the development of Baldwin Hills. Now, though, the voters would decide on the first full term.

"Damned if you do and damned if you don't," Ingram said. "That's what the coloreds get for being ambitious." He'd taken various shots of Bradley over the years, including the time when he was still a cop and was assigned to safeguard the singer and civil rights activist Paul Robeson when he came to town.

A crooked grin came and went on her face. "At least the CIA isn't involved, just good old-fashioned American capitalists. Which I suppose is the same thing."

"Go get 'em, Anita."

She was at a desk in a corner by the window assembling a few of her papers and putting them in a valise with her initials on it. "Stay as long as you want, Harry. Turn the lock and the door locks behind you."

He stretched, yawning. Ingram was tempted to hang around and laze away the day, waiting lustfully for her return. "Shouldn't I tiptoe out the back door so your reputation isn't ruined?"

"Little late for that, baby." She leaned over him studying his face, his chin held in her hand. "Say my name again."

"Anita," he said like cotton was in his throat.

"That's right." She gave him all tongue so as not to smear her lipstick.

He had another cup of coffee and turned on the portable TV she had on top of the bedroom dresser. The master of fitness Jack LaLanne was going through one of his exercise routines. He was always in a leisure jumpsuit, today's being sky blue in color with belted pockets on his chest and the same design on the buckle on the sewn-in belt at his trim waist. Watching LaLanne go through his paces and also visualizing the fabulous and fit nude form of Claire in his mind, he joined in and worked up a light sweat. Afterward he was hungry again but maintained discipline and didn't open her refrigerator. He left, making sure the door was secured behind him.

Downstairs he had to remember where he'd parked; he'd been too distracted when Claire had her hand between his legs, his fly zipped down. Finally it came back to him and he walked down West Thirty-Seventh toward the corner of Raymond Avenue. He was about to pass by a telephone pole, a handbill stapled on it. He stopped, the image on the flyer having gotten his attention. It was of several stern-faced men and women standing side by side looking out at the viewer.

They were Black Muslims, and the wording was about a picket of the White Front department store on Manchester. The action was to take place today at noon.

A few minutes later, dime in hand, Ingram made a call at a pay phone at a gas station, the driver's door of his Belvedere open and the engine running.

"Hey, Wes," he said, when the phone was answered by Wesley Crossman at the *Eagle* newspaper. "What do you know about this protest by the Black Muslims?"

"Nothing."

Deadline frenzy gripped the newsroom. As he talked to the editor, he heard reporters yelling for their copyedited galleys, cursing about getting a headline rewritten and the other joyous cacophonies of a weekly edition being composed.

With a dry chuckle he said, "It's happening today at noon at the, get this, the White Front."

"Don't know nothing. Just like them to not put out a press release," he groused. "It's happening today you said?" The rhythmic tak-tak-tak of typewriter keys being attacked came over the line.

He told him what he'd gleaned from the flyer. "How about it?" he asked.

"Okay, yeah, cover it. We'll find the room for a shot and a short piece. But get me a juicy quote and you got to have it over here before four."

"On it." Ingram hung up and got back in his car. Maybe he could kill two birds with the same stone, he figured as he drove away.

Back at his place he showered again, given his exercising with Jack, and shaved. He put on slacks and a light short-sleeved shirt; no coat, but took his snap-brim hat with him. He got over to the White Front not twenty minutes past eleven. Already there was a grouping of the NOI milling on a section of the parking lot. So far the only other newspaper represented here was a reporter for the Muslim's *Muhammad Speaks*.

His Speed Graphic strapped around his neck and his press credentials in his shirt pocket, he approached a huskily built man directing two others. He wore a dark suit, and his silver tie clasp contrasted with his black tie flat against his starched white shirt.

"Excuse me, brother," he began, "I'm here from the *Eagle* and wanted to know what brought this about."

The man regarded Ingram for a beat then said, "The white man and his continuing devaluing of negro labor. The plantation system is over."

Ingram had his steno pad out. "Could you be more specific? For the record. And tell me your name, please."

"I'm Kevin Abdullah and I've been authorized to speak for the Honorable Elijah Muhammad in this regard." He pointed at the arched façade of the discount chain. Several shoppers had paused near the doorway to see what was going on. "A salesman in this store insulted one of our women when she came in to purchase a simple vacuum cleaner."

"What did he say?"

"He was white, of course, and said there must be a lot of dirt in that mosque of yours what with the kind of people you all cater to." He looked evenly at Ingram, who wrote down the quote. "When contacted about this, the manager refused to discipline his employee."

Ingram made a note of that too. "I'll be back."

The other man nodded and resumed talking to the others. By now several station wagons had arrived with carloads of members. In the cargo area of the cars were placards on sticks. Ingram estimated at least three hundred were already outside and no doubt more were on the way.

Inside the store he took the escalator to the second floor and headed to the manager's office. He was intercepted at the door by a security guard.

"What do you want?" He was an older gentleman with a bent nose and a wooden matchstick propped in the corner of his mouth. His eyes were watery, and he made no attempt to hide his growing gut.

"I want to get the manager's side of the incident," Ingram said, showing him his credentials. The guard didn't strike him as an ex-cop, but he wasn't sure.

"This for a colored paper?"

"That's right."

"Then it's not real news, is it?"

"Can I use that in my article as the official outlook of the White Front corporation? They don't take their colored customers and the press that reports about them seriously?"

His face compacted. "All right, damn, hold your water." He went inside the office, closing the door behind him, then returned a moment later. Ingram saw past him into the inner office. The manager was standing at his desk, holding the phone's handset. The guard closed the door to his back.

"Mr. Peterson says he'll have something to say shortly."

"Looking forward to it." Ingram went back outside and walked around, taking shots and looking for a man with part of his left earlobe missing. He stared hard at the side of more than one head and got questioning grimaces for his intrusions. By now he counted more than four hundred men and women from the various mosques in the parking lot and out on the sidewalk. Standing off to one side, Kevin Abdullah reviewed his talking points on several index cards he shuffled in his large hands. Several police cars arrived, taking up position. Abdullah paused to watch this. A news van from local station Channel 5 also appeared. The officers exited their vehicles, conferring with one another.

Ingram took more shots and was about to break away to call Crossman to tell him this was going to be a longer article. It was then the manager, Mr. Peterson, came outside, a few steps from the front doors in case he had to rush back inside, Ingram surmised. The security guard stood next to him, along with a Black woman in a black-and-white-checkered skirt and black sweater.

A sergeant broke away from the other policemen and approached Abdullah. Ingram went toward the two as the TV newscaster stood on the sidewalk. He adjusted his handheld microphone as the cameraman set up his camera on its stilts. Various cables trailed from their equipment back into the van.

"This is an illegal assembly," the sergeant was saying to Abdullah.

"This is about justice and fair treatment. That's never illegal."

"Look, you need a permit to picket. You know this."

Ingram clicked away.

The sergeant turned toward him. "Get the fuck out of here."

"I'm press."

"I don't care if you're Old Man River."

"I have a right to cover this just like they do." He pointed his jaw at the newsman on the sidewalk.

The sergeant resumed talking to Abdullah. "I'm asking you to take your people and get out of here before this gets out of hand."

"Not until the manager talks to us about his failure to act responsibly."

"Jesus," the sergeant said, "give you people an inch and you take a mile."

Abdullah grinned. "We learned from the best."

The sergeant swore and walked back to his officers.

Abdullah started toward where Peterson stood but the manager retreated back inside the store. The security guard and the woman remained. Abdullah talked to her. Ingram took a few shots of them, then pivoted toward the cops. Not needing to look at his camera, by rote he took out the used roll and inserted a new one. He began taking pictures of the gathered cops.

"Didn't I tell you to get the fuck out of here?" the sergeant reiterated.

"Just doing my job."

"Do it elsewhere."

One of the police officers put his hand on his sheathed nightstick. "I've seen this nosy bastard around. Always taking snaps of misery and mayhem."

"Yeah, probably a peeping Tom too," another one cracked.

"He's got some nerve," a third officer added.

There were two Black officers present and they chuckled along with the rest of them.

"Brothers and sisters, how it warms my heart to see you out here today to represent that we will not tolerate bigotry and second-class citizenship." Abdullah stood in front of the store, though off to the side from the main doors. The Black woman he'd talked to was back in the store. The security guard remained posted outside.

"They sent this colored woman out, and I won't disparage her, for what choice did she have really? But they sent this lady out who works in the children's department to hear us out and report back to the white manager who leaned on her to come out here in the first place." His voice rose. "The manager who poked his head out like a turtle but doesn't have the courage to come out here and talk to me man to man."

Applause and yells of approval arose from the assembled.

"What do we do, Sarge?" The cop who'd had his hand on the hilt of his nightstick unsheathed it.

"Fan out, flank the Muslims. But no aggressive crowd control just yet."

The officers did as directed. Abdullah kept talking. Ingram captured it all, making sure to write his impressions down as well.

"What we are demanding is only right and correct," Abdullah said, moving back and forth in front of the crowd. "Oh yes, the city fathers give lip service to the imminent arrival of Reverend King, lauding him and his efforts to bring about our rights as citizens for our people down South. Pretending like everything here in the north, here in sunny Los Angeles is all milk and cream." He raised his arms. "Well, is it?" he called out.

"No," came the booming response.

"This isn't a matter for their put-upon lackey in the children's department. This isn't a matter of child's play. This is about adult business, this is about dignity and respect."

The crowd again reacted ebulliently. Toward the rear to one side of the gathered, shoving erupted between one of the officers and two members of the Nation of Islam.

"Get your hands off them," a woman said.

Several cops moved in, as well as several of the Black Muslims.

"Keep it together," Abdullah yelled from the front. "That's what they want us to do, provoke a fight so they can have an excuse to break heads and limbs. Don't succumb."

Harsh words exploded from both sides among the gathered. Ingram was jabbed in the stomach with a nightstick and reacted. Determined to maintain his focus, he managed to take a picture of the snarling cop, who now raised his baton to send it crashing against his skull. It was going to be the great shot he'd fantasized taking as he flinched for impact.

"Maybe we can still reach a civil outcome," a voice announced over a bullhorn.

The cop's eyes shifted and then looking back at Ingram, he seemed for the first time to see the camera in his hand. He lowered the baton, glaring at him. Ingram felt cheated instead of glad. A tall man in a gray pinstriped suit stood alongside a black Lincoln Town Car, holding the bullhorn. The car had stopped at the edge of the impending melee, four individuals having stepped out of it, including the man who'd announced his presence so dramatically. It was Tom Bradley. One of the others was Anita Claire. Now he was glad.

"I think if we can all take a deep breath, we might be able to resolve this," Bradley said. He wasn't using the bullhorn as he strode into the knot of blue, uniforms and suits and dresses. "Perhaps a conference of sorts can be brokered. What do you say, Sergeant Franks and Minister Abdullah? Shall we try dialogue?"

Ingram's experience was the cops in Los Angeles weren't shy about being caught on camera busting open a negro citizen's head. But Channel 5's film camera had been repositioned and was on Bradley, a candidate for City Council. That was a different matter.

"A call came into the reverend about this," Claire said, stepping closer to Ingram.

"Clever move by your candidate," he observed. "This'll show us natives he's no tool of the white man."

As if she hadn't heard him, she said, "I saw what that cop was about to do, Harry."

"All in a day's work."

She shook her head. "It shouldn't be."

"Remember, I'm Tarzan."

"Excuse me, you're Harry Ingram, aren't you? You're a photographer for the negro papers, right?" The newscaster thrust his microphone at him.

"Anita, if you please," Bradley said, holding up his hand and gesturing for her to join him.

"See you later." She and a small contingent including Bradley headed for the White Front doors.

"That's right," Ingram said to the reporter. He was off-balance being on the receiving end of questions. He wondered if he could turn sideways and disappear.

The TV newsman said, "My cameraman said he'd seen you around. Why did that officer attack you?"

"Why do you think?"

He moved the microphone back toward his own mouth. "What do you mean?"

"I mean the police treat colored reporters different than they do white ones."

"It's been my experience they don't have much love lost for white ones either."

As they talked, Ingram saw that Bradley, and the other man from the car who he assumed was Reverend Brookings and Claire were let into the store. The other woman who'd come with them stayed outside, talking to Abdullah. The members of the Nation of Islam and the police stood apart, glaring at one another.

About forty minutes later Ingram walked away briskly from the store in search of a pay phone. He found one and called in his update to Crossman.

"They're still talking?" his editor asked.

"Yeah. At one point they sent out the Black woman who works there to fetch Minister Abdullah to come inside. They've been in there ever since."

"Dammit, looks like I'm going to be here late again. You've got to get a quote from this Abdullah, Harry. The manager too if you can, but him for sure. Channel 5 still there?"

"They were packing up."

"Good. They'll have the newscast but end it with some jive like negotiations are ongoing."

"You want a quote from Bradley?"

"Think you can get it? Our readers know we've endorsed him, but still."

"Sure," he said confidently. He imagined he might get slapped by Claire for being so bold to ask to speak to Bradley and he decided he'd like that just fine.

Off the phone and back at the department store, he again studied the sides of faces of the Black males, looking for the former William Jones's missing piece of earlobe. He spotted the counterman he'd talked to at the cleaners the other day, but the other man looked past him. Ingram moved so as to not be in his line of sight. Probably seeing him in a different context, his face hadn't registered, Ingram figured as he continued looking at individuals among the crowd. Sure enough he spotted a man in sunglasses with a chunk of earlobe missing not twenty feet away, several people in between them. He was talking with another man, who was bobbing his head. The former Jones was a lighter hue than Ingram but not so much you would take him for being mixed race.

He had a carbon copy of the attorney's entire letter with him. But good sense told him if he went over to the ex–Mr. Jones now, he'd get about three words out before there'd probably be a reaction he might not be able to control. What if the counterman came over and wondered just what it was that Ingram was up to? Was he pretending to be a newsman to serve his papers and was what he'd said about a will made up? Was it a white devil's trap and he their Uncle Tom errand boy? Too, maybe the once–Mr. Jones would be embarrassed in front of his fellow members about this white man looking for him. Not that Ingram would announce the dead man's race, but his name and the fact that he left a will was a neon alert. No, he reasoned, it was best he do this out of the presence of so many Black Muslims.

Tom Bradley opened the double front doors of the department store. He stepped out, scanning about for the television crew, Ingram conjectured. But the man who was versed in containing his emotions, having risen in the ranks despite a prejudiced police department, showed no disappointment as he held the door open for the others to exit. Anita Claire was the last to come out and she smiled briefly at Bradley.

"Brothers and sisters," Minister Abdullah began, "thanks to the candidate and his persuasive words, the manager had a meeting with me that I will say in all charity was fruitful to some degree."

Wary murmurs rolled through the assembled. The cops looked from one to the other, unsure of what was coming next.

"While I did not secure the firing of this man, as should have happened, this insulter of our women, he will be transferred out of our community so as not to utter his vileness, at least as far as we, the so-called negro in America, are concerned."

There were whoops of approval and applause. Ingram started toward the minister, estimating this was going to be his only opportunity to get his quote whereas with Bradley, he might have a chance later today.

"Brother minister, I was hoping to get a quick interview with you for the *Eagle*."

Abdullah said, "Always have time for the fine publication Mrs. Bass steered as they continue to serve our people well."

Out of the corner of his eye, Ingram realized the man from the cleaners was staring at him. Well, there was nothing to do about it now. He asked Abdullah his questions for the article. By the time he was finished, the once–Mr. Jones in the sunglasses was gone, though Ingram had taken a surreptitious shot of him. Concentrating on putting together the article, he also got a statement from Bradley by simply going up and asking him. Given he was running for office, he'd stayed to work the crowd. Ingram wasn't sure if the Nation of Islam encouraged its members to vote, but nothing ventured and all that, he reflected.

"Got what you needed?" Claire asked him as the picketers and the police began to disperse.

"I can't be satisfied," he said, quoting bluesman Muddy Waters.

"Ain't just men who can sing that, you know."

He doffed his hat. "Yes, ma'am."

After she left, he opened his trunk and switched out the white bulb for a red one. He also taped his tarp in place along the edge of the trunk lid to block the light. Ingram then utilized the equipment and chemicals of his portable darkroom, including some bottled water, and developed his pictures.

Sitting in his car, he wrote out the story in longhand on a lined pad of paper he kept in the car. It took some effort, as this wasn't some sharpie shot dead and lying in the bushes, or two drunken women who went at each other with a clothes iron and a screwdriver. Those crime vignettes took little effort to bang out. The vivid pictures told those tales. But this time it was about an establishment in a Black neighborhood and the implications of having a mostly white staff who had no sense of the area they were in except that it was a colored part of town. He went over his draft, then rewrote it, doing his best to make it sound like the longer pieces he read in the *Eagle* and *Sentinel*—articles that told the facts, had a point of view but didn't hammer the reader over the head with it.

Driving to the newspaper, Ingram felt conflicted. Wasn't this the sort of story he should be doing more of? Work reflecting the plight and the striving of Black people, and not showing the race in the worst possible light? But those fights and shootings and stabbings were also part of life here. And, as he'd told the woman in Kinslow's rooming house, he took plenty of shots of white folks doing dirt to each other too. Though they were invariably poor and working people, just like their fellow Black citizenry. If he pursued the more uplifting stories, would that bring in more dollars eventually, get him in the white slicks so he wouldn't have to cobble together the money to pay his gas bill and buy a pot roast now and then?

"This is good, Harry, I'm impressed. A step above your usual." Crossman shook the typewritten pages. When Ingram had gotten to the paper, he'd commandeered an Underwood and banged out the story. They were standing outside the Classified Ads room, having wandered there from his desk as Crossman read. Most of the paper had been put to bed, Crossman holding open a space for the article on the protest.

"Trying to get it right, Wes."

"Well, keep it up. I'll put in your voucher."

"Thanks."

On his way out, Ingram passed by an open door. Keys were clacking away in there as an older man composed metal type at a battle-hardened Linotype machine. His aged fingers worked the keys nimbly.

"Chester," Ingram said, nodding to him.

The other man nodded back as he reached down to extract a line of cooling hot metal type.

Elated, Ingram next went to El Cholo's Mexican restaurant on Western Avenue. He sat at one of the tables in the bar area, a portable television set playing on a high shelf in a corner over the barkeep. It was a replay of the events at the White Front store. Briefly he saw himself in the background of one of the shots. He ordered a combination meal and had a margarita before it arrived, then another with the food. By the time he left the sun was down and he was in a mellow mood. As he unlocked his door the phone was ringing, and he hurried inside. He didn't think it was Claire but maybe her plans had changed.

"This Harry Ingram?" a man's voice said.

He told him he was.

"You were at the protest today."

"I was." The voice was familiar. "This the man from the cleaner's?"

"That's right, I'm Harold Ali. I saw you talking to the minister writing up an article. I called over to the paper and they said you did freelance work for them. But you told me you worked for a lawyer. Which is it?"

"I do both. I do work for a process service sometimes."

"Why?"

"Gotta make ends meet is all."

"No, I mean why do you deliver bad news to fellas just trying to get out from under?"

"Not always. Like this time, it's a letter requesting he come to the reading of the will, like I told you."

"Uh-huh." It got quiet, then, "How much you getting to find member William?"

Now we're getting to it, the shakedown. "A hundred," he lied.

"I want half."

"That's not very brotherly of you, brother."

"You want to find him or not?"

"You know I saw him today. It's only a matter of time until I find him." He could show the picture he'd taken of him around at the various mosques and Muslim businesses. But this could get him identified as a police agent, a snitch, and that would have all sorts of consequences for him beyond his immediate problem.

"Yeah, but I bet you need to get him down there sooner than later."

Ingram stifled a curse. "That's not acceptable, man."

"Then you're out of luck."

"So are you," he growled, about to hang up, incensed. Then he got clever. "How would you like to have the cleaners in the press? Minister Abdullah would like that, wouldn't he? Get you a star on your chest."

"You're just saying that."

"Am I?"

"When?"

"It could be in the next month." Or never.

"How do I know you'll follow through?"

"Tomorrow the *Sentinel* will be out with a front-page story about the protest at the White Front. But I need to see Brother William tonight."

"Why the rush, smart guy?"

"'Cause I don't think you can deliver, Mr. Ali."

"I should hang up in your face."

"That's on you, blowing an opportunity."

"Goddammit."

"I don't believe you should be talking like that, sir."

"You affirm I'll get the cleaners in the paper?"

"It might be *Jet*."

"That publication has women in skimpy swimwear stapled in the middle and not because it's for a beach story."

"Your customers come from the neighborhood and plenty of *Jet*s are sold at corner liquor markets where, and this might come as a surprise to you, they buy their liquor. You, me and the minister know that. Look at it this way: you'll be getting a chance of turning some of those lives around with the coverage."

"I don't like where this is going."

"Neither do I, yet here we are."

"I'll call back . . . maybe."

Ingram sat heavily. It would have been one thing if Harold Ali had laid it on the table that he wanted a finder's fee, fine. Like 10 percent, the usual. But to try and stick him up like this, might as well have used a lead pipe and knocked him over the head. But then again, he wasn't closer to getting to the former Jones or however he was referring to himself these days.

There was a throb at the side of his head from his margaritas, which added to his irritability. Ingram considered having another drink but knew better than to compound his woes. He also decided not to turn on one of his scanners as he wasn't really in the mood to break the positive spell of the article he'd written. To be back on the prowl once again chronicling some poor bastard's plight. Anyway, Ali might call back.

Though he'd turned on the TV, he wasn't paying much attention to the western show that was playing. He stared blankly at the screen. The phone rang again and he answered.

"Okay," Ali began, "he'll come."

"My place?"

"The cleaners."

"You sure? What'd you tell him?"

"That this was for the good of the NOI."

"That's not exactly accurate."

"You want him there or not? He'll hear you out."

"Fine."

"One hour."

"Tonight?"

"You want that fee you getting, don't you?" He hung up abruptly again.

Ingram didn't like the setup but he didn't have much choice. He splashed cold water on his face and popped two aspirins to stem the dull ache confounding his brain. Eventually he went downstairs to his Plymouth. The after-work traffic was over, and he got to the Shabazz Dry Cleaners No. 2 in less than twenty minutes. He parked in front, remaining in his car. There were no lights on inside the store. He took a deep breath, got out of his car and walked toward the establishment. Stepping out from the side of the building where an industrial boiler rested on a slab of concrete came Harold Ali. He looked unsteady.

"Where's William Jones?"

"He'll be here. And it's 2X now."

"Put your arms up," a man said behind him.

Ingram turned to see William 2X standing there. He still had on his sunglasses and was holding a length of lead pipe down by his side.

"That's not necessary."

"When it comes to people I don't know sniffing around for me from some lawyer, I don't take chances. I'm reformed, thanks to the Honorable Elijah Muhammad, but there are times when the old ways serve me best."

"I don't have a gun."

"That's not what we're looking for," Ali said.

"You asking for the money was a test," Ingram declared.

If he'd agreed, they would have been more suspicious if he went along with being jacked up too easily. Their reasoning being if he was a police agent he'd do anything to be in their good graces.

"We are quite aware of those who come to us in our skins but are agents of the devil employing tricknology," 2X said.

Ingram replied, "Don't you think we ought to conduct our business inside? Or are you two looking to attract attention? Like from a passing police car?"

The two exchanged a look and Ali took out a set of keys. He unlocked the security gate, pulling it aside in its track, then got the front door open.

"Who is this letter supposed to be from?" William 2X asked him, finally taking off his sunglasses to reveal pale gray eyes.

"The lawyer is representing the estate of Fordis Royal."

The other man stared hard at him.

The three went inside and the lights were flicked on. Ingram was patted down. The letter was taken out of his jacket along with his wallet from his back pocket. Harold Ali took out Ingram's driver's license and wrote down his address.

"In case this is some kind of trap," he said.

William 2X was reading the letter.

"I've done what I was asked to do." Ingram picked up his wallet and put his license back.

"Is it on the up and up, William?" Ali asked.

"Yeah, I think so," he said dryly, a faraway look on his face.

"Gentlemen," Ingram said, starting for the door.

Ali said to Ingram, "I guess you was jivin' about that article, huh?"

"Guess we was testing each other, brother."

In his car heading home, the driver's window partially

down and night air blowing on him, his headache had finally abated. Ingram made a decision. He had enough money from delivering the letter and covering the picket that he didn't have to chase work to make the rent and keep the lights on. It wasn't going to last but it might be long enough for him to do the one thing he'd set out to do, find out who had killed his foxhole buddy Ben Kinslow.

CHAPTER EIGHT

In the morning, after calling Doris Letrec to tell her the letter had been delivered, Ingram drove back to the mystic woman's house in Watts. He figured to brace her and Clovis, do whatever the hell it was they wanted him to do if need be, and get the information about Hoyt from them in exchange. When he'd come here with Edwards, he'd made a note of the street the house was on. It wasn't hard spotting it in the day given the ankh and cross staked in the lawn, the old pickup still in the driveway. After parking he went up the front steps, knocking lightly on the latched screen door. There was no answer. He leaned in closer and knocked again, this time with more force. Still no response.

He walked off the end of the porch onto the driveway and went down the side of the house, peering under drawn shades but seeing no one inside. There was a window in the back door, and he looked in on the kitchen where the woman had been cooking the time before. The room was tidy, no dishes piled in the sink, no occupants. The swing door was open. He detected no movement in the dining room. He started back up the driveway and found a white man in slacks and a loose bowling-style shirt in front of him.

"You friends with that gal calls herself Hanisha?" He was taller and broader than Ingram.

He knew this man, or rather knew his face. "Who's that?"

"Who's that, he says."

When he turned his head to the side Ingram recognized him—one of the two in the Dodge Polaris keeping watch at Kinslow's sendoff. The other one stepped into view. He had an open buck knife in his hand and Ingram was sure he'd been fooling with the latched screen door to get it open. The larger man was in his face.

"Whatchu doing around here?"

"I should be asking you that. This is a colored neighborhood and you two ain't hardly cops."

"You hear this sumabitch?"

"Got a mouth on him, that's for sure." The man stepped closer, tapping the tip of the knife against Ingram's breastbone. "Wicks asked you plain, boy, you don't seem to have no wax in your ears. What the hell you got to do with Hanisha?"

"She's my cousin is all. Came by to see her."

The larger man, Wicks, frowned. "That sound right to you?"

"All these darkies related some kind of way or another," the other one said derisively. "Their daddies planting their seed in whichever easy dame open her legs for the pipe."

Wicks was staring at Ingram. "I don't know," he drawled, "can't place him but I got the feeling I've seen this chump before."

"Shining your shoes, probably." Knife man swung his jaw toward the detached garage in back. "Let's whisper in his ear about it."

"Yeah, good idea."

Wicks made to grab Ingram and got punched in his face for the effort.

"Fucker," he growled.

Ingram tried to run but Wicks recovered faster than he'd hoped and latched onto his shoulders from behind, jerking him backward and upsetting his balance. Knife man joined in and hit him in the stomach, doubling him over. Together, holding him on either side, striking him several times, they dragged the struggling photographer into the garage, its double barn doors unlocked. They tossed him onto the floor. Ingram had gotten his wind back and as he tried to rise, got kicked in the side of the head by Wicks. He groaned and rolled onto his back, a fresh open wound on his temple. He lay there gazing up into the rafters, dust motes cascading on him like heaven's confetti.

Roughly one half of the garage had open floor space to allow for a vehicle. There were a couple of batteries and an old-fashioned toolbox on a shelf at the back of this section. The other half contained old furniture, grease-stained cardboard boxes and the like stacked about. Ingram was deposited on an upturned wooden milk crate. He attempted to rise again, anticipating hands on him and figuring to counterpunch.

"No, no," Wicks said, having produced a gun, waving it about lazily. "Sit your ass down. You ain't got no appointments to keep."

Ingram did as ordered. Wicks was gesturing with a Browning semi-automatic. At this range it could have been a .25, a pocketbook pistol, and he still would have complied.

"Where the fuck can we find Hanisha?" the knife man asked.

"Man, I haven't seen her or Clovis in a long time. Like I said, I had the day off and dropped by to say hi." He hoped using Clovis's name would make him sound more legitimate.

"Bullshit."

"It's the truth." Ingram gauged how best to counterattack these assholes.

Knife man regarded his companion. "What do you think?"

Wicks's expression was one of a bricklayer wondering why the wall he was building tilted to one side. "There's something about this gee I can't place." He grinned unpleasantly. "Ask him again, Morty."

"Sure thing," he said blandly. Morty plunged the knife into the bridge of Ingram's foot, shoe and all. The knife easily penetrating, he twisted the blade gleefully.

"Motherfuck," Ingram wailed, reflexively shooting up from the crate. But Wicks got behind him, putting an arm against his throat and using his other to tighten his grip. Ingram couldn't get a breath.

"Told you to sit down, didn't I?"

Morty twisted the blade again. "You better listen."

Blood seeped from the wound onto the garage floor, a series of warped and weathered boards. Ingram rocked and shook but couldn't get loose, couldn't alleviate the pain.

"Now about Hanisha," Wicks whispered in his ear.

"Okay, there is a place," he wheezed out. "Clovis, he might be there later."

"What, a whorehouse?" Morty cracked. He withdrew the knife, wiping it against Ingram's pant leg.

"Not exactly," he managed between labored breaths. "It's an after-hours joint, a blind pig called the Stockyard, craps, booze, cool chicks, you know." Wicks let go and Ingram bent over, coughing and hacking up bile onto the floor.

"That sounds like that self-righteous Clovis," Morty opined. He examined his knife.

Wicks asked. "Where is this place?"

Ingram cleared his throat. "Upstairs from a plumbing supply outfit on Hoover, not too far north of the Coliseum."

"What's the name on the outside?" Wicks asked.

"Fuck I know," Ingram said. "You can't miss it. The neon sign has this pipe getting screwed into another one then unscrewed."

"Subtle," Wicks said.

"What about laughing boy here?" Morty asked.

Wicks looked at Ingram with clinical distance. "What about him? We got what we wanted."

Ingram tensed.

Morty seemed inclined to argue but hunched a shoulder and folded his knife. The two departed.

Ingram sat on the ground, grimacing as he removed his ruined shoe. On a battered three-legged end table was a stack of old newspapers. They were not so aged as to crumble at his touch. He used several tripled-over crinkly sheets to stanch the flow of blood from his wound. He tore his sock into a strip and tied his tourniquet around his newsprint gauze. Ingram then limped out of the garage, one shoe on and the other in his hand, and headed toward his car. An older woman tugging a small cart of grocery bags watched him apprehensively as he got to his Plymouth.

"Christ," he said, his wounded foot pulsing as he pushed down the accelerator pedal. He was glad this car was an automatic and not a clutch like his last one. Gritting his teeth, he got the car going. Three blocks later, his wound bleeding from his exertions, he spotted a phone booth in the middle of a block and pulled over. He was going to need more than Mercurochrome for this boo-boo. Sitting inside the booth was a woman in a hat talking enthusiastically into the instrument. But she glanced through the glass to see this individual trickling blood on the sidewalk looking in at her. His appearance didn't upset her. She opened the accordion door.

"Mister, you need a ride to the hospital?"

"If I could make a call, I'll be fine."

"I'll call you back, Eunice," the woman said into the handset. "Man here looks like he needs some assistance." She hung up and rose from the built-in seat. "Here you go, sir."

"Thank you."

"It's the Christian thing to do."

"Yes, ma'am." He didn't add he was calling the biggest sinner he knew. He deposited his dime and dialed a number. The phone rang four times on the other end of the line before it was answered. "Strummer," he said into the handset, "there's a couple of rough ofays gonna show up tonight at your club."

"Who are they?"

"Pretty sure they work for Hoyt. They just gave me a going over. Sorry, but I had to give them something and well, you were the only one I could think of who wouldn't get rattled by these strokes."

"Gimme a description, will ya? You'd be surprised at how many white folks find their way into my establishment."

"Don't worry, I'll be there tonight. When you see me pistol whipping this smug smiling square-headed Oakie, that'll be your clue."

Edwards laughed. "Damn, soldier boy."

"Goddamn right." Ingram hung up, his foot throbbing worse as his adrenaline wore off. Ingram looked down at his red-soaked wrappings, realizing he wasn't going to stop his foot from bleeding. He needed stitches. As if he were auditioning for a chance to play the Mummy in a Creature Feature, Ingram got back to his car, trailing his leg and leaving smears of blood on the sidewalk. Along the way he'd picked up a discarded Sports section left on a bus bench. Stabbed foot propped on the car's bench seat, he redid his wrapping. He managed to not have an accident as he drove to the St. Vincent de Paul clinic on Avalon. He'd been there three years ago doing a photo shoot.

"Oh my," said a woman in slacks and a buttoned-up shirt when Ingram hobbled inside. She had a clipboard in her hand and stood in front of the receptionist's desk. There were other women in the waiting area, Black and Mexican American with their young children and an older colored man with his arm in a sling. The kids played with broken toys plucked from a wooden chest. There was an assortment of dog-eared magazines splayed on an end table, and worn comic books like the adventures of *The Black Cobra*, a do-gooder in a '50s style business suit, fedora and domino mask. There was also a comic book he'd seen before called *The Red Iceberg*. The cover of the anti-communist effort showed a grim Uncle Sam sitting on a boat as it approached a literal red iceberg with a hammer and sickle carved into it. Behind the iceberg were grave markers for the likes of North Korea and East Berlin.

The woman helped him to a seat. "A safe fall on it?" She was white, a few years older than Ingram, dark haired and dark eyed. She regarded him with genuine concern but not recognition. She wore a small gold cross on a light chain. He remembered her from before. He'd mostly been unnoticed with the camera and she'd been busy with patients that day. She'd worn traditional clothes then as well. He recalled the priest who'd showed them around, schooling them on the difference between a sister who engaged with the outer world and a nun who was cloistered. He didn't recall her name.

"No, Sister, two men jumped me and stuck a knife in my foot." He figured the closer to the truth the better. Anyway, there was no other way to explain the wound. He wasn't

Catholic, but lying to a nun seemed like it might bring bad luck. His foot could get infected and have to be cut off.

"Oh my," she repeated. "Hold on." She went to her desk and came back with a pair of surgical scissors. Acknowledging the wary looks on several faces, she bent down and helped him back to his feet. "We better get you inside."

She wasn't a stout woman, but plenty strong, Ingram noted, an arm around her for support as she guided him into an exam room. She sat him back down on a chair and proceeded to remove his bloody wrappings.

"Don't worry," she said as he flinched, "I'm a nurse and saw a lot worse in a MASH unit in Korea."

"I did too over there."

She briefly smiled up at him, then returned her attention to what she was doing. She cleaned his foot with an alcohol-soaked cloth and did a professional job of wrapping the wound in gauze and padding.

"That's going to need stitches. But first you'll need to get a couple of X-rays done and we don't have that here. I can send you over to California Hospital to get them."

"You can stitch me up, Sister—"

"Violet, Violet O'Shay. Anyway, stitches have to be authorized by the intern and he's not scheduled to be here until later today. You'll have to come back."

"What about those folks out there? They waiting on the doc too?"

"That's runny noses, and Mr. Iverson is just a check on how his bones are knitting after his fall. That sort of care I'm allowed to administer without direct supervision."

"Does it make a difference if I can donate to the church?"

"You trying to bribe me?"

"Yes, I am."

She was leaning against the wall, taking a pack of

cigarettes out of the pocket of her slacks. She shook one lose, angling the pack toward him.

"Cigars are my vice," he said.

Head back against the wall she lit up and blew a stream. She looked more like a torch singer between sets than a holy woman. "Why did the two men rough you up?"

He told her enough and added, "I was here before. Must have been three years ago, for an article about the clinic serving the poor folk around here. It was for *Ebony* magazine. I was the photographer." Crossman had written the article.

"You looking to get back at these men?"

"If I was a policeman, would you ask that?"

"You're not. But knowing how they act around here, yes, I would."

He believed her. "I intend to find out how they're involved. But I'm not crazy, Sister Violet, I go around assaulting white men, they'd bury me under the jailhouse."

She smoked, weighing what to do next.

"How about you call the intern and tell him, well, tell him what you think he'll want to hear then see if he gives his okay."

"I won't lie."

"I think we both know you have a ton more experience than some wide-eyed kid the church has assigned here, and you have to deal with his impatience with us natives. Looking to bug out for greener pastures when he can."

She let smoke drift up across her face. This didn't obscure the activity behind her eyes. "You ever see the movie *The Left Hand of God*? It's from a few years ago."

He shrugged. "Can't say as I have."

Sister Violet nodded. "Hold on." She left the room and soon returned with a cloth-covered dice cup, rattling the dice in it. She also had a deck of cards. "High hand or roll of the dice?"

"Wait, is that okay for you to do?" Ingram said. "Gamble, I mean. I don't want no lightning bolts zapping through the roof. And you just happen to have those laying around here?"

"A regular Redd Foxx you are."

It didn't surprise him she knew about the blue comedian.

"Besides," she continued, "the Bible says the love of money is the road to ruin, but as interpreted by many, it's vague on the subject of gambling. There is a reason the church puts on a weekly bingo game and conducts lotteries to raise money from time to time." She jingled the dice in the cup. "This is from our backgammon game, and cards are just cards, Mr. Ingram, even those used for spades. Best three out of five. What'll it be?"

Ingram wasn't a good poker player so not inclined to favor the cards. Dice he hardly played but what about beginner's luck? "The dice."

"You're on."

Using the compact countertop of the built-in, she rolled, a die falling into the sink but not down the drain.

"I'm okay if you want to count that," Ingram said. The total was nine.

"Brave man," she said.

He rolled a three. Ingram won the next two rounds and she the fourth toss.

"Here we go," the sister said as she jiggled the dice, the cup next to her ear, an earnest expression on her face. Out they flew, bouncing off the backsplash and coming up ten.

"Damn," Ingram cursed softly.

She snickered good-naturedly.

He took the cup and shook it vigorously. He tipped the cup and the dice jetted out, banging against the backsplash as hers had done. A six and five came up.

"Hot dog," he said.

Sister Violet said, "Sit on the table and stick your foot out." Rubber gloves on over thoroughly washed hands, she sewed his wound closed. "I pray that doesn't get gangrenous."

"You and me both."

"Even a heathen's prayers are heard." She put away her medical supplies, plopping the scissors in a jar of disinfectant.

"Especially in a foxhole." He eased onto his feet.

"Here you go, sport." She handed him a cane.

"Thank you." He started to exit. "If I'd come up snake eyes, would you have turned me away?"

"Every day has an element of chance."

They returned to the front together and the sister called in a mother with a child in a striped T-shirt. Walking with the cane eased some of his discomfort and he had a couple of aspirin when he got back home. She'd told him to keep the foot elevated as much as he could, but he had preparations for tonight to attend to. He did keep shoes off his feet, though, and went around his place in his socks. He had a pair of slip-ons he'd wear tonight instead of trying to wrestle a lace-up shoe over the gauze. From his closet he retrieved his .45 in the small steamer-like trunk box. He'd swathed it in Cosmoline, and secured a cotton cloth around the gun with masking tape. He undid this, feeling its heft in his hand. He wiped off the excess grease. Sense memory came back, how to take it apart and reassemble the gun, though it had been years since he'd held the weapon. He distinctly recalled his drill sergeant hammering to the recruits: *your sidearm is like a woman, treat her right and she'll always respond.*

"'Cause if your baby jams, then Joe Chink gets to jam a bayonet up your ass."

Words to live by, Ingram noted dryly, sitting at his kitchen table as he took the .45 apart. From his tool drawer he'd removed gun oil, a round-headed brush and a small can of solvent for cleaning off old deposits. Wicks and his buddy with the pig-sticker were looking for Hanisha and Clovis, who were in hiding. Why, and did it have anything to do with Ben's death? The phone rang and he plucked the handset free.

"You want a home-cooked meal tonight, lover man?"

"More than anything, honey chile, but I have to see a man about a horse this evening."

"Yeah, what's her name?"

"I'd ask you along, but it could go sideways." Might as well tell her what happened now, he reasoned.

"I'm a big girl, in case you didn't notice, Harry. What is it?"

He brought her up to speed.

"Jesus, Harry," Anita Claire said. "You sure you should be doing this? What I mean is at least wait until your foot's better."

"They figure me for a chump, Anita, who punked out to save his skin. They won't be expecting me to come back at them."

"Do you hear how you sound? Is this for your friend Ben or revenge for you?"

"I'm not going off half-cocked. But these two work for Hoyt or some damn body in the association. You wouldn't want me knuckling under to the capitalists, would you?"

"How clever you are. I think there's a way to do this with the velvet glove approach rather than a hammer."

"Meaning my head?"

"Yes."

She was into this. He was liking her more and more. "What do you suggest?"

THAT NIGHT at the Stockyard, the crowd wasn't shoulder-to-shoulder, but orders for the untaxed liquor were plentiful, and several sets of bodies were pressing closer together than public decorum allowed, slow dancing to music from the jukebox. Edwards had the machine calibrated so the music couldn't be played loud, and its speakers were often drowned out by the din of the patrons. No sense being too blatant about what was going on upstairs, he'd once told Ingram. He knew too that Edwards was paying off a desk sergeant at 77th Division to keep the beat cops off his back.

Sitting on a stool in the bar area was Anita Claire. She wore a clingy dress that wouldn't have her mistaken for a librarian. She drank a martini and noted the customers coming into the establishment—that is, the ones who got past the bouncer on the ground floor, who stood behind a steel door with an eye slot in it, like out of Prohibition.

The Stockyard had gotten its name because there was a mural on one of the walls in the front here—an idealized depiction of farm life. Anthropomorphic pigs and cows sauntered about in a green field in vests, spats and dresses, several with open umbrellas to ward off the sun. There was a barn and silo in the background of the panorama and a bull in a bowler and rolled-up sleeves commanded a puffing tractor. What had been in this building before the plumbing supply occupied the bottom floor was the subject of speculation. When Edwards worked out the deal with the Wertzendahls, the German Americans who'd bought the building in 1957, the second floor had been vacant for years, except the mural. The commercial realtor they'd worked with suggested it must have been a meat-packing operation, but that made no sense on the top floor.

"Carry a cow carcass up those steps?" Walter Wertzendahl had opined. "I think not."

Pressed against the mural in the gloom, a man and woman were kissing and caressing, his hand under her skirt. In the scene behind them a cow with big eyes lazed in the grass on a blanket reading a book. Claire, looking at the couple and the cartoon, turned her head as a man matching Ingram's description of Wicks came through the archway into the bar.

Wicks sat on a stool. He signaled the bartender by bending two extended fingers. He was the second white man to enter the bar and remain here. Others passed the bar to head down a short hallway to an alcove where a second bouncer controlled the hidden door mechanism to the casino area. The other white man in the bar was a pudgy individual in a gray suit who sipped beer and ogled the colored gals. Sweat had broken out on his balding pate and now and then as he talked to himself, he'd giggle.

Claire waited several minutes, not imbibing. Checking her watch, she took a final sip of her drink and set it aside. She rose and moved past the creep, quite aware his eyes were locked on her. Purposely she brushed Wicks's back and stopped. Assuming a tipsy voice she said, "Say, you was down at the It club, wasn't you? The night Shorty Rogers was blowing hot?"

Wicks checked her out up and down. "Naw, doll, that was some other guy. Too bad for me, huh?"

She shook a finger at him, tongue flicking out. "Yeah, it was you. Me and my friend you talked to." Like one of those hula girl figurines hot rodders bolted on their dashboards, Claire swayed side to side standing in place.

"That so? What friend was that?" Interest glittered in his eyes.

She grinned, wagging her finger again and maneuvered around a passing couple as she said, "You know, Hanisha." Stepping farther backward, Claire got more people between her and Wicks, who'd come off his stool fast at hearing the name.

"Excuse me," Claire said as she put her hand on a woman's shoulder, nudging her out of the way as she hurried past.

"Damn, girl, what's your hurry? They givin' away free foot massages in the back?" the woman cracked.

Claire reached the short hallway, Wicks not far behind. Two Black men exited the casino area in a good mood, one of them having won at the blackjack table.

"Hey fellas," she said to them, putting a hand on one of the men's arms. "What's your hurry?"

"Hey yourself," this one said. He wasn't much taller than her, but he had wide shoulders.

"I need to talk to her," Wicks said.

"Who the hell is you, gray boy?" the one who'd talked to Claire said.

"This ain't Culver City," his friend added. He was taller and thinner, mahogany skinned.

"Look here, me and this gal got business."

"That right?" wide shoulders said.

Claire had her back to the alcove, the two gamblers between her and Wicks. The bouncer, a beefy man who'd played tackle on the Rams for two years with Night Train Lane, was now in the hallway too. He was called Timmy T, short for Timmy Teeth, due to his loosening them in his opponents' mouths.

Claire slipped past him. The alcove was an empty room not much bigger than a janitor's closet. Inset here was a visible door. In case the bouncer had to turn someone away, he'd usher them through this door where there were descending stairs to exit the building. Claire took those stairs.

In the alcove Timmy T said to Wicks, "What's the problem here?" He stood over Wicks by two inches. The two other men left.

"Nothing, it's fine," Wicks said. He returned to the bar.

The stool where he'd been sitting was now occupied and his beer had been removed. He stood for a moment, hand in his pocket jingling his change as he was considering what to do next. Then in the archway he spied Claire, who'd re-entered the blind pig through the front so as to be seen. He started for her slow and steady as she turned away.

Claire was nearly at the bottom of the carpeted stairs, Wicks at the top, descending. She exited onto the sidewalk. Overhead the neon sign of the pipe being continually fitted and refitted hummed, its light momentarily bathing her in arctic blue and white. She then pivoted away and headed toward the far corner of the building. Wicks was hanging back just enough as newcomers walked into the unlicensed establishment. She made a left turn down a gap between the buildings. Hearing his footfalls, she could tell he'd picked up the pace. He arrived at the opening, stepping into the light cast from an overhead streetlamp, a pale yellow circle beneath his feet. Farther along the passageway was a gloom darker than the night around them. Claire breathed heavily as she waited. As Wicks entered the darkness, he was struck in the forehead hard. He rocked back against a brick wall, his eyes glossy.

Ingram brought the sap down again on the hood's head. This time the other's knees gave out. He slid to the ground, back against the brick wall. Ingram reached inside the hoodlum's jacket and removed his Browning from its shoulder holster. He handed the gun to Claire, who held it authoritatively.

"What does Hoyt have to do with Hanisha? She supplies the brown sugar, ain't that right?" he asked him.

"You're so smart, you tell me, asshole," Wicks muttered, trying to get his legs underneath him.

Ingram sapped him again.

"Shit, man," Wicks swore. Blood seeped from the top of his head, wetting his hair.

"Careful you don't kill him," Claire advised.

"He's got a thick skull." Ingram pressed his good foot into the man's chest. "Why'd Hoyt have Ben killed?"

"Who?" Wicks said.

"You know who the hell I'm—"

"Let him go," Morty yelled from the entrance to the gap, leveling a gun at them.

"Aw shit," Ingram stammered.

Claire fired the Browning. The bullet pierced the wall near Morty's head, raising brick dust as he ducked away.

She grabbed Ingram's arm to speed him along and they ran farther into the passageway, swallowed by the black. At Ingram's urging, they dropped to the ground, lying prone. Morty fired and missed, and Claire fired back as Morty helped his partner to his feet. He had to help Wicks along as they made their getaway, their footfalls receding.

"Damn, Annie Oakley," Ingram said appreciatively as they got up, dusting their clothes off.

"We couldn't just stand there and get drilled." A car roared away on the street.

"No, we couldn't." His heart accelerated, thudding in his ears, but it wasn't from fear.

A heightened sheen illuminated her face from within. "That was exciting."

"Yes, it was," he croaked.

They grabbed each other and the two could barely contain themselves as Ingram drove them to his apartment. He nearly hit a post behind his building as he parked. Claire had his zipper down and had unbuckled his pants as she stroked him. Her dress bunched up, he fingered her clit, yet they were not so far gone and managed to get out of the car and up the stairs. They only made it as far as the front room and made love there on the rug. He was glad he'd vacuumed it a couple of weeks ago.

At some point the pair finally made their way to his bed, discussing what they knew so far.

Claire said, "If your friend was killed because he was trying to blackmail Winston Hoyt, are his goons looking for Clovis and Hanisha for the same reason?"

"Maybe they have copies of the photos I have," Ingram answered. "Ben was working for Hoyt so he wouldn't have come at him directly. He could have used those two to work the scheme."

"What if they double-crossed your friend?" she asked.

"Hoyt makes the payoff. Instead of splitting the dough they kill him."

"You sound like you don't believe that."

"Clovis would have shot Ben or beat him over the head. That cat don't strike me as the subtle type to mess with the brakes."

"You aren't saying a colored man can't be clever, are you?"

"If you'd met him you wouldn't be saying that. That negro is direct like raw catfish left out in the sun too long."

"Could be with direction from your girl he's less so."

"Okay, maybe," he allowed, nodding. "Hoyt found out they were involved and wants to silence them too?"

"Or buy them off. You said you didn't find the negs, but they have to be somewhere. They might have them."

"Negs can be duped, you know. Kodak makes a film for doing it easily."

"Then all kinds of bodies could be dropping."

"Naw, I guess they'd want to keep this to themselves."

"I think so too." Nude, she got out of bed and left the bedroom to rummage in his refrigerator. She returned with a bottle of beer and got back in bed, draping a leg over his as he sat propped against the headboard. "What if it's something else?" she said. "Hanisha supplies the colored girls for their little parties, a little pepper to the salt for seasoning. Them chicks report back to her what they've seen and heard. Men like to brag when they're waving their dicks around. Spellbinding us impressionable women."

"Is that right?"

"Or so I've been told." She took a sip and shared the bottle with him.

He drank some. "Then there could be more photos than just what Ben had."

She snuggled beside him under the covers. "If he drove Hoyt to his little get-togethers, he could have met one of the women. He dated Black women, didn't he?"

"He did," Ingram acknowledged.

"Add to that—what if Hanisha had compiled names of those who partook? You said you thought you recognized a judge in one of the shots."

"Men like that can't have their reputations questioned. Especially if there's a photo with his tongue between a colored woman's legs." He caressed her as he said this.

"What exactly are you saying, Harry?" She kissed him.

"You know there was an article about this in *Dapper*."

"About what?" she asked, not so innocently.

He cleared his throat. "Oral sex, I believe was what they called it. Like what was good for the gander was good for the goose. Copies of the issue were banned in a lot of cities, there was even a bonfire of them down South. All that was officially. Unofficially, there was a whole lot of under the counter sales."

"Well, well. Did you learn anything from that article?"

"I picked up a few pointers." Feeling bold he added, "But I usually do best at on-the-job training."

"Hmmm," she said, kissing him, then lying back.

When morning came Claire was up early as there was preparation to be done for King's visit to town less than a week away. His advance men would be here in two days, she'd told him, putting in her earrings.

"You going to look for those two, aren't you?"

"I'd be lying if I said it hadn't crossed my mind. Problem is them being palefaces, I got no way to get to them. Strummer has a few contacts on the white side of town from his Dragna days, but something tells me that might be barking up the wrong tree. When I've asked him in the past about being in touch with any of those guys, he always shined me on."

"What about a Jewish gangster?"

"What about one?"

"My mom could be helpful."

"She's Jewish?"

"And if she is?"

"It's cool with me, baby. Anyways, I never dated a Jewish chick."

She chuckled. "She's not, she's of stern Lutheran stock, to be precise. But even out here there were trade unionists called on and their hoodlum relatives who broke legs and cracked heads, useful undertakings in certain campaigns. There might be a few of those guys she still knows. I'll call and ask her."

"That would be great."

"You might also want to try and find out what Ben was doing up on Mulholland that day."

"Probably an errand for Hoyt is what I figured. Or he could have been checking out a club in the Valley. That tall pitcher for the Dodgers, Drysdale, has a restaurant out there called the Dugout."

"They offer live music?"

"Don't know."

"Well, like I said, maybe you should find out." She came over to where he sat clothed on the side of the bed. "Bye," she said, her hand rubbing the back of his head.

"Bye."

She smacked red from her lipstick on his cheek and was gone.

Feeling spry, he returned to the Y and worked out. Afterward he was hungry and went to the Detour and ate heavily, probably negating his morning's labors. He did wonder how many calories you burned off having sex as he buttered his toast.

Around ten-thirty in the morning, Claire called him.

"Mom says come on out and see her," she told him. "Today around two would be fine. She lives out in Riverside these days."

"Lay the address on me."

She did, along with her mother's phone number. She added, "She does like to reminisce, so best not to be in a hurry."

"No sweat."

"I'll tell her you'll see her today."

Driving to Riverside, Ingram reflected on what Claire had said about her mother. She'd used the name Cynthia Hayes but that was a nom de guerre, Claire had emphasized. Her real name was Dorothy Nielson. Several years ago in the late 1950s, the anti-communist purges had come down hard on civil rights fighters like her, a public school teacher. She was hounded out of the L.A. Unified school system. But after changing her hair color and taking a false name, she'd been able to get a few jobs outside of teaching, like working for a freight outfit as a scheduler and as part-time as a bookkeeper at a go-kart track.

Curiously, when he'd asked Claire about her father, Solomon, she'd been less forthcoming. She did vaguely allow that Solly, as he was called, was around. She didn't elaborate and he didn't push it.

He did ask, though, "What do I call her?"

"You call her 'my queen.'"

"I'm on it."

"Dorothy will do. I think she might have gone back to her real name but I'm not certain."

"How come?"

She grinned. "Lefty parents aren't always that up front with their kids. I do know she has a driver's license and other identification in the false name." She'd obtained them through this shady guy she knew who'd been part of Mickey Cohen's crew.

Ingram arrived on a residential street lined with fourplexes and tidy California bungalows, like the address he sought. He parked in front. The house's postage stamp of a lawn was split by a walkway. The grass was yellowing but neatly trimmed. A dark-colored Buick of a few years' vintage sat in the driveway. Up the walkway he went. His foot was sore and stiff, and he felt self-conscious using the cane, but it was necessary. The door opened before he reached the steps. The woman backlit in the doorway was a dead ringer for her daughter, build-wise. She stepped out onto the porch.

"Miss Nielson, good to meet you." They shook hands.

"I'm sure Anita told you to call me Dorothy."

"Yes, ma'am."

She was darker hued than he had imagined until he realized she had a tan. There were light freckles on her face, and her eyes were a different color than her daughter's.

Inside, the home was neat and sparsely furnished. At least in this part of the house there were few framed pictures and the books on the small freestanding bookshelf lacked political titles. He smiled at one of the pictures, Anita and her sister as kids and their mom wearing a big floppy straw hat. Through an archway with pocket doors was the compact dining room that included a built-in sideboard of drawers and glassed-in shelves containing china and wineglasses. On the oval dining room table were laid out a pitcher and two drinking glasses on a place mat. There were two coasters as well.

Nielson pointed. "That's fresh lemonade made from the lemons growing in my backyard. Which, like the front, is not too large, just the trees and a few gopher holes. I suppose I should poison the little critters, but they're just doing what their nature dictates."

Ingram smiled.

She laughed heartily. "Yes, I guess Anita didn't tell you I'm losing my mind."

"No, Dorothy, she skipped over that part."

"Have a seat. You want cookies? They're store bought, though."

"Lemonade is fine." He poured for them both and placed each glass on a coaster emblazoned with the Blatz beer logo. They both sat.

"Here's to progress," she said, raising her glass.

"To progress." They clinked and he had a swallow. The stuff was exactly as he liked it, not so much sugar as to negate its natural sourness.

"Before we dive in, you should know that when Anita and Bea were kids, it was Anita who would talk her sister into questionable activities. Like skipping school to adventure across the city or thumbing a ride when they were teenagers."

"She seems pretty levelheaded now."

As if she didn't hear him, she said, "I tell you that so you understand that streak she didn't inherit so much as develop. Admittedly, though, they were raised somewhat unconventionally."

"You trying to scare me off your daughter?"

"Both my girls are pretty sharp. From what I hear you are too. But being able can trip you up. Figuring you're smarter than the ones coming at you."

"I understand you speak from experience, Dorothy. I'm getting to be quite fond of Anita. I wouldn't knowingly do anything to cause her harm."

"But you do want to find these two gangsters, who also, from what Anita told me, have a connection to Winston Hoyt, a Provider."

"A what?"

"You know him to be a member of the Association of Merchants and Industrialists. Well, within their ranks, there's an inner circle called the Providers. The AMI extols middle-class ideals. A chicken in every pot, a two-car garage and a barbecue pit in the back by the pool for weekend get-togethers. For white wage earners at least. Essentially mainstream Republicanism."

"And what is it the Providers want?"

She considered her answer. "They take the position—not unlike, say, the White Citizens Council—that progress is fine, as long as it proceeds at the pace they set."

"Don't get too uppity. Don't be in such a hurry," Ingram said.

She nodded. "I imagine Anita has told you some of what our family went through not so many years ago. The worst being betrayals by our comrades."

"You mean rats?"

"Not to put too fine a point on it, but a rat is someone who finks, as Lenny Bruce would say, for money or because they've been caught. But a sleeper is an agent provocateur, like a G-man who's been assigned to infiltrate, be your friend, and also nudge you into doing something illegal and dangerous."

"Hold on. You trying to tell me my friend was one of these infiltrators for the Providers?"

She held up her hand. "I'm not saying that. I never met him and what little I know suggests he wasn't. I am saying these two thugs might have been sent by whomever on an errand that is not what it seems to be. They could be more than what they seem to be."

Ingram flashed on Wicks and his Browning automatic, suggesting a background like his and Kinslow's. "Are the Providers hooked into the government?"

"I don't think they have a direct line to Hoover. But I know they played a role in undermining our efforts in L.A. In particular there was a strike at Ferris Aircraft in Santa Monica in '57. This was a big outfit."

"Still is," he noted.

"Solly was part of the strike team, the lead thinkers, we liked to call them, who developed strategy and tactics."

"Your ex?"

She nodded.

"There was a particular member, a man off the shop floor who wormed his way into my ex-husband's good graces. In the end it turned out he'd been sent into the plant, with the bosses' knowledge and aid, several months before, when the rumblings had begun about unionization. This man was responsible for not only telling the other side the strike team's discussions but convincing several to engage in sabotage to get them arrested. The head of Ferris Aircraft is a member of the association, and this was a page out of their handbook." She stared at nothing for a moment, then returned her attention to her visitor. "Anyway, I know Anita told you I can go on, but this was pertinent to what you're looking into, I believe. More than anything, the Providers see themselves as Old World patricians who know how best to engineer society. They seek to manipulate and forge the course of history, particularly here in Southern California. They help fund groups like the John Birch Society headquartered in Orange County. Have you heard of them?"

"I have."

"'If Mommy is a commie, you have to turn her in,'" she said, smiling. "Their perspective is Black people wouldn't be demanding things like equality and dignity if not for being whipped up by the reds. Three years ago, when the Democrats had their nominating convention here, the Providers made sure the politicians who they've contributed to pushed back on the idea of a comprehensive civil rights platform. They play both sides of the aisle."

"I covered the NAACP rally at the Shrine then," Ingram said. "Adam Clayton Powell was the star that day, not King. And when Kennedy showed up to speak, he was booed."

She said, "It was felt he wouldn't be a champion for civil rights like Humphrey."

"Yeah."

"But enough about recent history, what about the present, right?"

"Exactly." Ingram enjoyed more lemonade.

"The man I was thinking you might talk to is named Hamish Segal."

"Related to Bugsy?"

"No, not at all. Hamish is mostly retired now but I understand he keeps abreast of various goings-on. He and his brother came out of the schmatta trade in New York."

"The what?"

"Garments," she said. "His brother Hiram got involved in trade unionism while Hamish was more attracted to wearing flashy suits and diamond rings on his pinky."

"And this Hamish was helpful to you all at times?"

"Fighting fire with fire, yes," she said evenly. "Just because I'm a woman doesn't mean I'm all for turning the other cheek if you're knocking me in the head with a two-by-four."

"I heard that."

She sat back, putting one leg over another, folding her arms. "You're all right, Harry Ingram."

"Not sure how to answer that. Where can I find Hamish?"

"I think he still has an office of sorts in the back of Chin Low's in Chinatown."

"You're kidding."

"Nope," she said, straight-faced. "Let me make a couple of calls and see what I can do. Wicks and Morty are their names?"

"Yep, Wicks is a good-sized fella and his buddy Morty more the weasel type. But he does like his knives."

She pointed at his foot. "That limp of yours?"

Ingram, pouring more lemonade, nodded. He asked her about Howard Stockworth, the other name that had come up in connection to the Association of Merchants and Industrialists. In response she went away and returned with a pamphlet. On the cover was a stark black ink illustration of a paranoid, sweating man and a worried-looking woman. The title of the reading material was *How Unions Are Fronts for Soviet Russian Infiltration.*

"He wrote that personally. It was distributed to all the employees of his supermarkets," she said. "It was the second time an organizing drive had been attempted by the grocery workers of his chain. It failed."

He thumbed through the pamphlet and started to hand it back.

"Hold on to it, read what he has to say. It'll give you some insight on the Providers."

"Thanks."

When he returned to his car, the day had heated up and he seriously considered stopping at a watering hole to have a beer. But he kept going and got back to town, sweaty, hungry and thirsty. He parked and stepped into Whitehead's, his shirt clinging to a large wet spot on his back.

"Who's that?" Arthur Yarbrough said as he detected an unfamiliar gait enter through the back way. He was sitting in the office working an abacus. The beads were textured so the visually impaired could work them. In his friend's case, it was his way of keeping sharp, doing the additions and subtractions in his head.

"It's me, Arthur," Ingram said.

"What happened? I heard the tap of a cane. You break your toe or something?"

Ingram told him, taking a seat in the only other chair in the small space. To his left was a small bathroom with a stainless-steel sink.

"Damn, man, you might should stick to taking photos."

"You might be right, brother."

"Sounds like you could use a cold one."

"You read my mind." He started to get up.

"Relax, can't have you slipping in the store and suing."

"That would be going into my own pockets, wouldn't it?"

Yarbrough was already up and walking confidently to the cooler case. A shopper asked about the cost of nectarines as the squeak of cart wheels floated to the back. Yarbrough returned shortly with two cans of Pabst Blue Ribbon. He set these on the desk and removed an opener from a drawer. He punched triangular openings in the lids and slid a can across.

"Here's how," Ingram said, making his second toast of the day, clinking his can against Yarbrough's. "You don't know how I needed that." He slumped in the seat. They drank some in silence.

"Man, I had this crazy dream the other night," his friend began. "Seoul City Sue was out on the street calling to me through an open window. I go outside to look for her. Soon I'm down to my skivvies but I don't pay it no mind. I have to find her like she's a whatddaya call it for sailors?"

"A siren."

Yarbrough snapped his fingers. "Yeah, one of them. I can't resist her, Harry. I wind up on the train tracks. My foot gets caught in the rails and I hear that big freight bearing down on me. She's driving the train, leaning out and sayin', 'Are you lonely tonight, GI?'"

It was evident from the expression on Yarbrough's face that he was seeing all this in his mind.

"I stopped trying to get free and waited for her to roll right over me. But I wasn't panicked in the least. Like I was welcoming it."

Ingram took this in, then admitted, "Man, I was in the Lucky Clover a few days ago and swore I heard her in there." Ingram held up a hand defensively, even though his friend couldn't see the gesture. "I swear I wasn't tight. But I was so spooked, I was damn near searching under the stools for her."

"You think these are signs, like my grandmother would say?"

"Of what? An invasion by the Red Chinese? They gonna roll down Broadway singing 'When the Saints Go Marching In'?"

"And we'd be the chorus."

Ingram shook his head. "Who knows, maybe it's all this talk about the big one, the A-bomb wiping us all out. Got them kids ducking and cowering under their desks, like that would protect them from the radiation."

"I know war does funny things to people," Yarbrough said quietly.

They both got quiet again. There was an intermittent drip from the faucet in the bathroom.

"We ain't cracking up, are we? Like that soldier in that *Playhouse 90*?" Yarbrough had a television set. Ingram and a couple of the other friends would go over to his place and watch boxing matches. They'd take turns describing the action to him, filling the in-betweens of the announcer's observations.

Ingram hesitated. Finally, with as much conviction as he could, he said, "I don't think so, Arthur. Like we were, you know…" He couldn't bring himself to utter the term "shell-shocked."

"Look, man, you show up every morning, open up the store and keep the apples red and the grapes green, don't you?"

Yarbrough chuckled. "That's what they tell me. But what about you, Harry? Running after hoods and so on."

"It's about Ben."

"Would he do the same if it was reversed? Nosing around like one of them detectives on TV?"

Ingram drained his beer, wanting another. "It's me on this side of the grave, man. What else can I do?"

"Take those pictures of the good reverend when he's here and parlay them into a gig where they fly you around the country taking snaps of Lena Horne and Satchmo."

"My luck they'd strap me to the back of the Greyhound with a box of greasy fried chicken."

"Beats getting a knife in your foot."

"Oh, I don't know," Ingram said, rising with the aid of his cane and tapping it twice on the floor. "I might trade this one in for one with a big ol' brass ball for a top so I can knock in a fool's head when need be."

"See you, Harry."

"We gonna be all right, Arthur. We gotta be."

"What choice do we have?"

"Yes, sir."

Upstairs Ingram was pleased to find a bottle of beer behind the milk in his refrigerator. He opened it and for a change tuned the dial on his radio to KRLA. On-air was disk jockey Humble Harve. He said as he intro'd a song, "The hits just keep on comin', folks. Up next is 'Devil or Angel' by the Clovers."

The song began and try as he might to be in a good mood, he couldn't shake Yarbrough's words. "Goddamn Korea," he muttered, wiping at a tear.

CHAPTER NINE

Ingram arrived at Chin Low's on Alpine Street not far from Dodger Stadium, which opened the year before. There had been a fight about its construction as the sports venue displaced housing of mostly working-class Mexican and Mexican Americans in what was called Chavez Ravine. The man Ingram had run into at the party on Sugar Hill, Frank Wilkerson, had been involved on the side of the ones losing their homes. People did not go willingly, and the cops removed the recalcitrant by force after they were formally evicted from their rental properties. The worn wood frame buildings were bulldozed away, the dirt graded and tiered as if no one had ever lived there, tending their little gardens and sending their kids to school, hoping they'd get a better shake.

Ingram stepped into a cool dark area fronted by a walnut and marble counter. A large brass disk of intricate design hung behind the young woman there.

"Yes, may I help you?" she said. "Early lunch for one?"

"I'm here to see Hamish." He told her his name.

For a moment she regarded him as if there was a writhing octopus on his head. Her composure returned and she retrieved a conference phone from below the counter.

Pressing one of its buttons, she spoke into the handset in Chinese. She listened, responded and hung up.

"All the way back toward the kitchen, then left at the hallway, sir."

"Thank you." Ingram went through the padded leather swing doors, walking past diners. In the half-lit hallway, he was greeted by an older man in casual clothes with a golf club in one hand and golf balls in a wire bucket in his other hand. He had a round pleasant face and white-gray hair receding at the temples. There were heavy gold rings on the pinkie and ring finger of his right hand.

"Come on while I limber up, Mr. Ingram. Got a foursome coming up with money on the line and need the practice."

Figuring he wasn't going to get bashed in the head, Ingram answered, "Sure."

He followed Hamish Segal up a flight of stairs to a second-story private dining room. From there, they took more stairs to the roof. From this vantage point Ingram could see downtown and beyond—homes and old-style apartment buildings in the Echo Park area, Elysian Park with the police academy as well as the modernly designed oval of Dodger Stadium. Ingram darkly amused himself wondering if he were up here by himself smacking golf balls into the air and breaking somebody's window, how long would that last?

Segal stuck a tee in the tar of the roof and set a ball on it. "I owe Dot a few favors, so she called one in for this meet. I hope you appreciate that."

"I do."

"I asked around about you." He hit the ball with precision and force. "Would it surprise you to learn I know Charlotta Bass? I was around that time she announced she was running for vice president on the Progressive Party ticket."

"Not too surprised," Ingram admitted. A transcript of her

1952 speech had run in the *Eagle*. Ingram had read it in the newspaper's archives.

"That was something. A colored woman running for the second highest office in the land. Man. They didn't get much traction but still." He hit another ball he'd set up. This time he shaded his eyes with his hand to track its flight, and gave a satisfied nod of his chin.

"And anyway, I wanted to size you up since you're squiring Anita." He paused in setting up another shot, shaking the grip end of the club toward him. "I don't want to see any harm come to that girl."

"Neither do I."

"But you want to know about these lunkheads."

"I'm not inviting them over for tea."

"You kept your rod from the service?"

"Cleaned and ready."

"She can shoot."

"Anita?"

He fixed him with a look. "I taught her."

"Good to know."

"That's right, no tipping out on her." He smacked another one onto the imaginary fairway.

"I can't walk away now. I'm in too deep. Best to take the fight to them and not wait around to get my teeth kicked in."

"I can appreciate such thinking." He hit another one with a resounding thwack. "This Morty I don't know from Adam but this Wicks, him I've heard of. Trevor Wickland is his formal name, if you can believe that."

Ingram said, "A muscle for hire who's been around."

"Yeah, but like you, he was in the service. One of those fresh off the farm boys who couldn't wait to do or die for Uncle Sam. From what I heard he stayed in, looking to make a career of it, but something went haywire and he was bounced out, avoiding a sentence in Leavenworth."

"And he came out here?"

Segal nodded and swung again.

"How'd he hook up with Hoyt?"

"Not sure, but one story I've heard had to do with a rabbi needing hush money paid to this chipee and Wicks was used to make the payoff."

"The idea being if she kept squawking, the next time he saw her, it wouldn't be an envelope of money he'd be delivering."

"There you go."

"Wait, is Wicks Jewish?"

"Half or a quarter, something like that. You figure to trap him with a nicely prepared pastrami sandwich and a crisp dill pickle?" Thwack.

"Colored folks like pastrami too."

"You mean Johnny's on Adams?"

"Yeah, especially around two-thirty in the morning and you need solid food."

"Soak up that whiskey you've been sippin' on at Claudine's," Segal added. Claudine's Chalet was a nightclub in the area.

Ingram asked, "You know any of Wicks's hangouts?"

Segal paused his swing. "You plan on taking care of Wicks?"

"I'm not crazy enough to put a gun on a white man."

"Sure, I believe you." He hit another ball.

"I just want to get to the bottom of this, whatever this is."

"It could burn you. I know enough to know those Provider bastards don't play, Mr. Ingram. To them, Jews, negroes, Mexicans, they all best remember their place."

"I guess Wicks keeps that in mind."

Thwack.

Leaving Chinatown, Ingram followed up on what Claire had suggested, and took a trip back to Mulholland Drive, taking the ascent in low gear. When he got to the scene of the accident, he saw the guardrail had yet to be replaced. Ingram kept going. He didn't believe there was anything pertinent to be seen here. He turned down various residential streets, looking to see if he might find the house where the spy photos of the wild parties had taken place. He had copies of the photos with him and more than once stopped to investigate a particular house. But he struck out, not finding the place.

Ingram next piloted his car over the hills and into the San Fernando Valley. He drove along for a while, more or less aimlessly. He eventually stopped at a pay phone and sure enough, under nightclubs in the Yellow Pages, found a jazz joint he recalled being at a few years ago. It was called the Flying Potato and after consulting his map book for its location, he drove to the place. He parked and tried the front door but this time of day, the club wasn't open yet. He walked around back and saw the rear door ajar. Stepping through the doorway was a thickset man carrying an empty produce crate he added to a stack against the wall.

Ingram walked over. "You wouldn't know if a horn player named Ben Kinslow played here in the past, would you?"

The man had bushy eyebrows and hairy arms, a ring on each middle finger. His tight smile showed crooked front teeth. "Lot of cats come through here, man. On their way to the moon or nowheresville, baby."

"I hear what you're saying. How about a chick who went by Hanisha?"

His face lit up. "Now her, I remember well. She was a gas." He frowned and said, "Ain't seen her around in, oh, maybe since late 1960, come to think about it. Yeah, now that you mention her, seems to me I heard she'd gotten out of the biz, had a new hustle going I think. You looking to book them for a gig?"

"An article," Ingram lied, giving him one of his cards.

The proprietor studied the card. "Wow, dig that. I'm Gabe, by the way."

"Pleasure, Gabe. What about her manager, Clovis?"

He shook his head side to side. "Now him, I always said he was more anchor than propeller to her career, if you know what I'm sayin'."

"I do, I've met him."

He smiled again.

"You don't know if they stayed out this way, her and Clovis I mean."

"As opposed to the Black side of town?"

"Right."

"Can't say."

"I appreciate your time."

"Sure, man, take it slow."

"Righteous." They shook hands and Ingram started to walk away.

"You know," the club owner said, snapping his fingers, "Clovis had some kind of relation out here."

"Yeah?"

"Uncle, half-brother, something like that. I remember this because one night when she was headlining Clovis was giving me grief 'cause he wanted me to comp like a party of five including this relation of his. Like this is the Hollywood Bowl and not a little club eking out a living."

"That's Clovis. You remember this uncle's name?"

"No, sorry."

"Like I said, 'preciate your time, Gabe."

Ingram gave a half-wave good-bye. Driving away, he was pretty certain that the two had to be hiding out here in the Valley. He made a mental note to ask Johnny Otis if he knew Hanisha from her singing days.

"**MOM SAYS** you're all right."

"Of course." He grinned.

"Believe me, she can be quite judgmental, so that's saying something."

It was past ten in the evening and Claire had called first then dropped by with beer and takeout Chinese food. She also had her valise with her. Ingram had put a folded-over blanket on the floor and they were having their picnic in his front room, the jazz station on low. Miles Davis was blowing cool. On the coffee table was the pamphlet he'd gotten from Claire's mother, a torn piece of newspaper in it as a bookmark. He'd been reading it earlier.

"What do you think of the beer?" she asked. "It's from Mexico."

"I like it. I sometimes go over to the J-Flats to buy a Japanese beer I first had in the service. Kimchi too."

"What's that?"

"Spicy cabbage."

"You're such an international man."

"Ain't I though?"

At some point they cleared off the space and Ingram lay on his back, having stripped off his clothes. She had her hand around his erect member working him up and down.

Huskily he said, "Baby, I'm about to blow my top."

"Not yet you aren't."

He reached under her dress. She took it off but kept her underwear on. They made love with her straddling him. The lascivious words she whispered in his ear would make Redd

Foxx blush. Afterward he dozed there on the floor, his boxers back on and another blanket draped over him. Her valise open and papers about, Claire, wearing his robe, worked at his kitchen table late into the night.

CHAPTER TEN

Hamish Segal hadn't known where Wicks did his unwinding, but he did know that he wasn't exclusive to Hoyt. Or at least if you had a mind to employ his services, there was a used car lot on Beverly near Normandie where a message could be left. The outfit was called Gladfair Auto Sales. Ingram concluded it would be a waste of time to keep watch on the place, and surely nothing good would come of his going in there to ask for Wicks. He concluded for the time being, the smart move was continuing to look for Hanisha and Clovis.

"That's the thing, Harry," Edwards was saying over the phone. "I only know about them 'cause this chick I know knew her."

"You think she'd talk to me?"

"She's not in the free advice business."

"Didn't think she would be."

Soon Ingram was at Dolphin's of Hollywood, a record shop with listening booths on Vernon near Central. Like the racetrack, it was miles from the famous part of town. The LAPD used to station men in front to stop white kids from entering, listening and dancing to that jungle music. The woman who had been cooking the evening that Ingram and

Edwards had visited Hanisha had mentioned Clovis and a record shop. Edwards told him to ask for Sherry and to be there exactly at 12:50 in the afternoon, her break time. They talked out behind the shop on a small patio area.

"You gotta understand," Sherry said as he handed a ten across. "Bell's kind of the religious type." She was referring to the shop's manager. "She ain't no nun her damn self as much as she likes to gossip, but the less she knows about my after-hours activities, the better." Sherry wore a loose-fitting dress and to Ingram she looked like a showgirl only a year or so past her prime. He asked her about Hanisha. The story he and Edwards had cooked up to tell her was the two of them were looking to put on a shindig for some out-of-town Elks lodge members they were trying to get to invest in a tire store.

"Now look, if you're looking for some chicks to, you know, show these fellas a good time, I can line 'em up. But no whorin', get me?" She pointed an immaculately red-nailed finger at him. "We tee-hee at their stale jokes, rub their little bald heads, maybe even let them rest a hand on a thigh, but that's it. We help lubricate them and you make your sale. Now if one of those gals makes another arrangement, that's different. But I'm no pimp in high heels. Dig?"

"I appreciate what you're telling me, Sherry. But the thing is a couple of these guys was out here before and, well, they're kinda partial to Hanisha's girls, if you see what I'm saying. But of course, not leaving you out."

She made a sound in her throat. "Yeah, she got that mumbo-jumbo she spouts about the power between our legs and the way to spiritual enlightenment through the mastering of the chakra for us females, but she's just a hustler. Her and Clovis."

"How close are they?"

"They ain't that way in the sack if that's what you mean. Him and his tough guy act," she said derisively. "Back in their club days he figured he had to act like that."

"What do you mean?"

"He called hisself her manager, baby," she said, head cocked.

"Yeah, I heard she was a singer."

"Not much of one, but we got a couple of her records inside."

"Is Hanisha her real name?"

Sherry laughed. "Hell naw. When she was gigging, she got onto that spiritualist bullcrap she likes to spout and changed it to that highfalutin one-name jive." She laughed again. "Her country ass is Anna Mae Stanford."

"And Clovis is not what he pretends to be either?"

"He went to Pepperdine. And I don't mean he was a janitor over there."

"You know this how?"

The look she fixed him with was one of practiced exasperation. "All men like to brag on themselves, don't they?"

"But he could have just been telling you that to try and impress you."

"Oh, I know. See, though, I saw his picture in the yearbook. He showed me. And when we was talking then, he dropped that no-education talk he likes to fool people with."

"What's his last name?"

"Gonna check?"

"Do you mind?"

"No, you'll see I'm telling you straight. It's Clovis Mitchell."

He catalogued this, then asked, "So you can round up the party girls Hanisha usually gets?"

"Maybe," she said cagily. "If it was worth my while." She checked her watch.

"It could be," which wasn't quite a lie.

From inside something crashed to the floor.

Sherry said, "I better get back to work. But you want the honeys, and I'm talking about a few that are top heavy like battleships, Mr. Harry, I'm your girl." She handed Ingram a torn piece of paper with her name and number already on it. She figured to out-hustle the hustler, he concluded. "Call me and you won't be sorry." She kissed him on the cheek and returned to her duties in the record shop.

Leaving, Ingram considered driving over to Pepperdine, a private Christian-oriented college on Vermont near Manchester. He recalled meeting two men at different times who'd also seen action in Korea taking classes there. Maybe there were a thousand students enrolled at the college, but not many more, he estimated. And Clovis Mitchell had gone there? It wasn't just religious classes they offered, though certainly that was the core. But if he recalled correctly, you could study business management and even psychology there. It amused him to think of Clovis Mitchell in a suit and tie telling some patient their problems all had to do with a mother complex. Stopping at a light, Ingram laughed out loud at this, his window down. Several pedestrians gawked at the crazy man behind the wheel as he took off again.

Ingram sobered up, wondering how Mitchell had paid for the tuition. He had no idea how much it cost but he figured it couldn't be cheap. If the Providers were footing his bill, why? Because from what Sherry had said, it didn't sound like he and Anna Mae, now Hanisha, had found the pot of gold in the entertainment business—though that could have been the way they and Hoyt met. Her being a singer, it was plausible she'd have met Ben Kinslow at one of the local spots the last time he was living in town. Maybe even dated, he wondered. She was procuring for Hoyt and she recommended his friend to the rich man as his driver—all the while the three of them looking to blackmail the guy. Clovis might have taken those pictures.

THAT EVENING he kept an appointment he'd made regarding the missing diary.

"You were in the Abraham Lincoln Brigade."

"Yes, sir, I was."

"I'm not jivin' you when I say that was something." Ingram sat across from the wiry Charlie Sutton. He was a medium-built Black man with graying hair and an easy way about him. He was a partner in a print shop on Western Avenue that did letterpress and offset work. They were in Sutton's comfortable home on west Seventy-Fourth Street in the Hyde Park area. Overhead a plane rattled the windows slightly on its way to landing at the airport.

"Tell him what you did in the big war, honey," his wife, Joyce Sutton, said from the kitchen where she washed the dishes they'd eaten on.

"You were also in World War II? Damn."

"Yeah, part of the Balloon Busters," he admitted.

"The 320th?" Ingram said.

"You heard of us?"

"Had an uncle Elliot with them on my mother's side," he said fondly. "He died three days after Omaha Beach. I always remember him taking me to the corner store and buying me a comic book and jawbreaker when I was a kid."

The older man nodded appreciatively.

The two sat in the dining room. In the living room past an archway the Suttons' teenage daughter sat before the TV intently watching the *Ben Casey* doctor drama. A woman with big hair cried into a handkerchief as Casey, emoting empathy, laid the bad news on her about her husband's condition. Ingram refocused.

The 320th Very Low Altitude Barrage Balloon Battalion was the only all-Black unit to take part in D-Day, though other Black units were involved in the second wave, the mop-up. The job of the ballooners was to get their light balloons aloft on steel cables. The idea was as German fighter planes swooped down at 400 miles an hour, raking the troops with machine gun fire, they would slice a wing off on the cables.

"Charlie, you ought to write a book about what you've been through."

"That's what I've told him over and over," his wife said over the clink of a pot being set on the dish rack.

"Well, you know how it was," Sutton said.

"Anita told you I was in Korea?"

"That's the only reason I agreed to talk to you, Harry."

"No, it isn't," his daughter, Ophelia, piped in. "You love it when people drag these stories out of you."

Sutton smiled sheepishly and had more of his Pabst bottled beer, carefully replacing it on the coaster.

A beer on a coaster at his elbow as well, Ingram continued making notes. Sutton was the second name on the short list Claire had given him. The first person listed was out of the country at the moment. Ingram couldn't come right out and grill the man about the missing diary. He'd begun after dinner at a logical place given their shared background of being in the service. Ingram was genuinely interested in Sutton's experiences and figured he could turn this into an article for *Dapper* or *Ebony*. Sutton had various photos from that time, including one with him and writer Richard Wright, who'd covered the conflict.

They talked some more about the man's wartime

experiences, including being shoulder-to-shoulder with other Blacks who'd volunteered for the left-leaning Abraham Lincoln Brigade in the fall of 1937. This included his recollections about a man named Oliver Law, who Ingram hadn't heard about.

"This gee was from West Texas," Sutton was saying. "He'd been an enlisted man way before the action in Spain. He was smart and fearless and a flaming red."

"This is great," Ingram muttered as he wrote.

"Yeah, there was a sister named Salaria over there too, can you dig that? A nurse. Last I heard she married some ofay, I mean white guy," he chuckled.

"What about this Oliver Law?"

"He died leading his machine gunners trying to take Mosquito Hill."

Ingram looked up to see a somber cast to the other man's face. He recovered and on they talked, at one point going into the kitchen so he could dry the washed dishes and put them away. Ingram helped. They also had a second beer. This seemed like the time to ask him about his more recent activities.

"Not that I'm looking to put you on the spot, but what with being in the Brigade, that got you involved in the Party's activities?" Claire had told him Sutton not only often printed the informational flyers about their pickets but participated as well.

Sutton was putting away the dinner dishes in the cupboard over a toaster on the counter. "You mean I'm a dyed-in-the-wool commie? This all a bunch of hooey and you're really working for HUAC? To turn me in?" He was pulling a pack of cigarettes out of his pocket as he talked.

"Hardly."

Sutton offered a cigarette he'd shook loose.

"I'm a cigar man."

Sutton placed the end of the cigarette between his lips and drew it out of the pack in that way. The cigarette dangling from his mouth, he said, "Let's step out on the back porch."

The house was constructed such that this meant going out a side door in the kitchen. There was a concrete landing and steps as well as a railing made of plumbing pipe. Sutton cupped his hands and lit his cigarette.

"I came up in this piss-poor Southern town, Harry. Never had shit and headed for never having shit to hand down to those after me."

"I hear you."

"Anyway, when me and my brother got some size on us, we took the first thing smoking to get the hell away from there. Brian, that's my brother, wound up in Chicago and I landed in New York. I was doing the usual us colored folks find ourselves doing to keep a sandwich and coffee in my belly. Janitor in a medical supply outfit, hauling blocks of ice up flights of stairs in cold-water flats, man I did it all." He paused to blow a stream of smoke into the night air.

"Having those kinds of jobs brought me in contact with white people in a different way. Not having to take off my hat and bow and scrape or cross to the other side of the street like how it was expected back home. Hell," he began, a grin lighting his face as he lowered his voice before speaking again. "I even laid some pipe on this here white gal who was, you know, in the Party."

Ingram nodded knowingly.

"Yes, sir. Started going to their meetings, getting involved in what they called direct actions." He looked sideways at Ingram, tip of the cigarette glowing. "I liked that they didn't just give lip service to negro equality but laid it on the line.

Plus, well, I had my head in the clouds over that chick so, you know, the little head does the thinking a lot of times."

Ingram said, "There is that."

"Anyway." Sutton shrugged, tapping ash from his cigarette. "When the call-up came about fighting for democracy in Spain, despite the US dragging its feet what with that premature anti-fascist shit, like there's a particular time to be against oppression or not, me and some of the others I'd become friends with signed on."

"You want me to keep this out of the article?"

Sutton studied him for several ticks of the clock, then said, "I ain't too worried about them Birchers coming for me. Riding up here from Disneyland in their drop-top Caddies with John Wayne on a horse in the lead. Shit." He flicked the spent cigarette away. The tip sparked when it struck the concrete of the driveway.

He laughed and so did Ingram. It didn't seem like Sutton was worried about his past activities being exposed, the photographer reasoned.

"Let me level with you, Charlie," he said as the two stepped back inside. They sat at the kitchen table where they'd left their beers. The bottles were still cool, slick to the touch. The swing door to the kitchen was closed and Ingram made sure to keep his voice low as Sutton had done outside. "I'm going to do my best to get the story placed, but I had a different reason for coming to see you."

"Is that right?"

"Yeah, well, like you said, sometimes the little head does the thinking." Though his feelings for her were more than that, he realized.

"Anita is a good-looking, smart woman." Sutton tipped the neck of the bottle toward Ingram then took a sip.

"There's this diary the Berksons had. My understanding

is Don plans to turn these recollections into a book, a memoir." Lindon "Don" Berkson was Judy Berkson's father. "They was looking for it not long ago and couldn't find it."

"And I was one of the ones who hid some of his books in my shop," Sutton said.

Ingram spread his hands. He was surprised that Sutton hadn't gotten angry at his admission.

"I didn't swipe the diary. It don't make me no never mind. But since we're putting our cards on the table, could be your girlfriend has you intentionally looking in the wrong direction."

"You mean this Emil Freed?"

"Oh, no, not him. I mean Solly."

"Anita's dad?"

The swing door was pushed in a degree and Sutton's wife leaned in to address her husband. "Honey, how much longer are you going to be? Y'all want some coffee? I can put a pot on."

"We're okay, we're just about to finish up."

"Okay." The door closed.

Waiting a few seconds for her to retreat, Sutton continued, "I guess Anita doesn't know about her father. What got him in hot water with her mother, I mean."

"What's that?"

"He's a stick-up man."

"What?"

"I'm pretty sure he's knocked over at least two banks in the last six months or so."

Ingram was having a hard time grasping what was being said. "Is he that hard up?"

"He was inspired by the Bolsheviks. They pulled off robberies to get money for the revolution. Even using homemade tear gas or some such, supposedly."

Ingram pointed at him. "Were you in on these heists?"

"No," Sutton said, holding up his hands palms out. "But we used to have these study groups. Reading a book or tract, discussing how best we could use left victories, like even in Cuba, and how we might apply those lessons here. Talking down inequality and so forth."

"Yeah . . . ?"

"A couple of years ago, and this was when we had a few sessions in the back of my shop, there was one night, and it was just a few of us there—just the men, in fact. Including Solly and Don. Anyway, Solly was gassed up about what had happened to the Wells family."

"The *Sentinel* covered that." A Black family's white neighbors were drunk and threw beer bottles through the family's windows. Riled up, they then blew out the glass with a shotgun blast. The husband, Thomas Wells, wasn't cowed and borrowed another neighbor's shotgun to citizen arrest the perpetrators.

"Solly saw this as a sign. He was talking about tit for tat. For instance, going after cops if they beat another Black man in handcuffs to death."

"Man, that's reckless."

"Yeah, we talked him back from going off half-cocked, but Solly was determined that another picket line wasn't going to get it done. He made a point we should discuss at the next meeting how Lenin and his bunch came to the conclusion that ripping off the capitalists' banks was a revolutionary act. That if we organized ourselves, utilized military training and whatnot, we could use men and women like in Algiers to pull off successful robberies."

"That could have just been talk."

"Maybe," Sutton allowed. "Before the next session he called me and Don and asked us not to bring it up. It seemed like he'd petered out on the idea. But I don't think it was a coincidence First National got knocked over recently."

"Why do you say that?"

He fixed him with a look. "Solly had a janitorial service once upon a time."

"And he used to clean that bank?"

"I'm betting he did."

"I don't know," Ingram began.

"How does the robber identify himself?" Sutton asked rhetorically.

"Two letters, A.M., that and him robbing before noon is why they call him the Morning Bandit." Ingram recalled from the article he read in the *Herald Ex* that he wore a full face mask, gloves and newsboy cap. He used a sawed-off shotgun and didn't talk much. His note he'd hand the teller demanded the bills and was signed with an A and M.

"But what does that prove?" Ingram said.

"I think the letters are for Antonio Maceo, a Black general who fought with Fidel Castro and Che Guevara."

"Aw, come on."

Sutton hunched his shoulders again. "Dorothy figures the reason Solly hasn't been around is because he's taken up with another woman. Probably then Anita thinks this too. But Don and I talked about the bandit and we both came to the conclusion it's Solly."

"Hold on," Ingram said. "That diary was packed away before the Wells incident. So why would he break into Don Berkson's garage to take the diary?"

"Maybe Don said something to Solly, I don't know. And maybe he was worried Don was gonna include new stuff, if the plan is to do a book."

"He wouldn't rat him out."

"You're right," Sutton admitted. "Solly would know he

could trust Don to make sure he didn't put any of his old comrades on the spot."

Ingram didn't know what to make of any of this. He rose, circling back to more familiar territory. "I'm going to take a run at the article and will probably have a few follow-up questions for you if that's okay. I ain't putting in anything about the robberies."

"Didn't think you would. What are you going to tell Anita?"

"Nothing for the time being. You got my head spinning, man."

After he said his good-byes, Ingram stood outside on the walkway, hands on his hips. Had Sutton told him a fairy tale to throw him off? Was it just bullshit to cover the fact he'd stolen the diary? But he genuinely seemed not to care if his left-leaning associations were known.

Ingram dug out an El Producto from his sport coat's inner pocket, carefully extracting the cigar from its cellophane wrapper as if it were a stick of dynamite. Blocking his lighter's flame against the breeze, he lit up. He'd parked down the block and walked slowly to his borrowed car, trying to sort this strange tale out. Shouldn't he ask his girlfriend what she believed about her father? Had she tried to contact Solly in the last few months? If he was the thief, wouldn't he make sure to act normal around her and her mother and not avoid them?

Back home, he wrote further notes. The following day, once he'd prepped his equipment for the rally, he drove to the *Herald Examiner* building on Broadway in downtown L.A. It was a grand structure done in the Mission Revival style, designed by the state's first licensed female architect, Ingram recalled. He was about to go inside to look through recent issues in the newspaper's morgue, but checked his watch and decided on a new plan. He walked north up the next block to a bar and grill called the Driftwood. Sure enough, sitting on a stool smoking a Pall Mall, the remains of his lunch before him on a plate, sat Mike Piedmont. Ingram went over, passing other reporters en route.

"The intrepid Harry Ingram. What brings you down here today? And shouldn't you be getting your beauty rest for the big day?"

"'Fraid beauty rest won't help me now, Mike. Have you been covering the Morning Bandit story?"

"I have." Piedmont drank what was left of his tepid coffee.

"The cops working on any theories?"

Piedmont squinted an eye as he gazed at Ingram. "You got an angle on this, Harry?" He fired up another cigarette.

"I honestly don't know."

"Share and share alike."

Not looking to betray Anita Claire, he measured his next words. Have Piedmont showing up at the campaign office, now wouldn't that be grand?

"How about this? I'm not asking because I want to do a story. I'm not horning in, it's all yours to tell."

"But I get a name before anybody else."

"It could be just a lead. But if it gets to that, yes."

Piedmont had wheeled around on the stool, elbows set back on the bar top. "Cops ain't got squat. Over the last half a year, he's hit three banks in three different parts of town, always careful to be near a freeway entrance, of course, like any clear-thinking bank robber in our fair city. He's not greedy, apparently no monkey on his back, and he's also obviously casing these joints ahead of time. One of the banks, he'd cut the outside wires to the alarm. Which must have been done the night before. Smart guy is the only thing they know."

Which meant the law and Piedmont thought he was white. If it was Solomon Claire, that would be a reason he didn't speak much so as not to be identified as Black, Ingram conjectured. He asked, "Anything else?"

"That's the other thing that's clever about him," Piedmont said. "The first time he left on a bicycle and cut down an alley. But as the cops stopped chumps on their bikes, it became obvious he must have had a car waiting. Second time he zoomed off on a motorcycle, but again must have dumped it somewhere to hop in his getaway car."

Piedmont tapped ash from his cigarette into the cup's saucer on the bar. His plate had been removed. "But I saved the best for last. This most recent heist, he ran out and got in a waiting car, a Buick, the witnesses think it was. A dame at the wheel. Scarf on her head and wearing dark glasses."

He didn't say she was colored, Ingram noted.

Piedmont studied him. "That mean something to you?"

"Not sure yet." Dorothy Nielson had a Buick, but so did a lot of people. Still.

"But you'll deliver, yeah?"

"You won't be sorry."

"I tell that to the dames all the time," Piedmont joked. "And look how that turns out."

"I'll see you, Mike."

Walking away, Ingram was even more confused. He'd have to wait to go down this particular road until after the rally.

CHAPTER ELEVEN

The following morning the phone rang and he answered the call.

"Harry," he heard Doris Letrec say.

"Hey now."

"Got a sweet one. This is from Hamer, Nolvang and Jessup."

"No shit? Excuse my French." The law firm she mentioned was prestigious, what they called a white shoe outfit.

"You've been asked for in particular. Kind of like the Black Muslim assignment."

"No kidding?"

"That's right, and this one doesn't involve any legwork. The job is delivering a bankruptcy petition to a business partner. The partner is Black, and I was told they asked around and your name came up. The feeling is the one you're serving, his name is Byron Noomis, will be less on alert if it's not a white face coming to his house."

Ingram considered what this made him, using his color as subterfuge to keep another colored man at ease. He was about to voice an objection but Letrec spoke again.

"Your end is three hundred and fifty dollars. I've got the address to his home. He'll be there today."

The amount was enough to assuage his conscience. If he didn't do it, someone else would, and for sure there was no sense leaving money on the table. Get it done then get back on the hunt after the rally, he vowed.

Less than an hour later he was on his way to Altadena taking the Pasadena Freeway, the first one built in Southern California. Once off the freeway, he had to stop twice to consult his Thomas Guide when he got turned around. Ingram got reoriented and approached the street he was looking for. Rising behind the homes were the foothills of the San Gabriel Mountains. He'd arrived at the location in a roundabout fashion taking back streets, and he spotted a parked car he recognized—the Dodge driven by Wickland.

"Son of a bitch," he muttered as he slowed. The two weren't in the car, which meant they were waiting for him around the corner at the address he'd been given. He didn't have his gun with him, but he wasn't going to run. How had they identified him? It had to be Hoyt, or maybe one of the hoods had seen him on TV being interviewed. Dammit, that's what he got for hogging the spotlight. That meant Wicks and Morty knew where he lived. They'd lured him out here so as to work him over nice and slow in isolation, then dump his body in those hills for the coyotes to feast on.

Ingram double-parked briefly and got his tire iron out of the trunk. He'd worn a light windbreaker and taking this off, wrapped it around the tool. He had to park on the other street or they'd get suspicious. Anyway, his foot wasn't completely healed so it wasn't like he could escape by running. He doubled back and drove onto the street from the direction he'd have come if he hadn't gotten lost. He parked, and with his coat folded under his arm as casually as he could make it seem, he walked with his limp up the flagstone path to a humble Craftsman, its porch bordered in river stones as was the custom of houses out this way. He'd left his cane in the car.

The porch was constructed such that one of them could be crouched behind the low wall of the balustrade, waiting to ambush him. Instinctively he slowed his step but kept going, his senses on alert. There were shades down behind the windows facing him. It did not seem to him anyone was peeping out. Ingram went up the three steps, glad the porch was empty. He rang the bell.

"Yes?" came a voice from inside.

"Mr. Loomis, I have a delivery for you," he called out.

From the other side of the door, "Come on in, it's unlocked."

Ingram tried to steady his breathing. Hand on the knob, he dropped the pretense of hiding the tire iron and let his jacket flutter away. He put his shoulder to the wood. Counting to three and tuning the knob, he barreled into the house, the door banging against the wall. The one called Morty was standing there, looking surprised. He had a knife in a shoulder rig and another in his hand. Ingram hit him in the upper shoulder of his knife arm with the tire iron.

"Fuck," he rasped.

Peripherally Ingram was aware of Wicks on his left, his gun holstered over a blue striped shirt. Rather than try to get past, Ingram dropped the tire iron and grabbed Morty, spinning him around and propelling him into Wicks, who was unholstering his weapon. Morty collided with him and both stumbled backward into a round table with a doily and a lamp on it. As the lamp crashed to the floor, shattering, Ingram snatched up the tire iron again and drove the wedge end into Wicks's leg right at the side of the knee.

Wicks cried out and crumpled to the floor, using both hands to stem the blood pumping from the wound as Ingram withdrew the tire iron. Morty made to come at him with the knife but another swipe of the lug end of the tire iron connected solidly against his temple and this time Ingram staggered him. Ingram headed toward the kitchen and hopefully a back door.

"Get that slippery Black bastard," Wicks said.

Moving through the kitchen, Ingram noted they'd made preparations to torture him. There was a thick tarp on the linoleum floor under a wooden chair, rope to bind him and a roll of duct tape too. He half-ran out the back, raising and lowering his injured foot as fast as he could. It hurt like anything but fear of being caught kept him going. There was a patio, trim medium-sized lawn and an incinerator in the backyard. A wooden fence framed three sides of the yard, a gate allowing access to an alley. The remaining side was a hedge nearly six feet high separating this yard from the neighbors'. In his run-hop Ingram heard Morty rushing out the back door. Any second he was going to stick him with that knife.

"What's going on out here?" An older woman stood on her back steps, which allowed her a look into the yard over the hedges. She held a basket of freshly washed clothes, about to pin them out on the line to dry.

Morty turned his head. "Go on about your business, you old biddy."

The woman gaped at him.

Ingram used the distraction to turn and step in close to Morty. He jabbed the tire iron into the other man's stomach. But this time it didn't sink in as it had on Wicks and Morty sliced at Ingram's upper arm, tearing through material and muscle. Still, Ingram had done some damage. The hood backed up, grimacing. The material of his shirt over his navel was reddening.

"I'm calling the police." The woman dropped the basket and hurried back inside her house.

Ingram was out the gate and, in his hobble-skip-run, made it down the alley as fast as he could. It seemed at least he'd immobilized Wicks. Cutting through a rip in a chain-link fence, he was on dirt and soon scrambling up a gradual incline of a hill from which scrub brush, ice plants and high weeds grew. Discarded household items were strewn every-where as he ascended. He climbed past the ringer part of an old-fashioned wash tub. A doll's smashed head stuck out between rollers. Half of one of its plastic eyes glared at him.

Huffing, his lower body slashed by thickets, Ingram kept going. There was no turning around and no one would be able to help him. Off to his right were even thicker and taller patches of vegetation and some thin trees rising above that into the foothills. He plunged in, chancing to crouch down for several seconds to catch his breath and hope that he was hidden.

"You ain't getting away from me, Ingram. You gonna answer our questions about your buddies Kinslow and that broad Hanisha, then I'm gonna gut you, gut you good. Hear?"

Oddly Ingram pondered what sort of chakra hoo-ha Korla Pandit and Hanisha would summon if they were him. Up he went on all fours so as to minimize noise, like he'd been taught in the Army, and to ease the pressure on his foot. The day had suddenly become night, concussive blasts rend-ing the black in crimson and yellow. Ingram shook off the firefight, concentrating on his present predicament. Con-tinuing up, he reached a switchback, and getting to his feet on the inclined path, went to the right where it descended, breathing hard toward a bend of the hill. Hurrying as best he could, he could hear Morty charging through from below. Ingram got around the bend and found himself on a semicircular plot of earth, a small plateau cut into the side of the hill. From the other side of this area the path continued slightly upward but he knew that trying to run along that was doomed to failure. He stopped, sweating hard as he stood. As far as he was concerned, he was at a dead end. A panorama of houses and nature swept below him.

"Motherfuck," he muttered. This was it.

"You're a game sumabitch, I'll give you that."

He turned to face Morty, who had a knife in each hand. He made elaborate circular slashing motions, as if performing a circus act. There was a broad smile on his face as he closed in on Ingram. The trapped photographer swung the tire iron at Morty, who sliced the back of his hand open, causing him to drop the tool, cursing. Ingram backed up. Morty did his ballet of blades, closing in. Ingram coolly realized Morty not only wanted him alive but mobile—he had to get back down to flat ground with him. He grimaced as the edge of a knife cut into his cheek and the point of the other blade pressed against his rib cage. Morty was close to him, the two glaring at one another, breathing into each other's face.

Then, "Boo," Ingram said, shoving Morty hard with both hands.

The thug backpedaled, loose rocks kicking up from beneath his leather soles, his arms pinwheeling. Off-balance, he threw one of his knives, missing Ingram. Ingram drove his good foot into the man's sternum, sending him over and down the ridge. Morty didn't scream. He rolled down the hill, his body crashing through the undergrowth. He appeared again, coming to rest on an outcropping of rocks and hillside below. His neck broken, Ingram noted dispassionately.

Ingram stared at the aftermath of his deadly handiwork.

He'd killed before in the war, enemy combatants who happened to be Asian, and to his everlasting woe that child. He'd fought white men, could remember one ruddy-faced chump crumpled at his feet after the two had gone blow-to-blow like Emile Griffith and Benny Paret one night outside a bar on leave. But this was the first white man he'd killed. It occurred to him looking at Morty's corpse that he didn't feel particularly racked about this, no worse than any other time. Before, like now, had been in the heat of battle—even the horrible accident with the kid, an innocent. Well, he reasoned, as the sound of a siren floated up to where he was, if he wasn't careful or lucky, he'd have plenty of time to reflect on the nature of life and death sitting in a prison cell.

He started back down on his bum aching foot. Driven by the desire to survive, Ingram had found it easier to go up than descend. But he still wanted to survive. He figured out a way to stoop over to use the tire iron as a kind of cane. His hand was bleeding but not badly. Occasionally he had to scoot on his butt, but he made it back down. He came out of the brush the way he'd gone in, pausing at the slit in the chain-link fence bordering the alley.

"Shit," he swore, pushing the chain links outward with his head and taking a look. A county sheriff's prowl car with its big star in the center of each door was parked in the alley, not twenty-five feet away. He backed away. If a deputy walked this way, he was a goner.

"Hey," Ingram heard.

"What's up?" Footfalls sounded in the alley and then they stopped.

"There's blood on the rug inside the house here and signs of a struggle. There's a man's windbreaker on the porch. Like it was taken off and thrown down."

"Maybe that guy came up, saw who was inside, and took it off to get ready to fight?"

"Yeah, could be. There was a scuffle for sure. But sure looks to me like more than just a bloody nose was leaking inside." There was a pause accompanied by the unmistakable click of the top of a Zippo lighter being flicked open. How many hundreds of times had Ingram heard that in the trenches? The faint smell of smoke drifted toward him.

The deputy who'd been talking continued. "Neighbor where our caller used the phone says they both heard a car peel away. But only looked out then. They saw the rear of the vehicle, but neither can identify it."

"Is R&I running down whose house this is?"

"Yeah."

"Okay, so what do you want to do?"

"If this isn't nothing but two guys beefing over who knows what, the captain will ream us a new one if we call it in to the desk requesting a detective. No body, no gunshots."

"We got a negro in the yard here carrying a tire iron and a white fella with a knife after him," the other one noted.

Ingram imagined the other one blowing smoke in the air. "Like I said."

The second cop talked. "The colored fella might be the one that bled and then ran out to save his ass. He could be lying around the corner all cut to shit and whatnot. If we don't make the effort to find his corpse, you know what'll happen if a civilian calls it in. Which could be happening right now."

"Yeah, okay, you're tight. You take Gravalia to the next block and I'll walk along Aralia. One of us find a carved-up darkie, we come fetch the other one."

They both chuckled and walked off. Ingram counted to ten and chanced stepping out into the open. Wicks was gone.

Neither deputy had mentioned him, or the tarp and rope in the kitchen. Undoubtedly Wicks had taken those items with him. For now, he was one less problem for Ingram to contend with—but the hired muscle would be coming for him. Maybe even coming for Anita. His immediate problem was that his car was parked on one of the streets they were checking.

While there were Black people living out this way, he did have a pronounced limp and scratches on his arms and the cut on his face. The gate still unlatched, he went back into the house and cleaned up as best he could using a dish towel at the mirror in the tiled bathroom. His windbreaker had been laid on the couch. There were no papers or anything else in the pockets. He concluded it was best to leave it where the deputy had placed it. Besides, no sense taking the risk of being spotted wearing the jacket. The common garment had been bought at a JCPenney, therefore little worry it could be traced to him, other than maybe tracking it down to the ghetto by its batch number. Ingram used the dish towel to wipe the place down in case fingerprints were taken later. He also wiped down the tire iron and carried it into the backyard, holding it by the dish towel. He laid it beside the incinerator, not making an effort to hide it. Maybe one of the deputies would notice it was newly placed there or maybe not. He returned to the house and, folding it over, put the dish towel back in the drawer in the kitchen where he'd found it.

Before leaving, a curious Ingram checked in the bedroom closet. There were a couple of shirts hanging there and no items in the chest of drawers save a box of opened mothballs. The kitchen too had clean pots and pans in it with a few dishes and glasses in the cupboards. But there had been no boxes of cereal or pancake mix, and in the refrigerator, which was running, meaning the power was on, there was a half carton of eggs and a jar of strawberry jam. In the freezer were two full ice trays. The impression he had was the house was used but not steadily.

Cautiously he opened the front door. A young father smoking a cigarette was pushing a stroller and he waited for him to go past, then stepped out and walked along the sidewalk.

He was nervous about walking to his car, but he was certain waiting around he'd be arrested. It might be days before Morty's body was found, though Ingram was aware people liked to hike these foothills. He got to the corner and went along the side street. As he rounded the next corner, he spotted the sheriff's deputy standing mid-block talking to a woman on her lawn. They hadn't seen him, and he reversed course, backtracking along the side street again. Was the deputy coming this way or heading in the other direction? Ingram refused to be frozen by indecision and kept walking. He was back on the original street. On he went, aware of a curtain shifting in a window. He did his best not to favor his wounded foot, just a guy out for a stroll.

Down the other parallel side street he went, passing a mailman on his rounds. He got to the next block again and didn't see the deputy. He stepped up his pace. Down the block on the other side of the street, he saw him, a foot on the lower step of a porch as he talked to an older man standing in the doorway of his home. Just as the older man's head turned his way, Ingram reached his car. From this distance, with his head down and hands on the trunk obscured by the car's tail fin, he hoped it was harder to tell he was Black. Ingram opened the trunk, pretending to be busy in there. He again counted to ten and peeped around the lid. The deputy was walking away from the house he'd stopped at, his back to Ingram. He eased the trunk closed and got behind the wheel, holding his breath the entire time.

Keyed up, he depressed the accelerator too many times, flooding the engine. The odor of unburned gas was sharp in his nostrils. He should get out of the car and pop the hood, manually work the butterfly vents on the carburetor to better release the fuel vapors. But he was terrified of getting out and being spotted. He waited an agonizing thirty seconds and cranked the ignition again. Once, twice, three times the engine growled but didn't catch. He switched the ignition off and forced himself to wait, then tried again and this time the car started after yet another skipped heartbeat. He put the car in gear and began a three-point turnaround midblock. Good thing, as the deputy was now on his side of the street and walking this way. Keeping his cool, he righted the car and drove away, not sure if the cop was paying him any mind or not. But he made it to the freeway without a squad of sheriff's cars swooping down on him like jet jockeys buzz bombing enemy bunkers.

Driving, Ingram concentrated on what Morty had said about Kinslow and Hanisha. He interpreted this to mean they did know each other. Hoyt had tumbled to their scheme. Hanisha and Clovis hadn't gone on the run when Kinslow turned up dead. He supposed they didn't want to draw attention. But something had spooked them.

By the time Ingram got off the freeway, his anxiety and ruminations had given way to a pronounced hunger. But first he stopped to make a call.

"Is Anita Claire available?" he asked when the line connected at the Tom Bradley campaign offices.

"She's out, shall I take a message?"

"Tell her Harry called, if you would." He hung up. There was no particular reason Wicks would know they were seeing each other, but no sense being lackadaisical about a gunman out to get him, either. He drove to the Detour diner and sat down heavily on one of the stools at the counter. At this time of day, there weren't many customers.

"What'll it be today, Harry?" Winnie McClure asked him, eyeing the fresh cut on his cheek. She was one of the co-owners of the establishment. She didn't wait on tables or booths but she did take orders at the counter. McClure was a heavyset, solid woman with a handsome face and reddish-brown hair always worn short and straight like illustrations he'd seen of Peter Pan.

"Let me get some coffee, that strip steak you got medium-well, three eggs scrambled, home fries and toast. And grits too, please."

"Damn, you got a bunch of trees to cut down?" she said, writing down his order.

"Already have, Winnie. But I gotta keep my strength up for the next round."

"Okay, Paul Bunyan."

As she walked away, Ingram again fixated on Anita Claire and her well-being. He was going to have to tell her something, but how much of the truth was he going to reveal? If he got linked to Morty's death, she could easily be labeled an accessory—he knew enough about that from delivering legal papers. It would torpedo the campaign and he'd forever be known as the man who sunk Bradley's career. Rather than these prospects making him queasy, his appetite intensified. He made an effort not to wolf his meal down.

"I'd ask how was it, but I think I know." McClure surveyed the empty plate and the bowl the grits had come in.

Ingram used his last piece of toast to sop up the leavings. "Hit the spot."

"Good to know. Wouldn't want you to start chewing the roof beams." She took away the dishes.

His belly full, Ingram considered taking a room at the Y to lie low, but didn't like the idea of leaving his place unguarded for Wicks to break into. That would be making his photos vulnerable, and he'd be damned if he was going to see them stolen or destroyed. Back at his place, he again considered what he could do with his photographs and negatives. When he'd previously separated out his negatives, he'd put a grip of them in a Stetson hat box and the remainders in a Gladstone luggage bag with twin sewn-on straps, one of the few items his long-departed father had left behind. For the moment he'd stuck these in the hall closet.

Maybe he could arrange for his stuff to be stored at the *Eagle* or *Sentinel*, though he doubted either newspaper would go for that. The other clickers they used would have already asked. Too bad he didn't know anyone with one of those fallout shelters in their backyard. But could be he might pay an overdue visit to his mother, thereby storing his photos with her. Otherwise, it meant paying a monthly fee to store them in town, and who knew how long he'd have to do that?

Anita Claire called him back to say hi, and that for the next few days she was going to be too busy getting things ready for King's visit to see him.

"Of course, honey, I just wanted to hear your voice."

"What did you say?"

"I wanted to hear—"

"No, the honey part."

"Oh that. Slip of the tongue."

"I'd say something a good girl shouldn't say but I'm already getting looks speaking low into the phone. I miss you."

"I miss you too."

"Bye for now."

"See you soon."

"That's right."

Hearing that she was okay relaxed Ingram to a degree. He knew he better not get overconfident. He had some rope in his closet and used that to tie off the knob of the rear door in his darkroom off the back porch. He tied the other end of the rope to one of the legs of the utility sink. He debated moving his dresser to help block the front door but figured that might be going overboard. He did decide to sleep in the front room, though, gun handy. He also parked his car in front rather than his slot off the alley for a quicker getaway if need be. By eight that night he was worked up again, wondering if and how Wicks might come at him. He drank hard liquor, enough to take the edge off but not enough to spoil his aim. He relaxed again and by ten-thirty was asleep in his chair.

Until.

"Hey, Harry, your car's on fire."

Ingram came awake in a start, disoriented, still embodied in the dream he was having where he was flying on a magic carpet over snowy Pork Chop Hill in South Korea. He wiped his face as he again heard his name shouted up at him from outside.

"Your Plymouth's burning, Harry."

The gun in his fist, Ingram came out of his chair and out the front door of his apartment in a rush. He pounded down the stairs, several locks of his neighbors' doors turning as he passed. He reached the sidewalk and for an instant was transfixed at the sight of his car on fire. There was a line of flame from his hood up his windshield, across the roof then down the rear glass and the trunk. That meant someone had poured gas on his car then set a match to the trail.

As Ingram started toward the vehicle, a blush of yellow-white flame flared from the rear end, driving him back. The photo chemicals in the trunk had caught fire. Emerging from the glare came Wicks around the rear of the Belvedere, blasting away at Ingram. He was already diving behind the hedges. The people who'd been watching the car burn scattered for safety. Hitting the ground, Ingram returned fire. The flames whooshed hotter and brighter and Ingram couldn't tell if he'd struck his target. But there was no more shooting. Wicks must have run off, having failed in his ambush. The sirens getting closer, Ingram tossed his gun in the bushes next to his apartment.

Seconds later a fire truck blared around the near corner. A fireman in the truck's jump seat yelled out the window to no one in particular. "Get back, it's going to blow."

Sure enough, the car's fuel tank, strapped under the trunk area, blew, lifting the rear of the car up then slamming it down in a boom heard blocks away. In an odd twist of physics, the oxygen in the vicinity was sucked upward, extinguishing that part of the fire. The ruined back portion of the car was charred black and smoldering while the front end still burned.

Parked in the street, the firemen jumped off their truck, connecting the big hose to a nearby hydrant. They set about stopping the blaze before anything else burned. The Rambler parked behind Ingram hadn't caught on fire, but the windshield had been blown out from the explosion with other damage done as well. The onlookers had returned. Ingram knew more than one of them had seen him hide his gun, had in fact seen him shooting back at the white man shooting at him. But as they were Black and knew what kind of hell he could receive at the whims of the white-dominated Los Angeles Police Department, no one was volunteering information. He was also thankful the fire department hadn't been close enough to hear the shots. One of his neighbors, a man who worked for the city's Department of Water and Power, gave Ingram a knowing nod.

"What happened?" the fireman asked Ingram, who'd told him this was his car on fire. The other man was big armed and blond-haired with hazel eyes.

"Somebody torched it for kicks, I guess," he answered.

"You didn't fall asleep smoking in it, did you?"

"Nope. I was upstairs dozing and the next thing I know somebody's yelling about a car on fire." Ingram pointed toward his window. "I took a look and could see it was mine." When he'd heard his name being shouted a warning had gone off in his head. It had been Wicks yelling up to him to get him outside.

The fireman looked over to see his men finishing with the car. There were hosing down others as a precaution. He turned back to Ingram. "The police will want to talk to you."

Ingram shrugged. "Sure. I'll give you my name and everything."

The fireman was obviously surprised at his openness. His experiences in the ghetto had informed him people in questionable situations like this were usually evasive. "Okay, fine."

No police had arrived by the time Ingram had finished giving his information to the fireman and gone back upstairs. He didn't have full coverage on his Plymouth, so replacing it was on him. By the time he settled with the owner of the Rambler, his rate was sure to increase. Now he had to go to ground lest Wicks make another play for his hide. But for what remained of tonight until daybreak, he wasn't worried about another attack. He regretted not getting any photos of his car burning. That would have made the front page of the *Sentinel* for sure, as it tended more toward the sensational than the more politically inclined *Eagle*.

"Some One-Shot wonder I am," he mumbled before falling into a deep sleep.

CHAPTER TWELVE

"Don't forget to stop and get the curtain rods on your way home, Paul, they're ready," his wife said.

"I won't," Paul Westmore replied. "See you tonight."

"Have a good day."

"You too, dear." The front door quietly closed.

From his position he also heard the door of the Buick LeSabre parked in the driveway open and then, after a few seconds, close. But the ignition wasn't engaged. Westmore must have noticed the gate to the backyard was partially open. The car door opened again and closed; footfalls along the concrete approached. He got ready, sucking in a breath and holding it. Maybe Westmore figured one of the neighborhood kids must have hit a baseball into the back and hadn't bothered to close the gate again after retrieving the damn thing.

"Shit," Westmore swore, reaching the gate and seeing one of his patio chairs had been upended and moved onto his lawn. Focused on that, he stepped into his backyard to see what else had been upset.

"If you yell, I'll blow you goddamn head off."

Westmore turned to see an angry colored man holding a gun on him. He raised his hands. "Mister, I've got exactly forty-three dollars in my wallet. Take it, please, and leave us alone."

Harry Ingram said, "I'd like nothing more than to do that, Westmore, but I'm going to need something from you all right, just not money."

"How do you know my name?"

"You're with Hamer, Nolvang and Jessup, and you're the attorney named in the faked-up court papers that almost got me killed."

He gaped. "Listen, I—"

"In the pool house." Ingram flicked the gun in that direction. Taking up the rear, he marched the lawyer around the pool and into what was little more than a shed for changing and storing pool-cleaning supplies. There was a chair in there and Ingram had Westmore sit down. There was a small window of closed frosted louvre glass slats.

"What do you know about Winston Hoyt?"

Westmore frowned as if Ingram had spoken to him in a foreign language.

"I'm not fucking around."

"I realize that. Look, I know Hoyt golfs with one of the partners. I know that when I was told to execute the order, I did so knowing there was no such case, that is to say not active, at least. But I did as I was told. That's all I know, mister."

"You had your office specifically ask for me."

He'd been sitting with his hands partly raised. Now he set them on his thighs. "That was through the partner, not me."

Ingram considered going at the partner, but putting a rod on more than one well-off white man, and another lawyer at that, seemed to be pressing his luck. He said, "What do you know about that house I was sent to in Altadena?"

Westmore balked.

Ingram tapped the slide of the .45 against his temple. "You ever hear one of these babies go off? They're loud and leave a nasty hole."

"You seem like a reasonable man," he began. "You don't want to do anything you'll regret."

"The house?"

"It's a—you know—for assignations."

"Small words."

He shrugged. "Where the partners or certain clients can take a broad who isn't their wife."

"I bet the partner who's Hoyt's buddy lives out that way. Nice old-money South Pasadena maybe?"

Westmore's horrified look confirmed Ingram's guess. The house where the sneaky pics had been taken also popped into his head.

"Where does Hoyt live?"

"You can't get to him."

"Satisfy my curiosity."

"Santa Monica. On the beach."

"Do the Providers meet out there?"

Again Westmore fixed him with a frown. "You better leave that alone. Far alone."

"I'm hoping to get a membership card and secret initiation ring."

Westmore went silent. Ingram considered taking a page from a *Dapper* story and pistol whipping him to get him to talk, which brought a crooked smile to his face. If he learned where they held their meetings, he imagined bursting through a skylight like the Crime Smasher in the comics and interrupting their hoodoo ceremony praying to the skull of Thomas Jefferson or some such.

"Wait five minutes after I leave."

"Then what?"

"Then you can tell your boss to kiss my shiny Black ass." He quit the pool house and walked back along the driveway. He was stepping past the Buick when he heard Westmore's front door creak open behind him.

"Who are you?" the woman of the house called out. "What are you doing here and where's my husband?"

Ingram didn't look back at her as he jogged diagonally across the adjoining neighbor's lawn toward his borrowed car.

"Paul," yelled the wife. "Paul," she repeated. A neighbor on the far side of where Ingram was came to his front door. "What are you doing here?" she demanded of Ingram.

"What is it, Tricia?"

"That negro . . . person," she yelled.

Her neighbor, in short sleeves and tie, came out of his house to catch Ingram's eye as he drove away in a car he'd borrowed from Strummer Edwards, a humble Ford Falcon. In the rearview, Ingram saw the neighbor standing next to Tricia as they both stood on her lawn. Both were probably memorizing the car's plate as it receded. But Westmore would tell them not to worry, don't call the police. He wouldn't want anyone at his firm knowing about this confrontation. What could one half-crazy colored man do against the Providers? He chuckled.

In no hurry, Ingram drove from Hancock Park to his temporary digs, a comfortable room in the J-Flats. This part of town, on the edge of Echo Park, had gotten its nickname from the fact that when Japanese immigrated to L.A., they tended to come through here first as there were other family members around. There were a few Black families living in the area as well.

Not that Ingram was worried about getting run out of the J-Flats as he went along the aisles of the Fujiya Market picking up several items including ice cold Asahi beer. Through a connection of Josh Nakano's, he was holed up in a room of a large house up the hill from the market on Clinton. The place he was staying in was where the road curved, the freeway below. The widow who owned the two-story regularly rented out her top rooms to college students. She knew Ingram wasn't one, but hadn't asked any questions because of Nakano. He'd paid for two weeks in advance in cash. He was pretty certain he wouldn't be here that long, that one way or the other he had to bring things to a head—he'd be damned if he was going to always have to look over his shoulder for Wicks. He'd also moved out his boxed negatives, storing them for the time being in a locker at the Y. If he was alive after all this, he was going to secure them someplace more permanent for damn sure.

Leaving with his purchases, Ingram walked past a FREE-DOM RALLY sign taped in a corner of the market's display window. Back in his room he prepared his lunch: pickled mackerel from a tin with the spice furikake sprinkled on it, Japanese-style potato salad and a beer. In three days the rally was going down. He knew from Anita that King was already in town and staying with a friend in Sugar Hill. His meal finished, Ingram went outside with his beer, standing at the guardrail where the hill sloped down to the 101 Freeway below. Northwest of the freeway was a fenced-in plot of land containing the rusting hulks of trolley cars. Overhead a seagull circled the junkyard. The birds often came this far inland to try to pluck a trout from the stocked Echo Park Lake. Ingram's plan, such as it was, involved keeping his head down for now and taking his pictures at the rally. He polished off his beer and walked back inside.

"HARRY?" CROSSMAN said over the phone.

"It's me, Wes, heard you were looking for me."

"A big-headed white man came in here looking for you."

Wicks. "Shit. He get out of hand?"

"Well, he was pretty tipsy. Mind you, this was about two in the afternoon today. He waved around a hundred-dollar bill asking if anybody knew where you were. Him broadcasting you weren't at your apartment."

Crossman told him after Wicks left, he'd called Shoals Pettigrew, who he knew slightly. Ingram's childhood friend didn't know where he might be. But it was Pettigrew who'd called Edwards and Nakano, who in turn told Ingram the editor wanted to talk to him.

"Then what happened?"

"Well, we were ribbing this guy and I suppose a roomful of colored folks making fun of this square-headed ofay got under his pickled skin. He added a twenty to the hundred along with the pistol he pulled out."

Ingram's stomach tightened. "He hurt anybody, Wes?"

"No, he waved it around and insulted us and even blasted a round into the ceiling. Chester got him calmed down though, putting on the nice-negro act. Buttering him up, jus' us darkies down here on the plantation. He said he'd never liked you and would ask around as to your location. The white boy left a phone number and split. Bumping into the doorframe on his way out with his drunk ass."

Linotype operator Chester Howard was seventy at least. He'd been a typesetter at the paper for many years. He'd also worked for the *Sentinel* and the *L.A. Tribune*. He was a veteran of World War I, a former Black Rattler. Legend was he'd survived an attack by white vets in the violent Red Summer of 1919, when Black veterans among others were set upon and at times lynched. This for daring to think they could exercise the rights they fought for overseas back home. Howard kept a pint bottle and pearl-black .38 in a rickety table next to his Linotype machine.

"Wes, I'll take care of this. You think Chester would be up to calling this guy?"

"Harry, I can't believe I'm saying this, but maybe you should call the cops."

"They won't do shit about this, Wes. Only me."

"Okay ..." he drawled. "What do you want me to tell him to say? 'Cause you know that ornery old bastard will do it." He chuckled nervously.

"I'll call you back in about fifteen minutes. I gotta check something out first."

"I'll be here."

After he said good-bye, Ingram hung up the house phone. It was on a two-tiered table with the Yellow and White Pages on the bottom level. He chanced to look over to see the widow, Akane Ochi, standing in the doorway to her kitchen. She didn't speak much English, but she nodded at him, smiling. He nodded and smiled back. He started to dial a number. The widow had returned, holding a plate of fresh-baked chocolate-chip cookies toward him. He took two.

"*Arigatou gozaimasu,*" he said. It was one of the few phrases he knew in Japanese.

She said something in return and went away with her sweets.

Ingram didn't go through with his call. He replaced the handset, having decided not to talk to Anita Claire, to possibly hear her voice for the last time. Yeah well, he admonished himself as he walked out of the house, he wasn't dead yet. His injured foot barely bothered him as he descended the steps built into the hill toward the trolley yard.

NIGHT.

"You got a way about you, Ingram, yeah you do," Wicks called out, his replacement Browning down by his side. He'd stopped beside the bulk of one of the junked trolley cars. There was a section missing from its side, the metal having been haphazardly cut away by a blowtorch.

Wicks warily moved farther into the Los Angeles Transit Lines trolley graveyard. His leg wound had been stitched and wrapped tight. "Did you really think I was so far gone that when the old fella called me I was gonna be so excited I wouldn't realize this was a trap? That you wouldn't be ready for me?"

"I knew you'd come," Ingram said, deeper within the forest of rusting trolleys.

"You goddamn right I would." Wicks crept around the far side of the trolley, gun up as he inched forward.

When Ingram had gotten off the phone with Crossman, he'd walked over to the trolley junkyard to scout it out. The mothballed cars were bordered by a high chain-link fence. At some point those on the hunt for discarded treasure had used heavy-duty wire cutters to rend a slit in the fence for entry. He'd gotten in that way and Ingram was sure Wicks had entered that way too. It was nighttime, but Ingram had correctly guessed portions of the yard would be illuminated from the streetlights on the exterior. Ingram was also on the move. The facility not only contained decommissioned trolley cars laid out side by side, at times three across, but there were two areas containing decades' older trolleys that had been previously cannibalized, flattened to some degree and stacked by crane one atop another unevenly. Overall, there was an echo quality to sounds carried in here. The din of light traffic on the freeway beyond floated through the hulks, carrying to the antagonists as well.

There was a lone wooden building on the yard, a compact rectangular office with yellowed dingy windows and a door long since missing a lock. This was tucked in a corner and Wicks stood outside of it. He eased the door open with the muzzle of his gun, peering into the gloom. As the gunman stepped through the spiderwebbed doorway, he plucked the silken stuff off his face. At the sound of movement, Wicks whipped around, discharging a bullet as a cat scampered across the earthen expanse.

"Goddammit," he said.

The cat yowled, scampering onto a trolley's shell.

Wicks wiped a hand over his mouth and continued on.

Elsewhere in the manmade maze, Ingram rounded a corner where a bus missing a rim leaned on a wheel-less trolley. Quite a few of the cars in here lacked wheels. This rusting trolley was a chipped and fading yellow in color. The Yellow Cars had been operated by the Los Angeles Railway and were local. The Red Cars were operated by the Pacific Electric Railway and once upon a time took passengers all the way east to Riverside and south to Orange County. Taking a knee beside the bus, Ingram chanced using the penlight he'd brought along. He unfolded the hand-drawn map he'd made when he'd returned a second time to the yard before nightfall. He'd marked this particular trolley-and-bus combo on his diagram. There were layers upon layers of graffiti covering a number of the trolleys and yet right next to marked ones, some were untouched.

Ingram froze, sensing more than hearing something. He clicked the light off, waiting, holding his breath. He'd heard Wicks's shot but had estimated it was farther away. Sound was tricky in here, bouncing around like it did. He had best not get overconfident, he reminded himself. He touched the grip of his .45, feeling comforted, and went on.

WICKS ARRIVED at an uneven row of slagged trolleys and parts of such. He started to go around this heap, reaching his left hand out to make sure there was nothing sticking out to poke him in the eye. He eased along the row, slow and deliberate. Now and then he glanced up at the tops of the discarded bodies of the trolley cars, looking for Ingram.

A big truck's air horn blasted through the silence. Reflexively both men reacted, crouching down, their guns extended. Recovering, the two continued stalking each other under the pale moonlight.

Ingram lost his bearings, sure he hadn't gotten to the area he'd intended. Goddamn junked trolley cars in this tricky lighting all looked the same in the night. He was wary of using his penlight again. He liberated his pistol from his waistband and eased alongside of several cars. He first saw a flash from a muzzle, then what must have been a millisecond later, the retort. Ingram didn't have any idea how close the bullet had come as he fired back, hopefully driving Wicks to seek cover. And he was sure it was only him. He understood enough about his opponent that he'd want to handle this personally. It wasn't about avenging Morty—it was about his professional pride. This uppity spade had gotten the best of him and he had to pay for his temerity.

"How you doin', Harry? Did I nick you?" Wicks called out.

"Come and see."

"I might just do that."

Squinting, Wicks went along an aisle between some stacked trolleys, his pace quickening. His foot banged into a hard object. It skittered away, bashing against other metal.

"Motherfucker," Wicks cursed. He broke into a full-out run, a shot booming behind him and ricocheting. But he wasn't hit. He flopped onto his stomach and belly crawled in the dirt to get to the end of the row and slithered off to his right.

Ingram had no choice but to skirt down the same aisle Wicks had used, where he'd heard him scurrying. He had to press the attack. But he wasn't going to be overly eager and get his head blown off either. Involuntarily counting each step as he took them in his head, he went along, his gun leveled. There were patches of pale yellow illuminating the path between the piled cars, coming from one of the streetlights out on the sidewalk. They were near a section of the fencing. Ingram stopped, bending down, straining to hear. What was that? Where had it come from? He looked ahead but couldn't quite make out the end of the row. Was Wicks there, maybe flat on the ground to be less of a target, gun pointing this way? The noise from the traffic seemed to fade.

A barely audible tick caused him to look up. Silhouetted against the moonlight atop one of the artificial ridges was a damn cat prowling about. Yet just as the feline began to climb higher, the animal stopped, arching his back. Ingram reacted and dove out of the way as shots rained at him from above. The bullets sparked against the trolley car shells. Wicks had climbed atop one of the uneven stacks.

Ingram shot back, causing Wicks to scramble. Ingram banked from one side of the aisle to the other, his heart pumping furiously. Another shot from Wicks, but this time he was firing blind. This close, though, Ingram was certain where he was from the other man's footfalls. Wicks was moving as fast as he could over the irregular surfaces to get back to the ground. Reflexively he also noted the stockpiled trolley cars weren't meant to be climbed upon—they shook as he ran into them. Ingram hurried forward, tying to pace Wicks.

UP ABOVE Wicks fired the gun over his shoulder without looking. He was almost to the end of the row where the pile descended precariously. Ingram was also almost at the end of the row and could now make out Wicks's figure. He rammed his shoulder once, twice into the stack, causing them to jiggle.

"Fuck," Wicks blurted as he lost his footing and fell off, landing hard on his stomach, getting his wind knocked out.

Ingram dropped onto him, viciously cracking the butt of his pistol on Wicks's head. He groaned and Ingram got back up, now holding the Browning. "Get up," he said, breathing hard.

Wicks had rolled onto his back, glaring up at his captor. His face was bloodied. "What are you going to do, huh, Ingram? You gonna turn me over to the cops? Even if they believed you, then what? Think I won't be out on bail lickety-split before you can say Jack Robinson?" Sitting up, he grinned. In the wan light his teeth gleamed red from blood.

Ingram went stone.

"Then you know what, asshole? I'm gonna come back for you. First though I'm going to teach that old burr head who helped you a lesson and maybe whoever the fuck one or two of your friends are just for good measure. Like that gal you hoodwinked me with at the club. That's what it means to be me, Ingram. Something you ain't never gonna have, hear me? Never. Like that show, I'm a goddamn untouchable." He chuckled again.

"You mean because of the Providers?"

Wicks was sitting up now, hands splayed behind him on the ground as if at a picnic. "You too smart for your own good, Ingram." He hunched a shoulder. "But so what? You know the score. You're way over your head. You can't stop us. And you're just an uppity colored who don't know his place."

"I can stop you." And he shot him point-blank in the forehead.

Wicks flopped over onto his back again. Pointedly, Ingram had shot him with his own Browning. He used the hem of his sport coat to wipe off his prints and tossed the gun down to the dirt beside the dead man. In the dim glow of the streetlight, Wicks's eyes held their look of disbelief.

Ingram left the body cooling there among the junked trolleys and walked along the darkened streets. He didn't feel an urgency to flee and so he didn't. He wasn't sure if he'd be so calm if he heard sirens approaching but there were none close by. Boldly he returned to his rooming house and let himself in quietly. At the top of the stairs in the hallway there came the muffled strains of an LP playing in one of the other tenants' rooms. It was "St. Louis Blues" by W. C. Handy. After a belt from the pint bottle of Black Velvet he'd brought with him, Ingram stripped off his shirt and lay on the bed in his trousers. Just in case he had to be awake quickly and in motion, he reasoned. His head back on a pillow as Handy teased music out of his horn, he slept trouble-free.

CHAPTER THIRTEEN

To Ingram's mild surprise, the discovery of Wicks's body was kept out of the news. This he would find out later. The following day he stood at the guardrail at the curve looking down on a knot of onlookers gathered outside the junked trolley facility below. The coroner's men took the body out on a stretcher to load into a station wagon. It wasn't yet past nine in the morning. Several police cars were parked in or outside of the yard, the double gate having been opened. He stood there drinking his coffee. It occurred to him that as far as Hanisha and Clovis knew, Wicks and Morty were still looking for them. At some point Ingram calmly realized Hoyt would have to be getting himself another set of leg-breakers.

The widow Ochi walked up, standing beside him, also looking down at the activity. They stood there for nearly a minute in silence then she said, "Guess you'll be leaving." She walked away, Ingram staring after her.

He remained there and finished his coffee, visualizing the big event he was going to cover.

CHAPTER FOURTEEN

As anticipated, the Freedom Rally had a large turnout. The staff who oversaw the operations at Wrigley Field were of course there early, as were the local and state police. Chief William Parker, head of the Los Angeles Police Department, wasn't a fan of Martin Luther King, He considered him a self-aggrandizing rabble rouser and possible agent of the Soviets. Negroes needed to know their place and their pace as far as he was concerned.

Lately the chief had heard the chatter from colored preachers and the like for an end to the Cotton Curtain. This was essentially a color line as Blacks were not getting hired for the better-paying industrial jobs east of Alameda Street into the industrial corridor. Parker was concerned. The rhetoric had increased around this issue. That meant there would be more lip from negroes stopped for routine matters like a taillight out or congregating on a street corner. It was Parker's experience that when they got an inch in one area, they always demanded a mile somewhere the hell else. But as there was radio, TV and print media attention on the rally, he best show he was a responsible leader and have his officers on point.

Conversely Governor Pat Brown was a supporter of King

and was aware of Parker's views regarding the civil rights leader. He'd ordered the state police to be positioned as well to ensure nothing untoward happened to the reverend while he was in town. If that also meant keeping an eye on their brethren who were oft times more eager to use a nightstick on a colored citizen's head, then that was a bonus. Uniforms were stationed in the sealed-off clock tower to watch the field and prevent the structure from being used by a sniper.

Ingram had also been up early. Already that morning Reverend King had spoken at a special service at Ward African Methodist Episcopal Church to a packed audience. The governor and candidate Bradley were there as well. There were only a few photographers allowed inside, and Ingram was one of them. He'd previously been informed by Shoals Pettigrew, a member of the congregation, that this was happening.

"Remember when we were going to build our own submarine?" Pettigrew said to his friend. The two were on an open mezzanine level overlooking the gathering below. King was just finishing up. The hardware store owner was looking at a painting on the wall up here of dark waters lapping against a rocky shore, a cross glowing atop the rocks.

It took Ingram a moment to realize the painting had triggered the memory. He and Shoals had known each other since attending 61st Street Elementary. The school had a well-stocked library and both grade schoolers had spent several of their library periods paging through a picture-book version of Jules Verne's *20,000 Leagues Under the Sea*. They'd also made drawings of what their submarine, the *Fantastic*, would look like. The sub was named after Doc Fantastic, a comics character who headed a team of superheroes called the Danger Squad that included a non-stereotypical Black member. Their underwater wonder would be an improvement on Captain Nemo's *Nautilus*.

"We were going to sail to all those exotic islands Mrs. Alexander told us about," Ingram said. There had been a large world map in their room, and she would point to a particular island and tell them about its history, culture and so on. This was how Shoals got his nickname. Pettigrew was always going on in those days about visiting locales like Fiji; Hawaii, which wasn't a state then; and Madagascar.

"We were going to build robots for our crew," Pettigrew added. "For when we fought supervillains like the Octopus Master and Serpenticus." The latter was a giant anthropomorphized talking sea serpent with a genius IQ.

Ingram clicked off several shots of King gesturing with his hands. "And get Kent Richards to build us a force field belt so our crew wouldn't get eaten by sharks when they were in their diving suits." Richards' nickname was the bombastic Doc Fantastic. He could shrink his body yet had super strength, could turn invisible and was an inventor of all sorts of incredible gadgets. His superhero name was the rather bombastic Mr. Fantastic.

"Wow, Mrs. Alexander," Pettigrew said, staring into the past. "Man, I had a crush on her."

"Yeah, man, you did," Ingram agreed.

Applause filled the church from below, reminding the two of their duties in the present.

"I'm supposed to help with the reception with the Founder's Circle. See you later at the Field, Harry."

"For sure."

Descending the stairs, Ingram enjoyed the notion that he and Anita could steal away in a garage-built submarine from all this and live the life of vagabonds.

A few hours later he dabbed sweat from his forehead with his handkerchief as he walked around the outer ring of the seats that had been set up on the field. On the raised stage were various celebrities including Rita Moreno, Sammy Davis Jr. and Dorothy Dandridge, who was fanning herself with a folded-over program. Brown and Bradley were sitting up there as well. Actor Paul Newman in sunglasses, along with his wife and fellow actor Joanne Woodward, were now talking at one of the standing microphones.

Ingram snaked his way through a contingent of men in dark suits, holding up the press credentials he'd draped from his neck, obtaining a desirous angle on the stage. Sitting on a folding chair, studying a set of notes, was King, not more than twenty feet from him. No other photographer was around, and he snapped off several shots. There was a bespectacled man he didn't recognize sitting next to the reverend, but he made sure to get him in a few of his snaps. As he was lining up the next shot through his viewfinder, the images were blocked by a hand on a hip he recognized.

"You better not be trying to take a picture up under my dress, pervert."

"Hey, sweetie," he said, looking up. Anita Claire stood at the edge of the stage, bending down slightly toward him. She was in a white dress with black polka dots, cinched at the waist by a white belt. She had on an ostentatious wide-brimmed sun hat with a decorative sash encircling the crown. A gust billowed and she had to clamp down on her hat. How he wanted to be on the *Fantastic* with her.

"I wanted to make sure to tell you that there's to be a light reception for the reverend tonight at the O'Dells' in Sugar Hill. This will be after the fundraiser at the Lancasters'."

"How many damn appearances can this man make in one day?"

"As many as the cause demands, comrade. He's gotta be in Chicago tomorrow at their Wrigley Field for yet another event." She told him the address to the O'Dells', blew him a kiss and walked away.

Ingram had yet to come clean concerning his conversation with Sutton. He had told her he was pretty certain the man hadn't taken the diary. Ingram reflected on it, moving off to get more shots of the others onstage. In the last few days she hadn't asked him about interviewing the third person on her list. But then both of them had been busy, what with this rally coming up. On Ingram's part in particular, there had been the Wicks problem to deal with. He was still perplexed he wasn't more bothered by shooting the enforcer in cold blood.

"Him or me," Ingram muttered. A rationalization he'd made more than once in the last two days.

After getting the pics he wanted of those onstage, Ingram meandered about, spotting Pettigrew sitting with his church folks, Strummer Edwards by himself and Arthur Yarbrough with the woman Ingram had met at Kinslow's sendoff.

"How it going, Harry?" Yarbrough said as he stepped closer. Even with the voice of Governor Brown booming over the loudspeakers, his blind friend recognized the other man's muffled footfalls on the grass. "That foot must be feeling better."

"Like new."

"I heard that. Oh, pardon me," he said, turning slightly to his companion. "This is Millicent Mayfair. Millie was at—"

"Yes, I remember her." Ingram stuck out his hand. "Pleased to formally meet you."

"Same," she said. Her voice had a husky, smoky quality. Arthur was grinning like a goof at Ingram. The three turned their attention back to the stage as several musicians began a musical interlude. Up there was Johnny Otis on vibes, Buddy Collette on clarinet, Clora Bryant on trumpet and

Dexter Gordon on the sax. Reverend King had looked up from his notes to dig what they were laying down, Ingram observed.

When the musicians finished, Ingram made his way over to Otis, who was talking to Dexter Gordon. Ingram nodded at the tall saxophonist.

"Nice set, gents."

"Thanks, man." Otis dabbed at his sweaty brow with a handkerchief. He introduced Ingram to Gordon.

"Real quick, Johnny, you know a chick who goes by Hanisha?"

"Hell of a name," Gordon rumbled.

Otis grinned broadly. "Yeah, played a few sets with her around town. But I heard she got out of the business to do her soothsayer hustle." He chuckled.

"Do you know if Ben knew her?"

Otis looked away, then back at his friend. "Yeah . . ." he drawled, "seems to me Ben was in at least one of those gigs back when he was in town then."

"Did they, you know, go around together?"

Otis hunched a shoulder. "Don't know, why?"

"Just trying to fill in the blanks. Thanks." Ingram turned to go.

"I remember I heard she was doing readings or whatever you call 'em for a few heeled white women on the west side. Maybe Ben helped make that happen. But I don't know."

"I hear you. Thanks again."

Onstage comedian Dick Gregory was riffing at the microphone as Ingram again moved around, taking snaps of audience members laughing. After him a handful of other speakers came and went at the microphones until finally King came up to speak. First, though, he received a standing ovation that lasted over a minute. Ingram and Josh

Nakano stood together clapping a few yards away from the stage.

"I want to thank Governor Brown, Reverend Dockery and all the other fine people up here today who have brought me back to this fine city," King began. His next words were drowned out by more enthusiastic applause. When the clapping died down, he continued. "And you all out here today who believe that justice and equality are not simply lofty words but a clarion call to each and every one of us to do our part to bring about a nation that upholds its ideals set forth so long ago."

The crowd exploded again.

"I gotta tell my mom about this," Ingram said to his friend.

"Me too." Nakano grinned.

Soon Ingram said good-bye to Nakano to work his way among those seated to capture the beaming faces of the more than thirty-five thousand in attendance. "Birmingham or Los Angeles, the cry is the same, we want to be free," King proclaimed to thunderous applause. He looked out over the crowd. "Now is the time to transform the creative energy in this country to form a song of brotherhood to lift the country from the quicksand of racial injustice."

His words garnered another standing ovation.

When King finally sat down, his shoulders slumped and his head dropped, like a boxer who'd just gone the distance. But when his head came up, he was smiling, and waved to the people. When the stadium again got quiet, singer Aretha Franklin came to the microphone to end the event. As her powerful voice filled the air, Ingram was kissing Anita Claire in a shadowed recess under the stands of Wrigley Field.

"Guess I better get back."

"Okay," he said, their faces close.

"Either of those two hoodlums been around?"

"Not lately."

She pulled back farther, taking her hands from around his neck. "Those kinds of guys don't fade into the woodwork, you know."

"I hear you, baby. I'll figure it out."

"We'll figure it out." With a peck she was gone.

Ingram hadn't told her about the bushwhacking in Altadena, or Morty. She didn't know about his car being firebombed and him going into hiding. The last few days she'd been so busy getting things ready for King's visit, they'd only talked by phone. In this way he also hadn't had to let slip about his showdown with Wicks. The knife man, he could argue, was self-defense. His pulling the trigger on Wicks . . . a preemptive strike? That was only an excuse in wartime. Yet there had been no mention of either man's demise in print or over the airwaves. As to why, Ingram wasn't sure, but he was certain Hoyt was behind it. He supposed if pressed, the millionaire would send a killer after him to tidy up loose ends, so no sense calling attention to the two goons and Hoyt's own involvement. This meant, though, Ingram would have to strike first to make sure nothing happened to Anita. Was he seriously contemplating killing a rich white man? If by some miracle he remained alive after being arrested, he'd be sent to death row, waiting his turn to suck in the gas chamber's fumes.

But today the idea of death at the hands of the law didn't faze him. Today he had a job to finish.

Ingram and Eddie Burrows, the writer covering the rally for *The Nation,* had arranged a time to meet outside of gate 7. Ingram walked out to the parking lot to keep the appointment.

"Hell of a speech by King," Burrows said. People streamed past them exiting the stadium, then milled in the parking area, talking about the rally. Burrows was in short sleeves and from the streak of wetness on his back, he'd sweated profusely this day.

"August in D.C. will be even bigger, grander," Ingram said. He lit a cigar.

"Indeed. Are you going?"

"At first I had no interest, but now, yeah." Ingram nodded. "Even if it's on nobody's ticket, yeah, I might just go." If he wasn't sitting in jail, he didn't add. "How about you?"

"I want to, but looks like I'll be in Indo-China then. Vietnam, they're calling it now."

"Didn't Kennedy send some troops there?"

"Yeah, these tough bastards that eat nails for breakfast. They're called the Green Berets. The word now is he's stepped up our involvement on the sly to help out the French and keep the dominoes from falling."

"They sold us that bill of goods in Korea," Ingram said pointedly. Absently, he aimed and took a shot of Bradley talking to Governor Brown nearby.

"I'm tracking down something called Operation Ranch Hand."

"What's that?"

Burrows's eyebrows went up. "Not exactly sure. But apparently it involves a chemical spray to screw up the North Vietnamese's crops. A way to starve them out I guess." He paused, then asked, "You think there'll ever be a Black president of this country, Harry?"

"The Arctic gonna run out of icebergs?"

"No, really. Like King said. We can only aspire to be whatever we want to be when the roadblocks to make that happen are eliminated. Isn't that the goal?"

Ingram tapped ash off the end of his cigar. "Not sure why any colored man would want to be the president. The aims of the Confederacy are alive and well in plenty of white folks' hearts, Eddie. Black man as president, well," he hunched a shoulder, "that fella would be living in a glass house. Every step he took, every sneeze he made would be a reason to find fault with him."

"But think of how that could mean we've turned a corner when it comes to race and race relations."

"Huh," Ingram said, "right around that corner will be another white wall. Taller and harder to get over than the last one."

"I hope you're wrong."

"Me too."

IN HIS shirtsleeves, Dr. Martin Luther King Jr. sat in a club chair in a corner of the large living room. In a few hours he'd be driven from this home in Sugar Hill to the airport to take an overnight charted flight to Chicago for the rally he was speaking at the next day, Sunday—at that city's more famous Wrigley Field. He'd had a catnap between the rally at the stadium and the fundraiser with the Hollywood crowd that included Marlon Brando and Burt Lancaster. Ingram had skipped the event in favor of this one at the O'Dells' home. The O'Dells, Nan and Hal, were an older white couple who'd lived here since the 1940s. Unlike several of their white neighbors, they hadn't moved away when the neighborhood started changing. Claire had also informed Ingram the husband and wife were contributors to Bradley's campaign.

Inside the home all sorts of people talked and snacked. It was a small gathering and the house itself was only two blocks away from the previous time Ingram had been in the neighborhood, the last time he'd seen Ben Kinslow alive. He was the only journalist here and had already gotten several candid shots he felt certain he could sell to one of the white slicks.

"I'll be glad to get some sleep tonight," Shoals Pettigrew said to Ingram as they stood off to one side of the home.

Stifling a yawn his friend answered, "You and me both."

Despite a very long day, King was in good humor and chatted with several people who stood near him. Ingram drifted over to where Anita Claire and Judy Berkson were hovering near the spread laid out on the dining room table. Berkson nibbled at a cracker dabbed with a green blob. Given their trim figures, Ingram figured he put away more calories at breakfast than they did between the two of them all day.

"How you all holding up?" he asked them.

Claire briefly slipped an arm around his waist. "You losing weight, baby?"

"It comes from trying to keep up with you."

"You two are too cute," Berkson quipped. "Anita says you talked with Charlie Sutton." She'd finished her cracker and was eyeing another one with a small, boiled shrimp on it.

"Interesting cat. I'm going to legitimately write up an article on him. But as to the diary, it doesn't seem like he swiped it."

"And we only have two others, one of them away until next week." Berkson worried her bottom lip.

"We'll figure it out," Claire said. "Don really wants to write this book, huh?"

Her friend said, "He's already started to work on it. But the diary contains specific dates and such that will help him keep it all organized. He'd like to have the facts to write the fiction."

Ingram and Claire nodded.

Later, when it was just the two of them in the kitchen, she said to him, "I'll work with Judy and her folks to get his book in shape. My mom's got a pretty good memory and she can help fill in the gaps."

"You're not worried about the diary?"

"If it's gone, it's gone."

"You was kinda hot to find it before."

She laid a look on him he couldn't decipher.

The swing door opened and in stepped a white woman, athletic build, early forties, tawny skin and decked out stylishly in black capri pants, a buttoned-up shirt and matador shoes.

"I'll get you a beer and something to eat, Martin," the woman was saying. She smiled at Ingram and Claire and reached a hand to the refrigerator. That's when Ingram noted the sparkling bracelet on her wrist. The bracelet he'd seen in the photo among the ones Kinslow had stowed away.

"What is it?" Claire asked, catching Ingram glaring at the woman.

"Nothing, tired is all," he said, trying to sound casual, a hand on her shoulder.

Past her, the woman had removed a can of beer from the refrigerator and placed it on the tiled counter. She rummaged in a drawer for an opener, then used it on the can. She'd also retrieved a highball glass from the cupboard and poured an amount into it. From the way she moved about the kitchen it was obvious she'd been a guest of the O'Dells before. She smiled again at the two as she exited.

"Harry," Claire began.

A finger to his lips, he turned from her and opened the swing door a crack. In this way he could see into the dining room, where the food was laid out under overhead lights. He had set aside his Speed Graphic but had also brought along his compact Canon. He watched as the woman piled several dainty triangles of sandwiches on a small plate. Ingram held the camera level to his sternum. Just before the woman picked up the plate, she dropped a round white pill into the beer glass and swirled the contents to help dissolve the pill. She then left his field of vision to deliver her goods.

Standing in the kitchen, Ingram frowned at Claire, who looked at him questioningly. "I think that lady is trying to poison the reverend."

"What?"

"Come on." He tugged her by the wrist to the living room.

The highball glass and sandwiches were on an end table next to the club chair King had been sitting in. Ingram stared fixedly at the glass. The level of the head of foam seemed to be where he'd last seen it less than a minute ago. At the moment King was standing, a hand in his pocket as he talked to Reverend Brookings. The woman with the particular bracelet was talking to a man and woman across the room.

"Shit," Ingram mumbled. He whispered to Claire, "I'm going to distract Reverend King and you swipe his beer. In fact, spill it if you can so you have to replace it." He started off.

"Okay," she said softly to his back.

Ingram walked over and said to the clergymen, "Mind if I get a shot of you two?"

Brookings looked annoyed but King said, "Make it fast, will you? I'm about dead on my feet."

"Sure, of course." As Ingram lined up his shot, Claire was in position. But then King held up his hand.

"Hold on, I'm parched." He pivoted and picked up the highball glass with a flourish, as if auditioning for a TV commercial to sell its contents.

Like when he was in combat, time slowed for Ingram, his heart racing and throat constricted by fear and anticipation.

King winked at him, saying, "Now you wait till I put this down. Got to keep certain parts of my real self separate from my public image."

The words came to Ingram as if through a heavy scrim. He watched as King had the glass to his mouth. As he tipped it forward to drink, Ingram had two flashbulbs in hand plucked from his pocket. He threw them with force onto the hardwood floor. They exploded in audible pops, causing wide eyes all around.

"Sorry, nerves," he stammered.

As if reacting to the mini-explosions, Claire bumped into the reverend. "Goodness," she declared. Her action caused the contents of the glass to slosh over, wetting King slightly.

"Oh no," someone said.

"It's fine," the prophet of nonviolence said, wiping at his shirt with his hand. "I'm still thirsty though."

"Coming right up," the woman with the bracelet said.

"I got it," a man said, already heading through the swing door.

Someone else had fetched a wet towel and was rubbing King's shirt.

"I've got another one in my luggage," King assured his helper. "But the good Lord bless you for this beer." The man had returned from the kitchen and King eagerly took the offered libation, this time straight from the can. He had a sizable sip and sighed satisfactorily. "That's better."

The woman with the bracelet had her arms folded, her

mouth a thin line as she clenched her jaw. She stared hard at Claire.

With time to spare, King nonetheless said his good-byes about forty minutes later and was out the door, on his way to the airport. The woman had left before then. Ingram had glanced around the curtained window, and had noted the car she was driving. It was a sporty Jaguar XKE convertible.

Afterward at his place, Ingram and Claire unwound and debriefed.

"Maybe it wasn't poison," she wondered.

"What, a sleeping pill? He wasn't driving himself."

"Doesn't seem to me the Providers would want him dead," she said.

Ingram put his feet in his socks on the coffee table. "Four months before what's going to be the biggest gathering ever for jobs and justice for the negro? Could you imagine how defeated everyone would feel if he were to die?"

Claire observed, "Seems to me that would drive more people to Malcolm X's militant point of view. Cause riots and whatnot. King is for reform, not revolution. Him being cut down could make people way less inclined to wait for answers from Washington and more inclined to seek it in the streets."

Shaking his head he said, "We'd need a whole grip of white folks on our side to pull off that kind of action, baby. Unless of course there's a whole bunch of your running buddies' secret cells around. And I mean there'd have to be several high-placed ones in the armed forces and all." He imagined tanks rolling down Broadway, firing into buildings in the ghetto indiscriminately.

"The Bolsheviks built on a series of intense struggles over years, including maneuvering their allies into the governmental structure to pull off their coup."

"You mean the white Russians. There's a whole bunch of folks who look like my buddy Josh over there too, right? I mean I know they ain't Japanese. But where are they when it comes to the Soviets?"

She grinned lopsidedly. "Touché, comrade. Clearly there is work to be done all around." Her grin faded. "Are we conditioned, though, to accept that the negro's longing in America is always destined to be dialed down?"

The fact that Clovis Mitchell had attended Pepperdine occurred to him and he told her this, adding, "Maybe the Providers have their own Black leader they're grooming hiding in the woodpile. Somebody who will not be as forward-thinking as the good doctor. More like, I don't know, George Washington Carver. Separate is okay as long as we apply ourselves."

She made a derisive sound in her throat, snuggling next to him. On the coffee table were two squat glasses containing whiskey, neat, and the two surreptitious snaps Ingram had taken of the woman with the bracelet. They were still drying. One was as she was leaving the gathering, in motion on the walkway of the house, furtively illuminated by the porch light. The other was in the dining room, the white, round orb of a pill suspended in the air just as she released it from her hand. The frozen moment in time looked as if the two had rehearsed the shot.

Claire picked up the picture, waving it slightly. "We should at least find out who she is."

"Hell yes." He sipped his drink.

THE FOLLOWING day Claire made an inquiry to the O'Dells and found out the woman's name was Elise Duville. She was listed in the White Pages. When they drove to her house in Cheviot Hills, there was a FOR SALE sign staked in the well-tended lawn. They got out and walked up to the abode.

"Ain't nobody home but us chickens," Ingram cracked as the two of them peered in the front window, the drapes inside slightly gapped.

"You ain't never lied." The furniture was already gone. Back in the car she turned to Ingram and said, "The reason you haven't mentioned Morty and Wicks lately is they're dead, aren't they?"

"Yes," he said, staring straight ahead.

"I need to tell you something, Anita. It's been eating me up. Not what I did, but the not talking about it. I killed them both." Stammering he added, "Two different times. Before the rally. Both times they'd come at me." He told her about the ambush and Wicks coming to the *Eagle* to call him out. He didn't provide further details but would if she asked. Like still-life paintings, they sat there in front of the empty house. His hands were on the steering wheel, inert, seemingly without purpose.

"But Hoyt hasn't sent anyone else," she finally said.

"Not yet." He turned to her. "You know I'd do whatever I could to protect you."

"I'm a big girl, Harry. I've told you that."

"I know you are."

"Come on, I'm hungry."

A FEW days later Claire circled back with Nan O'Dell trying to unearth any other information about Elise Duville. They sat in the front room of the woman's house in Sugar Hill having tea.

"Why so curious about Elise?" O'Dell wondered.

"I think I might know a relative of hers, a girl I went to school with. Miss Duville gave me her phone number but it's disconnected."

"Hmm," the older woman said, sipping from her Spode china cup. "I know she's moved around a lot so that's not surprising." She regarded her guest.

Sensing she was holding back, Claire asked, "What is it, Nan?"

"Well, dear, I know a little about you and your sister's upbringing from Frank Wilkerson and was wondering if it was in one of those summer camps you'd met this relative of hers. Elise being you know, what's the term, a fellow traveler?"

"Really?" Claire said.

TWO NIGHTS later Ingram was alone at home and his phone rang. He answered it.

"Hello, Mr. Ingram," a pleasant voice said.

"Who is this?"

"Winston Hoyt."

His throat tightened but he said calmly, "What can I do for you?"

"Oh, I thought I'd check in with you. Particularly I wanted you to know I'd advised Wicks to leave you be, but he took it rather personally about his associate."

"They killed Ben on your orders," he said evenly.

"Such an unfortunate matter."

Ingram wasn't going to utter an unrealistic vow like he'd make him pay. They both knew that couldn't happen, given Hoyt's command of resources and his lack thereof.

"Hard decisions have to be made at times, Mr. Ingram. It's the nature of progress."

"The brass always says that shit and the soldiers do the dying. You had my friend killed because he knew you were going to try and kill the reverend."

"What are you saying about King?"

"Be cute. Your girl, Elise. I know who she is and what she tried to do."

"What are you saying?"

"You heard me."

A pause, then, "You are an enterprising sort, Harry. Credit to your race. Truly. This city with the proper guidance can be a model for the nation. Once you understand that, I believe you'll see what we are attempting to accomplish in its proper light."

"Look, if you're going to come for me, do it. None of this going on about good darkies and all that hoorah. But you leave my friends alone. Me and you, man to man."

"Be well, Mr. Ingram. I have no doubt our paths will cross again." He hung up.

For several moments Ingram remained still, evaluating Hoyt's words and the reactions behind them.

"I'M NOT going to walk around with a roscoe in my purse, Harry," Anita Claire added, "so you can do an article on me in *Dapper*, 'Tragic Mulatto Pistol Whips Rich White Man Half to Death.'"

They both chuckled. "Okay, Moms Mabley, I had to suggest it." The two were in his apartment and had been discussing possible repercussions from Winston Hoyt. They were sitting at his kitchen table eating smothered steak he'd made according to his mother's recipe. They also discussed his friend's murder.

Ingram said, "It must have been Ben was hooked up with Hanisha and that square head Clovis trying to work a blackmail angle." He imagined Mitchell skulking in the bushes to take the pics Ben Kinslow had.

"You said Johnny Otis told you she had an in to the whites," Claire said. "Who's to say she wasn't giving spiritual advice to Hoyt's wife, sister, someone like that? Hoyt himself for that matter. Plenty of men go to crystal ball gazers. Whatever, she found out something juicy and tried to cash in."

"Yeah, that could be it," he admitted. "Hoyt's boys weren't looking for Hanisha to give her flowers." It gave him pleasure visualizing Morty grinding that knife of his in Mitchell's foot. He forked in more steak, chewing enthusiastically.

"Anyway I think you're on to something about Hoyt sounding confused when you mentioned Miss Duville. After my tea with Nan, I went to see my mom. She recognized that family name, Duville. We looked through her pamphlets and what have you and found a picture in a booklet the Party circulated in 1938. Back then to score propaganda points over the States, the Soviets were pushing the idea that there was no racism in Russia, unlike here. There was a program to have various people, particularly Black folks, immigrate there, blue-collar workers, artists and so on." She chewed quietly on her green beans. "Of course the reality of life under Stalin was a whole other thing. Some of these people left, others wound up in a gulag."

"And some found paradise," Ingram said.

She nodded. "The Duvilles had been big muck-ety-mucks in the Party back then in New York, their daughter Elise a teenager. Part of the well-off who'd followed Lenin's edict and turned against their own class. Elise was part of a kind of one-way foreign exchange program where red kids were sent over there for schooling. The booklet was about that program and showed the smiling Duvilles in the picture. She was younger then of course, but we were pretty sure it wasn't the woman from the other night."

"Say what?"

"Yeah," she said, nodding her head. "Much different face and build."

"Duville is older," he pointed out. "And maybe she had work done on her face."

"Mom made a few calls, looking to see if the husband or wife were still alive. She found out Elise Duville died in a skiing accident in '56. She double-checked."

Ingram was several steps behind. "Wait, this program..."

Claire said, "For the selected, they got indoctrinated and sent back."

"To do what?"

"Elise Duville lived well because her folks had money. Could be she was supposed to be a sleeper agent but balked when her handler sought to activate her."

"The hell?"

"Or maybe it really was an accident. This other sleeper takes her place and infiltrates the Providers." Claire held her hands wide. "How best to know what the capitalists are up to?"

"But if anybody wants King to succeed, isn't it in the interests of the Soviets?"

"Again, maybe the pill wasn't poison. Maybe it was to knock him out and he'd wake up in the sack with a naked white woman draped over him as the photos were snapped. Blackmail him to, I don't know, be more radical?" She considered her words and added, "I don't know, that seems like a stretch."

"Yeah," he agreed. Then Ingram offered, "What if she wasn't a Soviet agent? What if she was a government agent, I mean ours? The FBI knew about her and when she died, saw an opportunity. The pretend Elise Duville probably hobnobbed with some radical organizations, gathering information before relocating here. It's no secret Hoover and his buddies ain't got no love for the likes of Martin Luther King. And you're the one that's talked about the CIA working overtime to overthrow leftist foreign leaders."

"Their charter says they're not to operate domestically."

"Shit, white men running those alphabet agencies all swim in the same pool at the club, don't they? Having their cigars and cognac later, laughing and joking, sharing ideas on how to keep the darker races down."

"Something like that," she said.

Ingram said quietly, "And if it was a setup, we know who took King to the airport the other night. Maybe he was supposed to make a stop first."

"Oh, Harry," Claire said, staring at him.

"YOU'RE TALKING crazy, Harry," Shoals Pettigrew said. The two were alone in his hardware store. "Your chick has turned your head sideways, man."

"Were you supposed to bring the reverend to some motel where they would take the pictures of him in the sack with some white woman?" Probably one of the women from those other pictures, he conjectured. "King doped up, not knowing what was going on. Then get him to the plane where he'd sleep through the trip. He'd wake up, not remember a goddamn thing. Figure the pictures wouldn't show up until after the March on Washington when they would have the most impact, completely gut the struggle."

"That's fantastic. You ought to see if you could sell your idea to Alfred Hitchcock."

"Shoals, for the longest time you've had a lien on your shop. I asked the lady at the process server I work for," Ingram continued. "She checked the court records, that lien was recently erased."

"You got it twisted, Harry."

"Do I?"

"I'm no Uncle Tom sellout."

"Then what are you, Shoals?"

His childhood friend was at a loss for words.

STRUMMER EDWARDS looked up from the Sports section he was reading. He was sitting at his desk in his off-the-books club, the Stockyard. Standing in the doorway was a man in a suit and tie. It took him a moment to recognize Clovis Mitchell.

"What brings you around?"

"Mind if I sit?" His demeanor too was different. "I have a business opportunity I'd like to discuss with you."

"You and Hanisha?"

"Yes."

"Sure, be my guest." As he did Edwards added, "This have anything to do with the favor you were gonna ask Harry?" He had a pistol in the drawer but figured he wouldn't need it.

"Things change," the other man said, smiling.

ANITA CLAIRE didn't ask Ingram about interviewing the other two regarding the purloined diary.

The Morning Bandit struck again, nearly getting caught this time, pursued by an eager young security guard who worked out at Muscle Beach and had recently applied to the Police Academy. But it turned out the Bandit had a third accomplice with him, also a woman. As the guard ran after him, about to shoot him in the back, this woman seemingly stepped out of nowhere and threw some type of chemical balled in a tied handkerchief in his face. The stuff exploded in a plume, causing him to cough and sneeze, his shots to go wild. The trio escaped.

INGRAM FRAMED the photo of the pill dropping into the glass and hung it on his wall. It was the most significant picture he'd ever take.

The next time Josh Nakano and Strummer Edwards came over for a domino game, Jed Monk had replaced Shoals Pettigrew. When they asked about the picture, Ingram told them it was a try-out for obtaining advertising work.

Other Titles in the Soho Crime Series

STEPHANIE BARRON
(Jane Austen's England)
Jane and the Twelve Days
  of Christmas
Jane and the Waterloo Map
Jane and the Year Without a Summer

F.H. BATACAN
(Philippines)
Smaller and Smaller Circles

JAMES R. BENN
(World War II Europe)
Billy Boyle
The First Wave
Blood Alone
Evil for Evil
Rag & Bone
A Mortal Terror
Death's Door
A Blind Goddess
The Rest Is Silence
The White Ghost
Blue Madonna
The Devouring
Solemn Graves
When Hell Struck Twelve
The Red Horse
Road of Bones
From the Shadows

The Refusal Camp: Stories

CARA BLACK
(Paris, France)
Murder in the Marais
Murder in Belleville
Murder in the Sentier
Murder in the Bastille
Murder in Clichy
Murder in Montmartre
Murder on the Ile Saint-Louis
Murder in the Rue de Paradis
Murder in the Latin Quarter
Murder in the Palais Royal
Murder in Passy
Murder at the Lanterne Rouge
Murder Below Montparnasse
Murder in Pigalle
Murder on the Champ de Mars
Murder on the Quai
Murder in Saint-Germain
Murder on the Left Bank

CARA BLACK CONT.
Murder in Bel-Air
Murder at the Porte de Versailles

Three Hours in Paris
Night Flight to Paris

HENRY CHANG
(Chinatown)
Chinatown Beat
Year of the Dog
Red Jade
Death Money
Lucky

BARBARA CLEVERLY
(England)
The Last Kashmiri Rose
Strange Images of Death
The Blood Royal
Not My Blood
A Spider in the Cup
Enter Pale Death
Diana's Altar

Fall of Angels
Invitation to Die

COLIN COTTERILL
(Laos)
The Coroner's Lunch
Thirty-Three Teeth
Disco for the Departed
Anarchy and Old Dogs
Curse of the Pogo Stick
The Merry Misogynist
Love Songs from a Shallow Grave
Slash and Burn
The Woman Who Wouldn't Die
Six and a Half Deadly Sins
I Shot the Buddha
The Rat Catchers' Olympics
Don't Eat Me
The Second Biggest Nothing
The Delightful Life of
  a Suicide Pilot

The Motion Picture Teller

ELI CRANOR
(Arkansas)
Don't Know Tough
Ozark Dogs

GARRY DISHER
(Australia)
The Dragon Man
Kittyhawk Down
Snapshot
Chain of Evidence
Blood Moon
Whispering Death
Signal Loss

Wyatt
Port Vila Blues
Fallout

Under the Cold Bright Lights

TERESA DOVALPAGE
(Cuba)
Death Comes in through
  the Kitchen
Queen of Bones
Death under the Perseids

Death of a Telenovela Star
  (A Novella)

DAVID DOWNING
(World War II Germany)
Zoo Station
Silesian Station
Stettin Station
Potsdam Station
Lehrter Station
Masaryk Station
Wedding Station

(World War I)
Jack of Spies
One Man's Flag
Lenin's Roller Coaster
The Dark Clouds Shining

Diary of a Dead Man on Leave

RAMONA EMERSON
(Navajo Nation)
Shutter

AGNETE FRIIS
(Denmark)
What My Body Remembers
The Summer of Ellen

TIMOTHY HALLINAN
(Thailand)
The Fear Artist
For the Dead
The Hot Countries
Fools' River
Street Music

(Los Angeles)
Crashed
Little Elvises
The Fame Thief
Herbie's Game
King Maybe
Fields Where They Lay
Nighttown
Rock of Ages

METTE IVIE HARRISON
(Mormon Utah)
The Bishop's Wife
His Right Hand
For Time and All Eternities
Not of This Fold
The Prodigal Daughter

MICK HERRON
(England)
Slow Horses
Dead Lions
The List (A Novella)
Real Tigers
Spook Street
London Rules
The Marylebone Drop (A Novella)
Joe Country
The Catch (A Novella)
Slough House
Bad Actors

Down Cemetery Road
The Last Voice You Hear
Why We Die
Smoke and Whispers

Reconstruction
Nobody Walks
This Is What Happened
Dolphin Junction: Stories

NAOMI HIRAHARA
(Japantown)
Clark and Division

STAN JONES
(Alaska)
White Sky, Black Ice
Shaman Pass
Frozen Sun
Village of the Ghost Bears
Tundra Kill
The Big Empty

STEVEN MACK JONES
(Detroit)
August Snow
Lives Laid Away
Dead of Winter

LENE KAABERBØL & AGNETE FRIIS
(Denmark)
The Boy in the Suitcase
Invisible Murder
Death of a Nightingale
The Considerate Killer

MARTIN LIMÓN
(South Korea)
Jade Lady Burning
Slicky Boys
Buddha's Money
The Door to Bitterness
The Wandering Ghost
G.I. Bones
Mr. Kill
The Joy Brigade
Nightmare Range
The Iron Sickle
The Ville Rat
Ping-Pong Heart
The Nine-Tailed Fox
The Line
GI Confidential
War Women

ED LIN
(Taiwan)
Ghost Month
Incensed
99 Ways to Die
Death Doesn't Forget

PETER LOVESEY
(England)
The Circle
The Headhunters
False Inspector Dew
Rough Cider
On the Edge
The Reaper

PETER LOVESEY CONT.
(Bath, England)
The Last Detective
Diamond Solitaire
The Summons
Bloodhounds
Upon a Dark Night
The Vault
Diamond Dust
The House Sitter
The Secret Hangman
Skeleton Hill
Stagestruck
Cop to Corpse
The Tooth Tattoo
The Stone Wife
Down Among the Dead Men
Another One Goes Tonight
Beau Death
Killing with Confetti
The Finisher
Diamond and the Eye
Showstopper

(London, England)
Wobble to Death
*The Detective Wore
Silk Drawers*
Abracadaver
Mad Hatter's Holiday
The Tick of Death
A Case of Spirits
Swing, Swing Together
Waxwork

Bertie and the Tinman
Bertie and the Seven Bodies
Bertie and the Crime of Passion

SUJATA MASSEY
(1920s Bombay)
The Widows of Malabar Hill
The Satapur Moonstone
The Bombay Prince

FRANCINE MATHEWS
(Nantucket)
Death in the Off-Season
Death in Rough Water
Death in a Mood Indigo
Death in a Cold Hard Light
Death on Nantucket
Death on Tuckernuck
Death on a Winter Stroll

SEICHŌ MATSUMOTO
(Japan)
Inspector Imanishi Investigates

CHRIS MCKINNEY
(Post Apocalyptic Future)
Midnight, Water City

MAGDALEN NABB
(Italy)
Death of an Englishman
Death of a Dutchman
Death in Springtime
Death in Autumn
The Marshal and the Murderer
The Marshal and the Madwoman
The Marshal's Own Case
The Marshal Makes His Report
The Marshal at the Villa Torrini
Property of Blood
Some Bitter Taste
The Innocent
Vita Nuova
The Monster of Florence

FUMINORI NAKAMURA
(Japan)
The Thief
Evil and the Mask
Last Winter, We Parted
The Kingdom
The Boy in the Earth
Cult X
My Annihilation
The Rope Artist

STUART NEVILLE
(Northern Ireland)
The Ghosts of Belfast
Collusion
Stolen Souls
The Final Silence
Those We Left Behind
So Say the Fallen

The Traveller & Other Stories
House of Ashes

(Dublin)
Ratlines

KWEI QUARTEY
(Ghana)
Murder at Cape Three Points
Gold of Our Fathers
Death by His Grace

KWEI QUARTEY CONT.
The Missing American
Sleep Well, My Lady
Last Seen in Lapaz

QIU XIAOLONG
(China)
Death of a Red Heroine
A Loyal Character Dancer
When Red Is Black

MARCIE R. RENDON
(Minnesota's Red River Valley)
Murder on the Red River
Girl Gone Missing
Sinister Graves

JAMES SALLIS
(New Orleans)
The Long-Legged Fly
Moth
Black Hornet
Eye of the Cricket
Bluebottle
Ghost of a Flea

Sarah Jane

JOHN STRALEY
(Sitka, Alaska)
The Woman Who Married a Bear
The Curious Eat Themselves
The Music of What Happens
Death and the Language
* of Happiness*
The Angels Will Not Care
Cold Water Burning
Baby's First Felony
So Far and Good

(Cold Storage, Alaska)
The Big Both Ways
Cold Storage, Alaska
What Is Time to a Pig?
Blown by the Same Wind

AKIMITSU TAKAGI
(Japan)
The Tattoo Murder Case
Honeymoon to Nowhere
The Informer

CAMILLA TRINCHIERI
(Tuscany)
Murder in Chianti
The Bitter Taste of Murder
Murder on the Vine

HELENE TURSTEN
(Sweden)
Detective Inspector Huss
The Torso
The Glass Devil
Night Rounds
The Golden Calf
The Fire Dance
The Beige Man
The Treacherous Net
Who Watcheth
Protected by the Shadows

Hunting Game
Winter Grave
Snowdrift

An Elderly Lady Is Up
* to No Good*
An Elderly Lady Must Not
* Be Crossed*

ILARIA TUTI
(Italy)
Flowers over the Inferno
The Sleeping Nymph

JANWILLEM VAN DE WETERING
(Holland)
Outsider in Amsterdam
Tumbleweed
The Corpse on the Dike
Death of a Hawker
The Japanese Corpse
The Blond Baboon
The Maine Massacre
The Mind-Murders
The Streetbird
The Rattle-Rat
Hard Rain
Just a Corpse at Twilight
Hollow-Eyed Angel
The Perfidious Parrot
The Sergeant's Cat:
* Collected Stories*

JACQUELINE WINSPEAR
(1920s England)
Maisie Dobbs
Birds of a Feather